MOTHER PUCKER

THE MOMCOMS

SWATI M.H.

KISMET PUBLISHING

ALSO BY SWATI M.H.

<u>Elements of Rapture Series</u>

Adrift

(Forbidden, single-dad, nanny, grumpy/sunshine, forced-proximity romance)

Ascend

(Marriage of convenience, single mom, forced proximity romance)

Ablaze

(Angsty, brother's best friend, one bed/one night, firefighter romance)

<u>Feel the Beat Series</u>

My Perfect Remix

(Single-dad, friends-to lovers romance)

My Beautiful Chaos

(Fake-relationship, second chance romance)

My Darling Neighbor

(Enemies to lovers, surprise pregnancy romance)

<u>Fated Love Series</u>

Kismet in the Sky

(Slightly forbidden, second chance romance)

Surrender to the Stars

(Enemies to lovers, hospital romance)

To all my ladies who love their men with a touch of alpha, a pinch of cinnamon, and a whole dollop of sweet. I present to you, Rowan 'Slick' Parker.

Then you walked in and my heart went, 'Boom!'

— PHILLIPA SOO & ORIGINAL BROADWAY
CAST OF "HAMILTON," 'HELPLESS'

CHAPTER 1
SHAY

I look at my watch for the fourth time in the past half hour, begging for time to speed up. There's so much I could be doing right now, rather than watching a bunch of overgrown barbarians on ice skates dash around after a tiny puck.

Even if they are a bunch of gorgeous, overgrown barbarians with nice asses . . .

It's a brutal game, and even in the short time I've been here, it seems like someone is always getting hurt. Why would anyone *willingly* play something so dangerous when there are so many more civilized sports like golf, or track, or . . . I don't know, egg throwing?

Sighing, I rummage for my phone inside my purse. I might as well make my weekly grocery list while I have the time.

My hand wraps around the thick G-spot wand I carry in my purse, brushing over the indentation before I find my phone and pull it out.

I have a collection of such toys nestled in the back of my nightstand drawer, but this purse-sized one always stays with me. It's a little overused and has seen better days, but it's reliable, effective, and practical. What more could I ask for?

"Chicken," I mumble, typing into my text app. "Flaxseed, Ezekiel bread, quinoa–"

I'm jostled, almost losing my grip on my phone, when my son Kai and the man–or rather, *manchild*–Beckett Langfield fist bump each other across my body.

"Did you see him score, Bossman?" my nine-year-old yells over the din of the crowd, using the nickname all the kids call Beckett. He's such a quiet kid in general, so I'm always a little taken aback whenever I hear his voice teeter over its normal soft volume. "Rowan 'Slick' Parker is going to be the greatest defenseman of all time. I just know it! That play was *ducking* fantastic!"

"Language." I eye my son before scowling at Beckett. Kai may not have *actually* cursed, but I know he meant to. He *thought* about it. Another teaching my best friend, Liv's, gazillionaire husband has so graciously bestowed upon my son.

I hear an 'oof' slide out of Beckett's mouth, indicating my best friend has likely elbowed him in the ribs from his other side. He pointedly looks at my son and repeats, "Yeah. Language, IceMan." He uses the nickname he gave my son when he moved into the Boston brownstone with me and my best friends, and Kai smiles.

I shake my head, tucking the long side of my asymmetrical bob behind my ear before going back to my phone, ignoring the chatter between my best friends and their kids. We're all standing in Beckett Langfield's private owner box at the arena, watching the Bolts play a preseason game. Well, technically, his brother owns the team, but tomatoes, to-mah-tos.

"Now, what else did I need to add to this list?" I mutter to myself, looking down at my list.

It's wild to think that only nine months ago, me and Kai

were adjusting to our lives without Ajay–from a family of three to a permanent family of two–and now, we're living with not one, but thirteen other people in the same house. My best friends–all single moms, like me, and women I couldn't survive without–their kids, and more recently, Beckett and Cortney. Cortney is my other best friend, Dylan's, fiancé, who also happens to be the catcher for the Boston Revs.

Many people might call us crazy for taking a part in what seems like an outlandish social experiment, but one of the best decisions I ever made was during our last girls' trip when we all resolved to move into Delia's enormous, but dilapidated, brownstone in Boston and do what we always planned to do ever since college–raise our kids together.

Men were never a part of the original pact, but since Liv actually fell in love with her then fake-husband, Beckett, and Dylan fell for her baby-daddy-to-be Cortney, we've just added to our brood.

It's been one wild and crazy ride over the past few months– a far cry from my and Kai's quiet, albeit lonely, life in Califor- nia–but I can't say I've ever had as much fun.

"Asparagus and kale." I twist my lips as I type into my phone.

I have no interest in ice hockey, or *any* contact sport for that matter. I'd much rather be sitting at home, reading a book or researching the negative effects of high fructose corn syrup. But since Beckett promised to take Kai to the Boston Bolts's game as a gift for his ninth birthday, and insisted we all make a night of it, I'm stuck in this overfilled arena, with obnoxious and drunk fans–who all look like they might have been on their way to a frat party but mistakenly ended up at a sporting event.

If it wasn't for the fact that it was Kai's birthday present, we would never be here. He and his dad may have watched the

Bolts religiously on TV, but I have no interest in condoning such a dangerous sport to my son.

He could break a bone, or worse . . .

And though he's been relentless in begging me–with his soft voice and those downturned, puppy-dog eyes, reminiscent of my late husband's–to let him learn hockey, I've been adamant about not giving in.

Though, I *did* give in to that large Slushie in his hands, full of all sorts of terrible sugars, artificial food coloring, and who the hell knows what else. I wouldn't have, but the kid used those puppy-dog eyes to Jedi mind trick me into breaking my resolve.

I let it go just this once, but I'll have to detox his body of all that nastiness with wholesome, healthier foods all week.

Come to think of it, I should add sardines, liver, and Brussel sprouts to my list.

I turn to look at Dylan behind me. She mindlessly smooths a hand over her pregnant belly before taking a bite of what I can only assume is a hotdog.

My nose wrinkles. "Dyl, do you know how many nitrates that hot dog contains? It's emulsified meat glued together with all sorts of disgusting chemicals."

Dylan's eyes glitter in my direction, speaking around her mouthful. "The universe told me to give the baby what she wants. And what she wants are nitrates!"

I roll my eyes, adding another essential item to my list. This one specifically for Dylan's detox. "I'm going to make you that oatmeal, turnip, and turmeric smoothie again. I know how much you loved it last time."

Dylan responds with something that sounds strangely like, " . . . loved it about as much as I love eating compost," but the sound of the buzzer and the crowd going absolutely berserk drowns out some of her words.

The Bolts have scored another goal, and while the players glide effortlessly over the ice, my gaze snags on the defenseman with the number sixteen and the name Parker written on his jersey. Even from where I stand, it's clear he towers over the players, both in height and presence.

I'd seen images of him on TV, since both my late husband and our son were crazy about him, but seeing him in real life today . . . he's like a gravitational force all on his own.

The man is well over six feet, with dark hair and golden, sun-kissed skin, despite the fact that he likely sees more ice than the sun most days. And from my *incredibly unreliable* recollection of his screen image, that skin is complemented with a golden-green gaze, thick eyelashes and brows, and plump, smooth lips that may have had me involuntarily licking my own.

But again, that was from my incredibly unreliable recollection.

My eyes trail him like slutty jersey chasers, watching his swift movements and complete focus. There's an assurance and decisiveness in the way he moves, guiding the puck with the precision of a surgeon, making me wonder if he applies the same sureness and control to everything else he does with those large hands . . . and that sculpted body.

And thinking about what he might do with his hands off the rink has me swiping my bottom lip with my tongue and clearing my throat unnecessarily. Annoyingly, I catch Beckett's eyes and his stupid knowing smile peering my way.

I don't know what that smug grin on his gazillionaire face is all about, but if he doesn't drop it, I'm going to smack it right off him. I quickly drop my eyes to my phone, wishing my short hair could hide my burning ears.

I just need to get laid again.

It's the only reason I was gawking at a man almost a

decade younger than me, and envisioning what his *stick* would feel like between my–

"Holy shh!"

"Oh, no!"

A collective gasp shifts the entire atmosphere in the arena and has me lifting my head to see what I missed.

I get up on my toes to get a better glimpse, catching Beckett swearing under his breath. "Duck! That doesn't look good."

"What happened?" I ask, my brows furrowed as I watch Rowan Parker shuffle to stand back up on the ice. He's limping on his skates, clearly not putting pressure on one leg as he walks over to the bench, but it's hard to tell how hurt he is.

"Something happened when he shot to make the goal, and he fell," Kai answers. "Didn't you see it, Mom?"

I shake my head in answer as Beckett fills in more details. "He lost his balance somehow when he swung, but my worry is, he fu–" Beckett catches himself, knowing all the kids are hanging on to his words, "ducked up his leg."

He takes his phone out and calls someone, likely his brother or the physician. "Hey, what's happening? How badly hurt is he?"

Liv and I exchange a concerned glance before I peer at Kai next to me, his previously bright eyes now veiled with worry. I place my hand on his dark hair, scratching the back of his head. "He's going to be okay, sweetheart. Don't wor–"

"I'm bringing my wife's best friend over to him now," Beckett states on the phone, cutting off my words and getting a glare from me. I really hope he's not talking about me. "Her name is Shayla Kumar, and she's a physical therapist. We'll have her assess him."

"Wha–" I say with a start.

What the hell is he talking about? Has he lost his mind?

Why the hell is he volunteering me? Doesn't the NHL have their own doctors and athletic trainers?

"She'll be there in a minute," he decides, hanging up the phone.

"Beckett . . ." Liv says, seeming just as confused. "What the heck are you doing?"

"I just talked to the team's physician. He's still stitching up Sanders, and the head trainer and athletic trainers are with other players. They could use someone to help take a look at Parker."

Beckett turns to me and I swear, if I didn't know better, I'd say there's a glint in his eyes. *A fucking glint!* What is this guy up to?

I shake my head vigorously. "I'm a physical therapist, not a physician or an orthopedist. If he's hurt, he'll need to get looked at by–"

"And he will," Beckett cuts in. "But right now, for the sake of the team, the physician could use another pair of hands."

I put my hands on my hips, recalling the all too observant smile he gave me earlier when he caught me ogling the muscle-bound stallion in skates. "Is that what the physician told you? That he *needs* another pair of hands? Because that seems highly unlikely, not to mention something that could get me into legal trouble." I look down at Kai to ensure he isn't paying attention, before I continue in a hushed tone, "Or is this another one of your ploys?"

Beckett reels back. "Ploys for what?"

"To get me to date one of the guys on your team again?" He's been trying to set me up with random people in his network for the past few weeks, and I've been thwarting all his efforts.

I don't have the time or energy to date. Not when I have

goals and *responsibilities*. Like raising my son, running my business, and growing old with my best friends. I don't need more.

Beckett gapes at me animatedly. "I would *never* take advantage of a situation as serious as this to find you a suitable man. That you could even *think* I was capable of such low-handed tactics, only so I could get you hitched and out of the ridiculous pact you and your best friends, including my beautiful wife, made is *beyond* hurtful."

He groans when Liv elbows him again, and my squint gets squintier. "You're a lying piece of–"

"Language," he interrupts me before I can finish, gesturing toward the exit. "Come on. I'll take you there myself. And as for legal repercussions, need I remind you my family owns the team?"

I take a breath before looking at Liv to see if she'll come to my defense. Instead, she shrugs, covering the side of her mouth to stage-whisper to me, "I mean, there are worse things than having to examine the man who's said to melt the ice just by being on it."

Five minutes later, and after letting Kai know I'll be back shortly, I'm standing outside the team's locker room, adjusting the strap of my purse unnecessarily over my shoulder. I don't know what Beckett said to everyone when he went inside ahead of me, but a minute later, everyone has shuffled out, except for the defensemen I'm here to see.

Beckett swings his head in the direction of the entrance, giving me the signal to go inside.

"Wait." I furrow my brows. "You aren't staying?"

He shakes his head. "I've gotta check on Liv and the kids. You've got this."

I give him another knowing look before he takes off with a barely suppressed smile. The man always has something up his sleeve.

Clearing my throat, I place my mask of professionalism on before stepping into the locker room. Truth be told, the mask no longer feels like one. The only people I let my hair down around are my best friends, but even they call me the "ball of nevers" for a reason. Because I tend to say no first, and then perhaps come around to saying yes, but only if I'm compelled to do so.

Sure, I've shown that silly side to my son when we're having pillow fights or when I'm tickling him to get him to laugh, but otherwise, the fun-loving, carefree girl I used to be stays buried—and that's exactly where she ought to be.

To the rest of the world, I'm a bit on the rigid side. Some may even call me anal, bordering on obsessive. While I wouldn't say I'm ritualistic, I *am* regimented.

I try to eat only healthy, organic food, limiting my intake of anything processed. I'll have a glass or two of organic wine occasionally—*and one other little vice I refuse to acknowledge at this moment*—but I consider that a reward for being "good" throughout the week. I try to sleep at least seven hours a night, workout at least five times a week, and get all my annual exams done on time.

Because sometimes a missed annual exam can mean the difference between life or death.

I wasn't always a "ball of nevers".

My best friends know that better than anyone else. I was

the crazy one of our group in college–staying out until the sun came up, drinking until Delia could wiggle the cocktail glass from my grasp. I was the girl who rolled into physics wearing pajama bottoms and a sweatshirt, smelling like last night's bad decisions and minty toothpaste.

It all changed after I met my late husband, Ajay. And though I still miss his presence in my and my son's life, I've finally come to accept his loss after three years. I've also come to accept that our marriage was far from perfect, and that somewhere in the middle of it all, I became less of the person I used to be and more of the person *he* wanted me to be. Some-where in the middle of it all, I forgot how to have fun.

But despite the fact that I've come as far as I have through therapy and the support of my best friends, neither they nor Beckett Langfield can convince me to take a leap for love again.

Not after what I endured right along with Ajay. Not after the way I watched him lose his battle with the C-word I've sworn to eliminate from my vocabulary. Not when I know the universe doesn't give second chances, despite what my astro-logically-inclined best friend Dylan believes.

That's not to say I haven't had a casual hook-up here or there.

I don't use the Tinder app on my phone often, but when the *need* arises and all I want is to feel a stranger between my legs for a night–instead of my collection of hand-operated toys, one of which is sitting in the safety of my purse right now–I haven't shied away from finding someone on there.

But emotion and attachment? Commitment and love? Those are words from my past that I don't plan to reinstate into my current dictionary. Not when my son needs me more than ever, not when he's my only reason and focus.

I take another step forward when my eyes fall on a stretch of sun-kissed skin. The sinewy muscles in his bare back flex and strain like they're both uncomfortable and content at the same time. He keeps his tattooed forearm above his head, leaning on it while keeping the weight off his injured leg.

Noting a glint of silver from his necklace, my eyes caress his broad back once more before trailing down to his tapered waist. Have I ever seen a more beautiful ass on a man? I honestly can't recall.

He's one hell of a prototype for physical human perfection. A colossus amongst ants. Sheer strength and beauty wrapped into one enormous form. And if my heart is galloping this fast from just ogling his back, then I might be in danger of heart failure when he turns around.

"You like what you see, Doc?"

The rumble of his voice hits me square in the ribs before my body jolts back to reality, as if his voice had an electrical charge. How did he know I was checking him out?

I'm not one to be flustered easily, but I'm finding myself at a loss for words. "Shit. Um . . ."

At my mumbled attempt to regain my composure, Rowan 'Slick' Parker turns around to study me with hooded eyes. A smug grin plays over his ridiculously plump lips while his eyes stay fixed on mine.

He holds up his phone, showing me that it's on camera mode. "Watched you walk in and check me out like you were fixin' to make me your next meal." His smile grows before he slicks his lips with his tongue. "And while I'm usually the one to do the *eating*, I'm not entirely against being offered up on a platter for you, Doc."

CHAPTER 2
ROWAN

Fuck, that hurt!

And where the hell did that sharp pain come from? One second, I'm in control of the puck, fucking dominating the game, despite the fact that we're short two of our best players, and the next, I'm face-planting on the ice.

Pain skyrocketed through my thigh, and I swear I saw stars. And they weren't the good kind, like before shooting my load while balls-deep inside some faceless girl; they were the shitty kind of stars that tell me I'm going to be out of the game if I don't fucking fix it.

Fuck!

I'm in the locker room with our assistant trainers and the team manager, waiting for the team's physician to get done stitching up Sanders when Beckett Langfield storms in. His family—specifically, his brother, Gavin—owns my team, the Bolts, while Beckett owns the Revs, one of the best baseball teams in the US.

"You okay, Slick?" He eyes my cautious stance as I lean

against the locker, leaving my weight on my uninjured leg. "What happened?"

Our assistant trainer hands me an ice pack and velcro strap, and I pull it around my thigh, placing the ice pack over where I can feel my thigh still burning. "Overextended swing, I think. Fucking felt like my thigh caught fire."

"Shit." Beckett runs a hand over his face, clearly worried about my injury. "Alright, well, I have someone who can help. She's my wife's best friend and a physical therapist. So, until you can see the physician, she might be able to help you out."

I give him a nod, wincing as the pain radiates all around my thigh. My phone vibrates on the bench, and I glance at it before picking it up, leaning against the locker with my forearm above my head.

I already know who the text is from. The man who never misses watching one of my games, but who also never misses the chance to tell me how royally I fucked something up, too.

No matter how many media reports claim I'm the best defenseman in the Eastern Conference, or how I'm the ticket to the Bolts winning the Stanley Cup this year, I'm always a fuck-up in my dad's eyes.

Why? Because Anthony Parker *was* the golden boy of ice hockey for almost a decade until he fucked up his knee and could no longer play.

DAD

> Work through the pain, son. I did it for years, and you can, too. Don't fucking leave your team hanging. The season's about to start so, man the fuck up.

My nostrils flare as I clench my phone in my fist. *Man the fuck up?* Is that what he did when he left my mom and me for his then-coach's twenty-year-old daughter? Is that what he did when he yelled in my face in front of my entire high school hockey team for losing our last game, telling me what a "fucking disgrace" I was?

Is that what he thinks *manning the fuck up* means?

I clench my jaw tight, opening up the camera on my phone to selfie-mode and wiping his text from my memory. I should block his number, but I'm a masochist. Or maybe I'm still just that kid under his dad's shadow, hoping one day I'll live up to his expectations.

Yeah, that's some Freudian shit I don't need a therapist to reveal to me.

I take a quick grinning picture of myself, like I always do before and after games, posting it for my fans on Instagram with a caption under it. It's what they want to see, so it's what I'll give them.

```
Hold up while I turn this pain into power.
Coming back stronger. #ComingfortheStanley
```

Beckett mutters something to the other two people in the locker room before they shuffle out. Not even a minute later, I hear footsteps inside the entrance.

My camera is already flipped to selfie-mode, so I position it to watch the short, fit woman hesitate inside the entrance. She's wearing a thin, cropped light blue sweater and tight denims, her pink phone case peeking out from her front pocket.

Her dark eyes study me, traveling the length of my back leisurely before she licks her lips. Her gaze snags on my ass and a smile lifts the corners of my mouth.

Well, this is interesting.

I've never had problems getting attention from the opposite sex. I'll admit, it comes easier when you have the attention of millions of fans, a ridiculously hefty contract, and are in top physical form, but I'm also not out looking for it.

Sure, I've hooked up with a few puck bunnies over the years, but no one's ever taken my focus for more than a night. I keep things temporary and transactional–that's just how I like to work . . . or rather, *play*. Taking my eye off the puck for longer than that isn't an option.

Because I don't make the same mistake twice.

The woman, who still hasn't moved, continues to watch me from her spot at the entrance. She's an adorable little thing, pocket-sized in comparison to my six-foot-three build, but there's nothing slight or inconsequential about the way she holds herself. She radiates confidence, sophistication, and–if I'm not mistaken by the glint in her eyes–fire.

I'm an intimidating man, in spite of the grin I'm always sporting, but I have a feeling she's not one to cower.

She tucks the longer strands of her hair behind one ear, a large gold hoop dangling from the lobe, and I notice the ink on the inside of her wrist, though I can't tell what it is.

I also notice the lack of a wedding ring.

"You like what you see, Doc?"

She freezes, her eyes becoming huge saucers, and even though her skin color is a deep brown, I imagine her cheeks are burning.

She fumbles for a response, finally blinking out of her stupor. "Shit. Um . . ."

She shifts from one foot to another before I gingerly turn around, leaning my shoulder blades on the wall behind me and holding up my phone to show her how I caught her. "Watched you walk in and check me out like you were fixin' to make me your next meal."

A soft gasp leaves her lips and a confident hum runs through me, like I just caught the cat pouncing on the canary.

I run my tongue over my bottom lip, satisfied with the way she watches the movement. "And while I'm usually the one to do the *eating*, I'm not entirely against being offered up on a platter for you, Doc."

She seems to regain her composure, straightening her back, before her eyes sharpen on me, clearly not loving my directness. "Mr. Parker, I'm sure you're used to women–*puck bunnies*, I believe you call them?—kneeling at your feet, but I assure you, that won't be the case with me."

My smile widens as a vision of her doing exactly what she claims she won't, plays in front of me. "We'll see."

She clears her throat, clutching her purse a little tighter to her side, as if it's threatening to run away from her. "I was told you were hurt and in need of someone to look at your–" she looks down to the way I'm standing, "leg, which is why I'm here. My name is Shayla Kumar, and I'm a physical therapist. Now, if you're done using up the space inside this room with your overinflated ego, I'd like to begin my assessment. Are you ready for me, or do you need more time to get over yourself?"

A soft, rumbling laugh flutters in my chest. I like this girl's sass. In a world where most women only want my time, my fame, or my money, this woman doesn't seem to give a shit about any of it, nor does she give a shit about putting me in my place. "Not sure if I'm ready for *you*, Doc, but I do think I'm ready for you to examine me."

She keeps her expression neutral, stepping forward and not remarking on whether she caught my innuendo.

After asking me a few things about my physical history and pain level, she has me stand on both my feet. I gingerly do so while she makes her visual assessments. I wince when she asks me to squat, because yeah, that hurts like a motherfucker.

Her slender throat bobs as she swallows. "I'm going to need to see where the strain is exactly, so would you mind undressing?" And before I can do as she asked, she jumps to clarify. "Uh, only down to your underpants, please."

My brows rise and my smirk follows. "My *underpants*?"

Shayla sucks in her cheeks, her blush evident. "What I mean is, please just take off the rest of your hockey gear, aside from your underwear, and lay on the bench."

She turns around while I do as she asks, though I take off the uncomfortable boxers I'm wearing with the jock built in, and put on a pair of gym shorts from my locker. I move slowly to avoid another shot of pain traveling up my leg. Then, placing both my palms on a nearby bench, I scoot onto it before laying down, wincing when pain thrums through my leg.

Shayla drops her bag onto another bench before shuffling closer, but right as she does, we both hear a vibrating sound coming from inside her purse.

Her eyes flick to it before they find mine, and I swear the tops of her deep brown cheeks turn pink.

I risk a glance at her pocket, where her phone is tucked in, before my brows fold. Maybe she has another phone inside her purse for work? "Do you need to get that?"

She scurries to her purse, opening it and fiddling with something inside, but the mortification on her face worsens. A frown pulls on her mouth, and I hear clicking noises, as if she's pressing something to turn it off, but the sound only increases to a long, pulsing buzz.

"Shit."

She continues to jostle the contents inside her purse for a few more seconds before she gives up with a huff and shoves it back on the bench while the vibration continues.

The corner of my mouth lifts. Who is this woman, and why the fuck do I find her so intriguing? Nothing about her comes off as comedic, but just watching her over the past few minutes–from the way she got caught ogling me, to the way she's now glaring at her purse with disdain, as if it's her new enemy–has me silently chuckling.

"Do you . . ." I try to wipe the smile from my face, tilting my head once more in the direction of her purse. "Do you need help with that?"

"No," she says curtly, but it only has me chuckling more. "It's fine. Now, I'm going to need you to extend your injured leg."

I do as she asks while she watches my face contort as the muscles in my thigh contract.

"I'd like to examine you using my hands. Is that okay?" She tucks her short hair behind her ear again, avoiding my eyes.

Oh, she's making this way too easy.

"It's more than okay, Doc. In fact, I think I might like that very much." I smirk at her with intention, loving the way she tenses.

By now, I think I've figured out the source of the incessant vibration. And based on the humiliation that seemed to take over her otherwise confident persona, I'd bet I'm right.

My eyes rake down her body from head to toe before she bends over me, my eyes snagging on the sliver of skin between her jeans and sweater. She's fucking exquisite. From the way her waist cinches, to that firm ass I got an eyeful of when she bent over her purse, I can tell she doesn't shy away from the gym.

I smile bigger, noting the increased pulse on the side of her slender neck before catching a glimpse of tiny stars tattooed right behind her earlobe, almost blocked by her large golden hoop.

I've never been one to note these things on women–hair, jewelry, or ink–but it seems my brain has decided everything about this woman is noteworthy.

Except, I can't understand why.

I decide to goad her a little more. It's too fun. "So, just your hands or . . .?" My lips twitch when she stiffens. "Are there any *tools* inside that vibrating purse of yours you want to use to help relieve the . . . pressure?"

Shay's eyes snap to mine, and I'd bet she's positively sweltering under that sweater. "I don't know what you're talking about, Mr. Parker, but I'd appreciate if you'd let me conduct my assessment."

I smile, knowing we both know exactly what's in her purse, and damn if that doesn't make my cock perk up. The vision of her using it, touching herself . . .

"Conduct away, Doc."

Her slender hands wrap around my thigh, and despite the fact that I'm in pain, a shudder rolls down my spine and my cock thickens inside my shorts. And when she presses her fingers into a few tender muscles on the inside of my thigh, I have to clench my jaw to refrain from releasing a groan.

Think about something else.

My fourth grade teacher, old Mrs. Merdock, wearing a bikini.

Coach's balls when he comes out of the shower.

Yup, that did the trick. My dick feels nice and un-bonery now.

"Have you ever injured your groin before?"

Well, that was a short-lived reprieve.

Dick's springing back up again, seeming to like the word *groin* on her lips. There should be nothing, and I mean *nothing*, about her question that should make me hard, but tell that to the metal rod inside my shorts.

I eye her with amusement, hoping to send signals to my erection to chill the fuck out, but it's no use. Not when the vision of her using that buzzing tool in her purse on herself fans at the edges of my fantasies. "If you're asking if I've ever broken my dick, then I can assure you, I haven't."

She rolls her eyes, purposefully shoving her fingers into my muscles and making me grunt. I get the feeling that was purely for her benefit.

"You clearly haven't been with the right woman, then," she mumbles almost inaudibly.

I lift my brows. Say what now? *Did she just imply that the right woman would break my dick?*

"What was that?"

Jesus Christ. Should I want her hands on me, knowing her weird ass fetish, or should I be making a run for it, regardless of my current groin situation?

She shakes her head before speaking more clearly, "What I meant was, have you hurt your adductor muscle before?"

I smirk, wondering if I'm out of my mind for feeling aroused by the direction of this conversation. "Is that what you meant? Because I could have sworn you were talking–*thinking*, perhaps–about my well-functioning dick."

Shayla digs her fingers into my thigh hard, and I practically growl from the pain, but a laugh tumbles out of me just the same. I'm happy to see I finally get a smile out of her, too.

I decide to answer her earlier question. "My muscles have been a little tight over the past few days, but I've never hurt it this badly before."

She asks me to bend both my legs at my knees, and I try to do so with a slight wince, when Shayla's hands catch my leg– one on my thigh and the other on my shin–to guide it up. They're soft but sure, and despite the fact that they look delicate, they're surprisingly strong.

She puts a fist in between my knees and asks me to press against it, noting the way my thigh trembles. When she helps me lower my leg again, her pinky grazes the boner that refuses to disappear–despite her insinuation that she could break my dick–making me take in a quick breath.

Shayla's eyes widen for a second, and she pulls her hand from my thigh like she's touched hot coals. "Sorry, I . . . uh . . ." She clears her throat. "It looks like you have an adductor strain, though I recommend getting an MRI to be sure. But, as long as you haven't torn a muscle, which doesn't seem to be the case from my observation, you'll need four to five weeks of physical therapy and rest."

I stare at her for a moment, processing her words and trying to forget about my boner. I knew I'd be out for one game, but I hadn't expected that long. "I don't have four to five weeks to rest, Doc. The season is about to start, and I can't miss any of those games. *We* can't afford for me to miss any of those games. That fucking Cup is going to be ours this year."

Shayla stands before holding my elbow to help me into a sitting position. And though I'm perfectly capable of doing it on my own, I don't mind having her hands on me a little longer.

She scoots back, putting a bit of space between us, before picking up her vibrating purse. "I understand that, but that is the risk you run with dangerous sports. Your body will need time to heal. I would suggest one week completely off the ice, and then your physical therapist can help you get all your movement back and strengthen those muscles by designing a plan that works for you."

"Isn't that what you are? My physical therapist?"

Her eyes narrow. "No, I'm just here as a favor to Beckett Langfield and happen to be a physical therapist, but–"

"Well, I'd like you to be my physical therapist." I voice the request before I've even had a chance to think about it.

"That's . . ." Shayla shakes her head. "That's not really how it works."

"Why?"

She takes an exasperated breath, as if I've asked her why two plus two is four. "It . . . it just doesn't, Mr. Parker. You'll have to find someone else. I'm sure your team has some physical therapists who could help you."

I rise to my feet, fumbling slightly as I take a step toward her and she takes a step back. "I don't give a shit. I'd like *you* to help me."

"I . . . I can't."

I add in a sweetener to help her come up with a better answer, but for the life of me, I'm not really sure why I'm even insisting that she give me the answer I want. "I'm willing to pay you whatever you ask for. Fuck that, I'll pay you your yearly salary for each session."

A gasp leaves her lips, her head reeling back in confusion. "Mr. Parker–"

"Call me Rowan." I give her another smug grin, knowing she's considering my offer.

"Okay. Rowan, that isn't a good idea."

"Why?" I ask again.

"I have a full list of clients and–"

"Transfer them to another therapist."

She scoffs, "Mr. Parker–"

"Rowan."

Another audible breath. "Rowan. That's not how I conduct my business, and that's hardly your decision to make."

Her eyes trail up and over my chest, taking in the little divot at the bottom of my neck, flaring when they drop to my pecs. For the second time today, I find her studying me like I'm something to be cataloged and dissected. And in spite of her words, I know she's attracted to me.

A frown pulls her lips as she finds my knowing smirk

before she looks away. She hates that she can feel whatever this pull is, too.

I risk another step forward. "I'd hate for you to be the reason the Bolts lose their chance to win the Cup this year."

She wraps her arms around her chest, giving me a condescending look, despite the fact that her purse is still buzzing. "That's a little presumptuous, don't you think?"

"It's not presumptuous when it's factual."

"How very humble of you." *Fuck, I love that sass.*

My eyes lock onto hers, and I take another step toward her. Her arms drop as her back meets the locker behind her, and my chest widens, taking up the little space between us. "Aside from not having a humble *bone* in my body, Doc," I enunciate the significant word, placing one hand next to her head, "I'm also a persistent and decisive motherfucker. And what I've decided is that you're the only one I want."

"Mr. Parker—"

I trail my finger over her purse before dropping it to the top of her phone in her pocket, making her stiffen. "Oh, and Doc? We both know *exactly* what's vibrating inside your purse." A smile stretches across my face. "Feel free to bring your toys to our sessions . . . we'll get good use out of them."

CHAPTER 3
SHAY

"I honestly don't understand how you keep getting into these situations because of your vibrators," Delia wonders with dismay, taking a sip of what is probably her second cup of coffee this morning, and it's only half past seven. "First, at the airport, when you were on your way to our girls' trip, and then last night at the game with none other than Rowan Parker."

"I think the universe is telling you it's time you find a man." Dylan joins in, putting a couple of cherries into her mouth, which I'm happy to see after the unnatural garbage she consumed at the game last night.

Liv giggles, shutting the fridge door after getting some creamer out for her coffee. "Did you guys hear that he asked her to bring her toys with her to use during their 'therapy' sessions?"

I roll my eyes at the way she makes quotes around the word. "Firstly," I point at Dylan, "the universe has the wrong girl, because I'm not looking for a man. Secondly," this time I look at Liv, "he can ask whatever he wants; there still won't be any therapy sessions."

I pour two glasses of the spinach and sea moss smoothie I blended for me and Kai into our cups and lift the blender jug as an offering to my besties. It still has enough for another cup. "Any takers? It's super yummy and packed with all sorts of vitamins and–"

"That looks worse than the swamp sludge you've made before," Delia says, stepping away from the kitchen counter like I've just offered her a blended alien, and not a nutritious breakfast alternative. "I'll pass."

When my eyes land on Liv, she takes a healthy sip of her coffee. "I'm good."

Dylan just lifts her bowl of cherries, the stacked rings on her middle finger glittering. "I've got all the healthiness I can handle right here, but Cortney might want it. He'll be up here in a minute."

I take a sip from my glass, making a humming sound. "Seriously, you guys have no idea what you're missing."

"I'm sure," Delia deadpans, getting a squinty-eyed glare from me.

"So, why won't you treat Rowan for his," Liv can't help but snicker, "penis injury?"

"Not that I give a shit about men or their penises–given I had my girls without the help of either," Delia proclaims pointedly, indicating her demon, ahem, *high functioning*, twin girls, who will likely cause a nuclear missile crisis one day. "But I'll begrudgingly admit that this particular penis could potentially spawn humans of near-perfect physique and, therefore, should be saved."

Ladies and gentlemen, I give you Cordelia Masters, my no-nonsense, *get-to-the-point-or-get-the-fuck-out* best friend.

I huff. "This is not about his penis. I just–"

"Not about whose penis?" Beckett asks, entering the kitchen. He gives Liv a hurt expression. "Livy, I know I suggested we get some rest after the fourth time I took you last night, but you know my dick is perfectly–"

"Ew! I'm going to stop you right there, man-eating-billionaire," Delia screeches. "No one needs to know about your erectile dysfunction."

"Listen, Medusa," Beckett starts, referring to the name he's given Delia. "You–"

"Beckett." Liv raises a brow, giving her husband the look that tells him to rethink what he's about to say or he may *actually* get erectile dysfunction tonight. Liv looks at me with an exasperated expression before taking a breath. "Now, what were you saying about that therapy you were going to start with Rowan?"

"I wasn't–"

"Well, that's great to hear," Beckett interrupts, not letting me continue. "Gavin messaged me last night to ask if you could officially take over Rowan's physical therapy." He refers to his brother, and the owner of the team, before raising a curious brow in my direction. "Apparently, Rowan's agent called him. Seems Rowan really liked your style."

"That's cool," Cortney says, coming into the kitchen and placing a kiss on Dylan's temple. Dylan hands him the extra glass of smoothie, and he takes a sip, nodding to himself. I give Dylan a smug smile, to which she rolls her eyes. *Hmph!* At least someone appreciates nutrition around here. "So, you'll be taking over Rowan's PT?"

"The universe certainly believes she should–" Dylan starts.

"Guys!" I yell. "Why aren't you hearing me? I'm not going to be Rowan Parker's physical therapist. I've already rejected his offer."

"Good! You don't need him or his stupid offer," Delia chimes in with a huff. "Men. They always assume they're doing you a favor."

"Why would you refuse to work with him after he gave you such a great offer?" Liv asks, giving me a confused look and ignoring Delia's comment. "Shay, do you not realize how that money could set you and Kai up?"

"There's been this soft lavender aura around you since last night. I can tell something incredible is about to happen in your life," Dyl adds matter-of-factly, rolling the rose quartz around her neck in her fingers.

"Mom?"

All of us turn toward the soft word, spoken from none other than my son, who is standing at the foot of the stairs. He's dressed and ready for school. And though he's home-schooled, provided by his aunty Dylan—because I'm too scared to send him to a public school where he could get hurt on a playground—he still sets his alarm and gets ready as if he's going to regular school.

Kai searches my face, and I know he heard more of that conversation than I wanted.

"Hey, sweetheart. I have your favorite sea monster smoothie ready for you," I say, referring to the tall glass of green liquid and the name he recently gave it.

Kai brushes off my words. "Rowan Parker wants you to be his physical therapist, and you said no?"

My friends shift out of the kitchen, all finding other places to go so Kai and I can have a moment alone. They've all come to realize how reserved and shy he is. It's not often that he displays his feelings so openly, so I suspect they're giving us the time to talk privately.

Taking his hands in mine, I bend to meet Kai's eyes. "Honey, I'm already busy enough with the clients I have.

Treating Rowan would be a lot more than I can manage. I would need to go to his place downtown, sit in all that traffic . . . It would be too–"

"Please, Mom." Kai's downturned eyes, so much like his father's, fill with tears. "The Bolts are top of the division! They could totally get a spot in the playoffs, but they need Rowan. And if he's asking you to help him, then that means you're the best of the best. Just like he's the best of the best. You have to help him, Mom. You *have* to."

My heart sinks, and I know that, regardless of how I feel, I can't let the sweetest kid in the entire fucking world–who also happens to be my son–down. Rowan 'Slick' Parker isn't just a hockey player to my son; he's a god amongst men.

It's been so hard for him without Ajay. I know how much he still misses watching hockey with his dad–things I haven't been able to replace–and with the Bolts being his favorite team, I know how heartbroken he'll be if I say no to helping his favorite player.

"Fine," I sigh, "but you can't beg me to take you over to his place, Kai. Rowan would be my patient, not a friend, so don't beg to see him or–"

Kai's arms wrap around my neck, pulling me to him before I can even finish. His little face nestles into my neck. "Thank you, Mom. I promise, I won't beg to see him, but could you at least get my jersey signed?"

I wrap my arms around my boy, running a hand through the back of his thick, black hair. "I'll think about it. Now, how about we get some sea monster juice you love so much?"

Kai groans, "Fine."

I settle next to him at our green kitchen bar, handing him his smoothie and Ezekiel toast.

The kitchen is relatively usable, minus the fact that sometimes we don't get hot water on tap and some of the cabinet doors are missing. It also has these ugly yellow floors, but I take comfort in the fact that at least we have mostly functioning appliances.

Delia inherited this ramshackle place from her great-aunt not too long ago. And given the fact that she's thrown out or sassed practically every contractor who's had the balls to even come within a few feet of it, I'm just happy we've made the situation work. To be fair, a couple of them *did* leave us in the lurch on their own, so it's been tricky all around.

But because of all that, we still don't have drywall up in a few places, the floorboards are in need of replacement, and our plumbing problems rival that of a sinking ship.

It's a miracle we're all still living here–*or living at all*–and haven't torn each other's hair out or gotten, I don't know, asbestos poisoning!

I say the last statement in jest because, for the amount of grief we give her about her impossible standards on the house repair work, Delia would never put any of us in harm's way by insisting we live in an unsafe environment.

Though, did I mention we have raccoons in the chimney? Ah, yes, Junior and her three babies, Newton, Shadow, and Slick. Our kids banded together to come up with their names when our previously, thought of as male raccoon turned out to be a female, who gave birth to her babies in our chimney not long ago, and we were told by our local wildlife control center that we couldn't remove them for six months.

Any guesses as to who came up with the name Slick?

Kai kicks his feet on the barstool, slowly eating his toast. "Mom?"

"Hmm?"

"Liam said ice skating lessons are starting next Monday . .

." He refers to Dylan's teenage son, who Kai looks up to like a brother. "Is there any way you'll let me take them?"

I place my glass on the counter and turn toward him. "Sweetheart, we've talked about this. Ice skating isn't a safe sport. People injure themselves all the time on the ice, not to mention those blades on their feet are sharp. In group classes like that, there are always too many people who aren't paying attention. What if someone skates over your hand on the ice after you've fallen?" Just the thought of something terrible happening to my little boy has my stomach flipping over. "What if–"

"It's okay, Mom." Kai's shoulders sink and he goes back to his toast. "I get it . . ." He nods slowly, his eyes focused on his toast. "No sports."

My eyes connect with Dylan's across the room, and I know she heard most of that conversation. With her homeschooling Kai, she's gotten to know him well and has been urging me to let him explore the things he's made several mentions of– particularly, skating and hockey–but I've been fighting it.

But something cracks inside me, seeing the look on his sullen face. This is not what Ajay would have wanted for him. He would have wanted his son to live, learn . . . thrive.

I'm just about to suggest that maybe I can find him a private skating instructor when there's a loud knock on the door that draws all our attention.

Finn, Liv's five-year-old son, rushes toward the sound with his Nerf gun, his purple tutu bouncing, ready to open fire on anyone on the other side.

"Finn! Come back here!" Liv yells after him. "What have I told you about opening doors for strangers?"

"To open it only when I have a gun in my hand!"

He's almost at the door when Cortney catches him around

his middle, picking him up so Finn's feet swing in the air, trying to kick at him. "Pretty sure your mom would never say that."

He puts Finn down, opening the door to a delivery man. He's just finished signing for whatever has been delivered when Finn blasts the poor man with a few Nerf balls, laughing hysterically.

We hear Cortney apologize to the bewildered-looking delivery guy before carrying a small box inside. He raises a brow in my direction. "It's for you."

I point to my chest. "For me?"

"There's a card with it," Cortney adds, handing me the box and the card.

"What's it say?" Delia asks, getting up from her spot in the living room.

I tentatively turn the thick black envelope in my hand, my eyes tracing my name in a surprisingly graceful script on the front.

Walking away from the kids with my best friends in tow, I read the card stuffed inside, while Dylan, Liv, and Delia curiously peek over my shoulders. They have no concept of privacy, these three.

Liv giggles. "Oh, he's good. I hate to admit it, but you're screwed. Pun intended."

Delia gasps. "The nerve of this guy! He even put his address and number on the bottom. What a presumptuous A-hole!"

And Dylan gets an all too knowing smile on her face as if she predicted this.

I don't need to open the box to know exactly what's in it. And the initials of the gorgeous, albeit pompous, hockey player gives away who it's from. The note says everything to clue us all in.

Thought I'd get you a replacement for the tool you keep inside your purse since you seem to have broken the other one . . . perhaps from overuse?

Say yes.

Thought I'd get you a replacement for the tool you keep inside your purse since you seem to have broken the other one . . . perhaps from overuse?

CHAPTER 4
SHAY

"He's just another patient." I tell myself as I drive into the roundabout in front of the high-rise building Rowan Parker lives in a week later.

Broad men dressed in suits line the entrance of the building, along with the valets. They must be part of the security team for the celebrities who live here.

"He's like all my other patients." Just a tad more attractive, slightly taller, and well built. So what if he makes my vagina want to break out the party kazoos and confetti? I'm a mother and a professional, dammit! I refuse to be rattled by his finely-crafted ass and his plush, cushion-y lips.

I give my name and information to the valet before handing him my keys and heading up the short, white, marble stairs. My breaths feel caught inside my lungs as the doorman opens the enormous door, allowing me entrance into the modern lobby with a black-and-white checkerboard floor and opulent chandeliers.

My stomach does a somersault.

I've been inside a number of highrises back in San Francisco, but it's *why* and *for whom* I'm here that has my stomach feeling topsy-turvy.

Scrubbing my hands down the front of my pants unnecessarily, I give myself a moment of reprieve before I walk to the front desk to check in.

The brunette gives me a wide smile before handing me an envelope. "This is your permanent keycard to the private elevators around the corner, Ms. Kumar, and your keys to Mr. Parker's home. Feel free to come in and out of the building as you please. You no longer have to check in with us since you're on Mr. Parker's approved guest list."

I survey the black keycard and keys dubiously. Sure, I'm now Rowan Parker's official physical therapist, but having my own keys? That seems like something a celebrity hockey player would give to a friend, not someone he's only known for a few days, wouldn't it?

"Um, thank you?" I don't know why it comes out as a question, but the woman doesn't seem to mind.

I won't lie and say the enticing gift delivered to me last week didn't get my attention. The man obviously knows exactly what he's doing.

It could have been a simple bouquet of flowers or nothing at all, but a gift like *that*? He's not just determined, he's bold. Reckless.

All the things I haven't been in a long time.

All the things I told myself I'd never be again.

However inappropriate his gift might have been, it had me chuckling. Giggling like a kid on a sugar rush, actually.

Once in the privacy of my bedroom, a gasp slipped through my lips when I'd examined the contents inside the box. Because while I knew what I'd find in it, I had *no idea* it would be *a twenty-four carat, gold-plated G-spot vibrator!*

I'd set it on my bed, as if it were a newborn baby, before

staring at it like it was from another planet. Then, I'd promptly pulled out my laptop and searched for it online to find out how much it cost—because, *who wouldn't?*—and I swear, the price tag had my eyes bugging out of their sockets.

Fifteen thousand dollars?!

For a vibrator?!

In one small exchange—off an assumption he made as to the buzzing inside my purse that night—the cocky bastard had decided to woo me with an extravagant gift of the most lewd variety. I mean, talk about the balls on this guy! I didn't know if I should have felt offended or flattered.

But holy shit, a gold-plated vibrator?! Oh, how the filthy rich lived, stuffing fifteen grand into their hoo-has.

I've just pressed the button for the private elevator inside a smaller, more secluded lobby, when my phone vibrates inside the front of my pants.

Ajay used to ask me why I even carried a purse if I was always going to tuck my phone into my front pocket or hold it in my hand, but I like having easy access to it.

JEENA

Guess who broke his arm skateboarding today?

I didn't have many friends back in San Francisco—or none I felt close to—but Jeena was one even my guarded personality couldn't fend off. The woman knew exactly how to get me out of my shell and have me laughing until my stomach hurt.

I only met her a few years ago when my best friends and I decided to do a girls' weekend in Napa, and Jeena was our tour guide. She got about as drunk as we did, and before long, she was going into detail about her husband's 'potatoes'.

"They're large." She blinked at each of us for effect—to really

hone in the point—with a wineglass held in her hand, swaying a little. "The largest, meatiest, and juiciest."

We figured he was a farmer, and she was just enthusiastic about his recent potato harvest. It was only some time later that we found out the potatoes were actually a euphemism for a part of his body she was rather fond of.

Needless to say, the girl was a hoot, and before long, Ajay and I started hanging out with her and her husband, Wayland. I never could look Wayland in the eyes, though, because well . . . *potatoes.*

And even though their oldest son, Wynn, was a couple of years younger than Kai—and a hell of a lot more rambunctious—our boys got along great.

And when Ajay died, and I had no one nearby, it was Jeena and her family who lifted me up and stood by me while I slowly picked up some of mine and Kai's broken pieces.

So, while I'm closest to my best friends Dylan, Liv, and Delia—because of the years we've known each other—there are things Jeena has gone through with me, like holding me while I hit rock bottom, that even my best friends haven't.

The elevator doors open, and I click the send button to fire off my text before I lose signal.

ME

My guess is either you or Wynn. It wouldn't be Wayland or Weston because, like his dad, Weston takes measured, careful steps. You and Wynn, however? Only the two of you are capable of getting yourselves into a cast.

I read her reply as I step out of the elevator and into another beautiful lobby in front of Rowan's front door.

JEENA

I'm mildly offended you would think that. But
I'll happily accept a sugary treat as an
apology.

Another text follows before I can type my reply.

JEENA

Never mind. Your form of sugar would be to
send me papayas or some other unsatisfying
healthy shit. Please refrain from sending me
any treats, unless they're made with a shitload
of high fructose corn syrup and processed
sugars.

I shake my head, smiling. The woman is a sugar fiend if I'd
ever met one, and no amount of me sneakily trying to change
that has been successful.

ME

Am I wrong?

JEENA

Well, no. It's Wynn.

ME

Is he okay?

Jeena's reply has me smiling bigger, even though I feel bad
for her little boy.

JEENA

Given he's currently trying to jump from one
couch to another, I'd say he's fine, physically.
What's happening inside that head of his is
another story entirely.

I don't even realize that the smile is still on my face when I
lift my finger to ring the bell. Before I've even pressed it, the

door flings open and the most gorgeous man, wearing nothing but his very form-fitting boxer-briefs, grins at me from the other side. His tattooed arms are splayed up, holding the doorframe.

My eyes drop to what can only be considered an anaconda–or another snake of the large, and perhaps, venomous variety–inside the front of his boxers. They stretch to their ultimate potential around his massive thighs before my gaze crawls up to take in the rest of his body.

It's obscene, really.

Pornographic, even.

A body like that–rippling with tight muscles, and his smooth, creamy skin with just the right smattering of hair so he looks like a man and not some hairless mutant–should not exist. It's carved so perfectly, it seems to ridicule other men for their scrawny limbs and lack of armpit hair.

"Glad you like what you see, Doc."

I'm snapped out of my daze when I meet his smiling, mischievous golden-green eyes. "Mr. Parker, please put on some clothes. We won't be attending a nudist convention today."

If it's even possible, his grin widens. "Since you practically *begged* me to strip down to nothing last week, I figured I'd be an overachiever and do it before you asked this time."

"How very proactive of you, but I didn't beg."

"Oh, you most definitely begged. You said you wanted to use your hands and break my di–"

Before he can finish, I turn around to head back to the elevators, making my point crystal clear.

"Wait!" Rowan's large palm wraps around my forearm, and it's as if a live wire, buzzing with a heart-stopping current, has entrapped me. My entire body feels tingly from head to toe, making each hair stand on end.

With his brows pinched, Rowan stares at the spot where his skin touches mine, before he drops my wrist and brings his hands up in surrender. "Okay, I'll put some gym shorts on. Will you wait for me inside?"

I reluctantly nod before entering his penthouse.

My eyes bounce from the floor-to-ceiling windows in his living room, with the most incredible views of Boston Harbor, before traveling across the light teak wood floors, and the modern furniture in pops of orange and blue. I release a soft snort as I take in the high-end chef's kitchen, with the massive knife block and smaller appliances sitting on the beautiful marble countertops. Guarantee the man hasn't used half the tools he's got displayed here.

The penthouse is exactly where I'd expect a twenty-some-thing, uber-rich sportsman to be living. But, I'll give it to him, the bold pops of color all around are a surprising addition.

Rowan comes back, wearing his team's signature gym shorts and a white undershirt. I hadn't noticed the compression sleeve around his thigh earlier–probably because I was too busy focusing on his anaconda–or the slight limp to his gait.

Still, his clothing isn't an improvement over him being practically nude, since I can clearly make out the edges of his pecs and abs. And with the way the undershirt hugs his arms, it's like his biceps are purposely trying to be indecent.

"How are you feeling?" I gesture toward his thigh. "Have you been icing your thigh like we talked about?"

I spoke to his team doctor a few days ago and was sent over his medical records. Based on his recent MRI, I was glad to see it's only a strain and nothing major.

He nods. "Feeling pretty good, actually. It's a little tight in the mornings."

I glance back down at his thigh, admiring the sheer girth of it before I clear my throat and break my gaze from it. The man has a tenacity for catching me staring at him like he's a gluten-free, high-fiber protein bar I'd like to sink my teeth into.

My gaze lands on the wall behind me, with three large hand-painted pictures–a red sports car, a jet ski, and a pair of skates with a hockey stick. Under the paintings is a large display of trophies and his old jersey from when he played for the New York Mayors.

"Can I get you something to drink?"

For no reason at all–other than the fact that his voice hits me somewhere inside my stomach–I jump, turning around to face him again. "Um, water. Thank you."

When he goes to the fridge to get me a bottle of water, I point at the paintings on the wall. "Are you a speed demon off the ice, too?"

He hands me the bottle before putting his hands in his pockets. "I would have asked the artist who did those to paint me a motorcycle, too, but *technically,* I'm not supposed to be riding those."

I take a swig of water, interpreting his answer to mean yes. "Why do I get the feeling that *technicalities* don't seem to phase you, Mr. Parker?"

"Rowan," he reminds me. "And yeah, the technicalities that matter to me tend to stay on the ice." His eyes sharpen on me. "Otherwise, I firmly believe that rules are made to be broken."

I hold his gaze for a moment before I remember why I'm here. And then I remember the other reason I'm here–to return his *very gracious* gift.

I open my purse to get it out. My face feels hot as I hold it between us. "There are some rules I definitely won't break, and one of them is stretching the boundaries of our *professional* relationship, as doctor and patient," I clarify, in case he forgot. Hot, cocky men with anacondas as pets seem to do that. "So, as uh . . . *thoughtful,* but assumptious, of a gift as this was, I can't accept it."

Rowan takes a step forward–his towering frame making my head tilt up to look at him–and suddenly, my hand feels slightly shaky. "It's not assumptious when it's a fact, Doc. And *that,*" he flicks his gaze to the box holding the world's most expensive dildo, "is yours."

"It's not a fact, and I can't accept this," I respond, squaring my shoulders.

Rowan's lips twitch. "Are you denying that there was a malfunctioning vibrator in your purse during the time you were using your hands on me?"

I squint at him, knowing full well he said the whole 'hands' bit to get under my skin. "Yes."

He takes another step closer, and now the length of the box is the only thing that separates us. I can smell the soft notes of his cologne–sage, apple, and spice–and it's undeniable that I love it.

No, I don't. I hate it.

"The pulse thumping rapidly against your neck, the way your eyes are dilated, and the fact that you can't seem to hold that box steady says you're a liar. And I'm willing to bet that if the reward was worth it, you'd be a rule-breaker, too."

I swallow, feeling tiny droplets of sweat bead at my hairline.

Rowan's mouth grazes the shell of my ear and my thighs clench automatically. "Want to know what the reward for breaking all your rules would be, Doc?"

Goosebumps scatter over my neck where his face still hovers. "I . . . I don't . . ." I seem to have lost all my English-speaking capabilities.

Rowan chuckles softly, the vibration of it traveling down to my core before he leans back, giving me enough space to catch my breath again. "You can deny it all you want, Doc, but we both know you took that *gift* out for a test drive. And aside from the fact that I *won't* take it back . . . I *can't* take it back. You know why?" He lifts a brow but doesn't wait for my response. "Because your initials are engraved on it."

CHAPTER 5
ROWAN

A little voice inside my head asks what I'm doing.

Why am I pushing this woman's buttons? Why do I crave her reaction–the little gasps she makes when I've caught her off-guard, the rapid blinking, the most delicious spread of goosebumps along her dark skin? The kind I want to leave my nose on and inhale until I've gotten my fill. The kind I want to taste, crawling my lips up the side of her neck until I feel her shudder against me.

She's wound up as tight as a steel wire, and damn if I don't want to see her fray just a little. Or maybe I'd like to see her unravel completely.

A crease forms between her brow, about as adorable as the tiny little mole on the top of her cheek. "My initials? But I didn't see . . ."

She doesn't finish her thought, but the way her eyes widen in shock–knowing she's been caught, knowing my assumption about her taking the little toy in her hand on a joy ride was correct–has my smile resembling the Cheshire Cat's.

"You didn't see it there?" I lean back down toward her,

practically touching her large hoop earring with my lips and relishing in the way her chest rises and falls beneath me. "Is that what you were going to say, Doc? That you didn't see it there when you held it in your hand? When you skimmed it up your thigh, feeling the metal warm against your skin? When you felt it buzzing between your wet–"

"Rowan." She takes in a hurried breath.

I grin, pulling my lip in between my teeth. "It seems we're finally on the same page. I like my name on your lips."

She clears her throat, seeming to regain her composure. "Shall we get started, then?"

I swing my arm out in a welcome gesture. "I'll lead the way, if you want to follow me to my home gym."

Shay tucks her purse tighter under her arm before following me in quick, short steps.

Once she's sufficiently looked around at the equipment inside my workout room, she picks out an area next to my bench, placing both the small and large medicine balls and some resistance bands near it.

Putting her purse down nearby, she lays with her back on the bench.

"So, the first exercise I want you to do is called a supine groin stretch. I'll show it to you now, and I'd like you to do it for thirty seconds on each leg."

My eyes roam the length of her body lying on the bench. "You sure you don't want to start with a massage? I could really use a *groin-ular* massage."

Shayla glares at me, and I can't help the grin that spreads over my face. At this point, my smile seems to have become a permanent fixture around her. "Positive."

"You sure?" I urge again, hoping to really irritate her. "I feel like that'll help increase blood flow to the area." I point in the general direction of my groin, though it's possible it was a little closer to my dick.

Shay sucks in her cheeks, and I get the feeling she's trying to suppress a smile. "Pretty sure you don't need any more *blood flow* to that area than you've already got."

She proceeds to pull her knee into her chest, and I ogle her ass like a starving animal. Jesus Christ, it's so fucking round and firm, my dick begs for a peek. I shift, hoping the loose material of my shorts hides my erection.

"I'll walk you through all the exercises for this week, and then I'll create a plan for the following weeks. In general, I'll only need to see you once a week."

"Once a week?" *Oh no, no, no. That will not work.* "I thought we were meeting more than once a week until I'm fully healed."

Shayla sits up. "Once I create your weekly plan, there should be no need for us to meet more than that, other than to see what sort of progress you're making in your healing."

I wrap my arms around my chest. "Well, I'd like to see you more than once a week, especially when I'm playing home games."

She gives me that authoritative look I've seen from her a couple of times. The one I find so fucking cute, but the same one I'd like to wipe off her face if I ever get her under me. "Let me reiterate that playing hockey in your current condition could exacerbate the issue and potentially cause additional problems."

"Noted," I say, leaning back on my heels. "And let *me* reiterate that not playing when the season is about to begin, and my team's entire focus is on getting to the playoffs, is not an option, either."

She sighs. "Well, then I insist you stay off the ice this week as well. You'll need to do your exercises every day from here on out, but you won't need me here more than once a week after this week."

"That's non-negotiable. I'd like to see you three to five times every week until I'm fully healed." *And I'm not above pretending to be injured for longer, even if I'm completely healed.* "And I'd like you to travel with me for away games."

That same voice in my head that was asking me earlier what I was doing is now blaring and screaming.

What the fuck are you even doing, Parker?

It's fine though. I've ignored it multiple times before and haven't had to pay for any consequences. I respect it for being there as a cautionary voice of reason, but that doesn't mean I have to listen to it.

Shay comes to stand in front of me with her hands on her hips, her head tilted up. "That's not going to happen Mr. Parker. I have responsibilities, along with other patients. So, I'm afraid you'll have to find another therapist."

She starts to pick up her purse—*damn this woman and her ultimatums!*—and I rush after her, grabbing her wrist again. "Okay, fine. What about the next set of away games?" She starts to object, but I bulldoze past her. "We're flying out to California at the end of next week, from Saturday to Tuesday. Three games in four days. I'll take your advice and rest another week, but I'm really hoping you could be there in case I re-injure myself."

She gives me a pointed look. "Which is why playing so quickly after an injury isn't recommended. Plus, you'll have the team doctor there."

"I'll be careful," I promise her. "I won't get back on the ice until our first season game at home mid-next week. But I'd like you at the away games at the end of the week."

She purses her lips, but I can see she's at least considering my offer.

My thumb runs along the inside of her wrist, and I look at the tattoo inked there—a blue cancer ribbon. My gaze snags on it, not able to disconnect. Is she a cancer survivor or perhaps it was someone from her family?

Shay follows my gaze to the place my hand is still holding her tiny wrist, before clearing her throat. "My husband."

I drop her wrist as if I've touched a hot stove. *What the fuck?* I thought . . . I thought . . .

She smiles sadly, reading my thoughts. "He lost his battle to cancer and died three years ago."

And suddenly, there's a hazy gloom over the back-and-forth banter and tension between us. How could I have been so stupid to have not considered that the woman had her own past . . . her own story? I was solely focused on my assumptions.

"Wow. I'm sorry, Shay." My frown deepens. "I should have asked if–"

"What?" She lets out a soft, mirthless chuckle. "If I was a widow? If I had any children? If I was even ready to move on?" She pulls the strap of her purse over her shoulder. "How could you have known?"

She turns to exit the room when I find my voice again, finally processing her words. "I'd like to know."

What in the world? When have I ever cared to know more about a woman since Audrey? When have I ever pushed–*begged*–for another moment with anyone since?

I decided all those years ago that I was going to focus on me and my career. Nothing else would get in the way because no one was worth the time, the heartache. Because at the end of the day, anyone you let get too close could, and would, have the ability to rip your chest open, too.

Up until this moment, I was true to that path . . .

She turns around, her suspicious gaze taking me in. "What?"

"I'd like to know . . ." I take another step forward because the distance between us doesn't settle well for me. "Do you have any kids?"

Her gaze bounces between my eyes, as if she's trying to pick apart a puzzle. The woman is guarded as all hell, and it's going to take everything I've got to pierce the iron shield she stands behind.

"I have a little boy named Kai." A tender smile lifts the corners of her mouth and fuck, it's so incredibly beautiful. "He just turned nine."

I stay quiet, giving her the space to continue.

"You're his favorite hockey player, actually. He even named one of the raccoon babies inside our chimney, Slick. You were my husband's favorite, too . . ."

She trails off, not finishing her thought, and I take that as my cue to erase the gap between us. I have no clue what she means about raccoons in her chimney–*is that some strange metaphor for something?*–but I pull her hand down, holding it in mine. "I'm honored to be."

She stares up at me, not saying a word.

"And . . ." *Fuck, what am I doing?* I honestly don't know, but I can't seem to stop, either. "What about your last question? *Are* you ready to move on?"

Her eyes drop to my lips, and if I thought it was the right time, I'd kiss her. It's the only thing I want to do at this very moment, but the one thing I know will have her bolting out of here like her beautiful ass was on fire.

That she even showed up at my place today with the stunt I pulled sending her that dildo is shocking enough; the last thing I want is to push my luck any further.

She quickly untangles herself from my hold. "I'm sorry, I should–"

"Don't go." I hear myself say. "I'll work with whatever amount of time you give me."

"Rowan–"

"If you really don't want to come along for the games in California, I understand . . . but maybe just think about it?"

A smile graces her lips. "Fine. I'll think about it."

"And keep the gift." I wink at her. "Just call me the next time you take it out for a spin."

Her eyes sharpen on me, but this time, her smile stays put. "There won't be a next time because there wasn't even a first time."

"Uh huh, sure there wasn't," I deadpan, knowing she is a bold-faced liar. "Now, if you're ready, Doc, I'd like you to show me the other exercises you'd like to watch me do so you can ogle my ass like the hungry she-wolf you are."

She rolls her eyes, but a small giggle leaves her lips. *Holy shit! A giggle just left her lips! Dare I ask . . . is this progress?!*

"Your ego needs its own zip code, Mr. Parker." She pulls the corner of her bottom lip into her mouth as if contemplating her next words. "I do have one request before we continue."

"Name it," I say without hesitation.

She pulls out a small Boston Bolts jersey from her purse with my name and number on the back of it, along with a Sharpie. "Will you sign Kai's jersey? He'd be beyond the moon about it."

I swallow, taking the material in my hand. I hadn't quite processed the fact that I'm her son's–and her late husband's–favorite player, though I told her I was honored. And as true as those words were, my chest suddenly feels constricted.

I place the jersey on the bench and sign the back of it before handing it back to her. But before she can take it, I pull it back and hear myself say something I never thought I would. "Would the two of you like to come to the first season game at our arena next week? I have a couple of family and friends tickets."

Her eyes bounce against mine again, her gears turning for a long moment. "You know what? We'd love to."

I grin. "Now what was it you were saying about these so-called 'raccoons' that live inside your 'chimney'?" I put air quotes around the significant words. "I'm happy to 'sweep' your 'chimney' whenever you need, Doc. Just say the word."

CHAPTER 6
SHAY

I stare up at the exposed wood beams and metal pipes in the ceiling over my bed, cradled in shadows. Only the dimmest light flutters in through my window from the streetlamp outside, revealing the side of my dresser and the framed picture I keep atop it of Ajay and Kai.

I try not to think about whether I managed to dust enough to get all the residue from the rafters above. God knows how long it's been there, given how ancient this house is.

It was one of the first things I did when Kai and I moved into the brownstone—clean my room, along with the one he shares with Liam from top to bottom. I wanted to take zero chances breathing any kind of toxicity into our lungs.

Unfortunately, there was no other way to position the bed so it wasn't directly under the gaping hole, and after trying at least five different ways, I gave up.

Truth be told, I no longer hate the gaping hole. Somewhere in the midst of living here, it's become a familiar sight, surprisingly soothing and welcome. What isn't welcome? The loud vibration inside the walls, complete with some strange squealing, whenever someone flushes the toilet above us.

I turn to my side, squishing my pillow under me to get more comfortable, and look at the window Delia had to get replaced recently. I can't help but chuckle, thinking about the impetus for it from the summer.

Dylan had asked the kids to paint over the old windows, and they'd gone to town with their creation. To no one's surprise, Kai painted hockey sticks in the dining room. But it was Finn's vision of a tree that did Beckett in. It looked like . . . well, it looked like a penis, and it made Beckett lose his shit. He said he wouldn't be caught living in a house with dicks on the windows.

I'd been tempted to ask, "What about living in a house with a billionaire dick *behind* the window?" But I refrained since said billionaire also got Delia a big discount on the windows since he "knew a guy".

A voice in my head says I hadn't just refrained because of that; I'd refrained because I've actually started liking the guy. Sure, he's grumpy and high-maintenance, but below the dickish persona is a man who loves my best friend dearly, and who I've started to consider a friend. I'll never tell him that, though. No need to inflate that substantial ego.

And speaking of substantial egos . . .

Another smile forms on my lips as I think about my interaction with Rowan yesterday. I should hate that he's so relentless and pushy. That he finds ways to make me smile, even when I'm determined not to. And that everything about him—from his involvement in a dangerous sport, to his love for fast cars, to even that box of doughnuts and the can of Pepsi I saw sitting open on his kitchen counter—should keep me away. Far, far away.

I mean, does he have any idea how much sugar, trans fats,

and caffeine are in those things? Why not substitute with herbal tea and Ezekiel bread instead? They taste just as good, and are so much healthier.

My eyes widen as a thought enters my head. *I should make him my sea monster smoothie!* The one my besties rudely refer to as swamp sludge. But if Kai likes it so much that he practically gulps it down in three sips and does a weird victory dance afterward, like he's trembling from head to toe, then I'm sure Rowan will love it, too.

In any case, to get back to where I'd started this thought, I should hate all these things about him, but I don't. No matter how much I try.

And I can't wrap my head around *why*.

Perhaps he reminds me of the type of person I might have been had I not married Ajay.

A woman who worried less and smiled more. A woman who took the time to enjoy the moment, rather than rush through it because she felt like she had to do it all herself. A woman who didn't feel so unseen.

A lot of times—and God, it feels horrible even verbalizing it in my own head—that's how I felt when I was with Ajay.

Unseen. Inconsequential. Frivolous.

The world revolved around him—his startup, his career, his travels. It revolved around his next marathon, or the next mountain climb with his friends. It revolved around placatory apologies for coming home too late and forgetting our anniversaries.

And while I loved my husband dearly, I often forgot about my own desires. There was simply no time between running my own practice and taking care of Kai almost solely on my own.

And the more time went on, the more Ajay seemed to

forget that there was a second person in our marriage–or that he hadn't seen her smile in months, perhaps years.

I lay in bed for another moment before releasing a resigned breath, knowing sleep is far beyond the horizon at this point. But there *are* two things within my reach that might help me relax . . .

And they're both in the safety of my nightstand drawer.

Where they both ought to be.

I chew on my thumbnail for a moment, gathering my thoughts. Neither option is one I want to use. One has soured me from all other vibrators in my possession, and the other will give my nerves an hour or two of reprieve, but will have me feeling like a piece of hypocritical shit for days after.

Fuck it. Let's start with option one.

I stretch my arm across the mattress and open the drawer, feeling for the smooth metal with my fingers. I keep it in my hand for a moment, feeling the weight of it, my core already prepping for the feel of it.

Rowan wasn't wrong. I'd taken the thing on a ride multiple times at this point, and it lived up to every cent of that fifteen-thousand-dollar price tag.

I bring my new, ridiculously expensive toy to the middle of my thighs before turning it on, feeling the vibration against my skin. Rolling it further up, I feel my back start to arch and my toes curl against my mattress.

My eyes close and I pull my bottom lip in between my teeth, humming at the pulsing sensation now at the center of my thoughts. God, this feels so good. So fucking good.

I bring up the image of my go-to face–Henry Cavill as the Witcher–pretending it's his cock between my legs. Pretending it's his blue eyes piercing into mine as he fucks me like the monster slayer he is.

Except, his blue gaze keeps transforming into a golden-green one, and I have to shake off the image.

Ugh!

God, the irritating hockey player is even forcing himself into my fantasies!

I try again, pulling up another image of the white-haired, likely unshowered and unkempt, hunter.

"Keep the gods out of it," Henry, in full Witcher costume, growls inside my head, his lips thinned with that restrained ire I love so much.

"Yes," I agree in a whisper, placing the vibrator between my folds and feeling myself loosen up. "No gods, just . . . just us."

"I believe in the sword," he growls again, but somehow, his voice sounds different, like it's dripping with charm and honey. His lips look different, more plush. His skin, golden-toned.

To my utter dismay, Henry has completely turned into Rowan wearing the Witcher costume.

Whatever. It makes zero sense why the man keeps infiltrating my thoughts, but I'm going to go with it.

"Yes," I hiss, feeling myself getting wetter, despite the irritating imaginary man hovering above me. "Give me your sword. I love your sword."

"Whose sword do you love, Mom?"

My eyes fly open, my hand halting in place as I quickly gather my whereabouts and turn off the buzzing toy, shoving away Rowan's smug face. Why is it that his aggravating smile haunts me even inside my head?

Quickly stuffing the vibrator under my pillow, I tilt my head up to look at my confused little boy standing inside the entrance to my room. "Kai-bear? Are you alright?"

Kai shuffles over the wooden floor before he crawls into bed with me, and I scoot to give him more room. "You were having a nightmare about swords."

I nod, feeling my ears heat. "Yeah, it seems I was."

"You said you loved someone's sword. Who was it?"

I swallow. "The Witcher."

Kai tucks his head into the pillow next to mine, and I take the opportunity to relish the scent of eucalyptus and ginger wafting in the air around me. It was from the dye-free, chemical-free shampoo I'd ordered for him recently.

"That makes sense," he responds through a yawn. "He has a pretty cool steel sword."

"And how would you know?" I ask, gently caressing the top of his cheek with my thumb. "You aren't allowed to watch that show."

He shrugs, his eyes closing. "Liam told me because he watches it."

I hum. I love the bond between them, though I don't know how I feel about them discussing the show. "I should have guessed. Did you have a nightmare, too?"

"No. I just wanted to be here in case you had another one."

I stare at him, my heart and my eyes filling simultaneously.

This tiny kid, who wants nothing but to make sure his mom is okay. A kid forced to give up his own dreams because his mom said no, all because she's too scared to let him chase them. That same kid still finds room in his heart to come check on her, to protect her in case she needs him.

"Mom?" His sleepy voice has me blinking away tears.

"Yes, sweetheart?"

"Have you thought about the ice skating classes? They're starting next week." When I stay silent, considering his request again, he continues, "I'll be extra careful. I'll even wear those ugly knee and elbow pads you got me—the ones I used to play catch with Uncle Cortney sometimes." He yawns again. "He said he could teach me baseball if you were okay with it, but . . ." His downturned eyes plead with me. "I just want to learn how to skate, and when I get really good at it, then maybe you can think about letting me play hockey?"

My throat closes up, my heart at war with my brain.

How long can you keep him in a bubble, Shay?

How long can you protect him, keep him from experiencing the world?

He might reluctantly accept your decision now, but he'll end up resenting you later. Is that what you want? For your only son—the person who matters more than anyone else in the world—to resent you?

You can't shelter him forever.

I'm just about to tell him my decision, and how Rowan gave me tickets to watch his game, when I realize Kai's eyes are closed and his breathing has evened. Poor kid couldn't keep his eyes open another second longer awaiting my decision.

I slip out of bed a few minutes later, leaving Kai in the throes of deep sleep. As softly as possible, I open my night-stand once more, reaching further back where I've kept it hidden since the last time I used it a month ago, and pull out the second thing I was hoping to resist.

Throwing my robe over my pajamas, I stuff the white box inside my pocket and tiptoe out of my room and through the side door. During the daytime, my patients use it to come see me inside my home-office next door.

The early October chill makes its way down the back of my robe, ruffling my short hair, and I shudder, pulling my robe tighter around my body.

It's only four, still too early for the house to be up or for the streets to be busy, but it's the perfect time to relish in the quiet.

Taking a seat on the concrete steps, I pull out the white box from my pocket before looking this way and that to make sure no one is around.

Dylan already caught me smoking on the beach during our

last girls' trip, so I'm not too concerned about her, but no one else knows.

My chest feels heavy with the weight of my gruesome secret. A secret I've kept from some of my closest friends for the past three years, but a secret I'm not ready to divulge quite yet. I have to believe I'll kick this need before it gets worse, and by then, they won't even need to know.

I'd smoked a couple of times in college after a late-night bar hop, but I hadn't touched a cigarette from the moment I'd met Ajay. He hated the thought of anyone purposely filling their lungs with toxins, and I hated the thought of him thinking any less of me, so I put all my partying ways behind me and started anew.

But then he died . . . and so did a part of my purpose.

I had Kai to live and care for, but who was I besides a mother and a medical professional now that I wasn't a wife?

One dark night bled into another, and I found myself finding comfort in the rush of nicotine as it hurried through my system. I told myself it was only temporary, until I found my bearings in a life without Ajay.

Well, I'm here now, with most of my bearings . . . yet I'm still holding this flip-top box inside my palm.

I chuckle mirthlessly at my own ridiculousness. On one hand, I'm scrubbing dust and dirt off old ceiling rafters so we don't fill our lungs with toxins, and on the other hand, I'm *purposely* filling my lungs with carcinogens.

I can't even imagine what Delia and Liv would think, what with all the sermons I dole out about putting only nutritious things into our bodies. They'd see me in a completely different light, and that's a light I'm not ready to have shined on me just yet.

Hi, I'm Shayla Kumar, PT, DPT, five-foot-one, and I'm the world's biggest hypocrite and fraud.

Sliding my thumb on the side of the lighter, I place the cigarette in between my lips and lean toward the flame. The familiar soft hiss of the paper burning inside the fire gives me that same false sense of comfort it always does, knowing that, at least for a short moment, it'll just be me and my secret.

I inhale softly at first, focusing on watching the red cherry brighten at the end, before dropping the lighter back into my pocket.

Clasping the cigarette between my index and middle finger, I let out a balloon of smoke around me before taking a longer drag.

And then I wait for the shame.

The shame of living this dual life.

The shame of not being the mom I want to be—*that I yearn to be.*

The shame of disappointing my son and allowing my fears to overrule logic.

The shame of wanting someone I shouldn't. Someone who's not only my patient, but also my exact opposite.

And it comes.

Because it always does.

The self-loathing and self-deprecation, the feeling of inadequacy and defeat. The guilt of doing the very thing I'd look down on others for doing.

It ensnares me from head to toe, tightening its hold around my ribs and my stomach. But I *still* take another drag from the fucking cancer stick in between my fingers. I can't stop, even when I want to. I hate it, even while I love it. And I find myself succumbing to this duality every now and again when the water rises too far above my head and the only thing that helps me breathe is the very thing that depletes the oxygen in my lungs.

Yeah, how's that for heavy?

As always, I start by defending my actions to no one but myself.

You're so good about what you put into your body ninety-nine percent of the time. This one time won't kill you.

It's a temporary vice—one you can chuck at any time. Everyone has a vice, don't they? So what if this is yours? Temporarily.

Give yourself a break! You've only smoked a few cigarettes this month. You'll smoke a little less next month.

But then, it's my guilt—my conscience—that always wins.

Just as it's doing at this very moment, while I turn into a teary, sobbing mess.

I sob into my sleeve, feeling utterly defeated and sorry for myself for being a fraud in front of my friends and my son.

I project this poise and perfection on the outside, but on the inside, I'm the kind of mess most people would be better off staying away from.

My cigarette wobbles between my fingers as I bring it back to my lips, taking a puff and releasing the smoke on another garbled cry. My tears bite my cheeks as the cold breeze dries them on my skin.

I'm just in the middle of sniffling and running my nose over my sleeve again when I hear a crunching sound on the grass to my side.

Goddammit! Can't a girl get railed by her gold-plated vibrator, or get a decent smoke in for once in her life around here?!

I quickly rise to my feet, throwing the cigarette on the concrete step. Tightening my robe, I turn toward the sound, when I come face to face with a man holding a baseball bat in position to strike.

A scream forms somewhere inside my lungs, but before it has a chance to escape, the man lunges at me, placing his gargantuan hand over my mouth.

CHAPTER 7
SHAY

"Shh! Don't scream! You'll wake up the entire house, and I really can't have Livy in a bad mood because she didn't get enough sleep."

I blink rapidly, trying to catch my breath as Beckett's face comes into focus. "Beckett?!" I mumble under his fingers. "What the fuck? You almost gave me a heart attack!"

"I gave *you* a heart attack?" he retorts, dropping his fingers. "For the past ten minutes, I've been thinking someone was slaughtering cats out here based on the *dreadful* sounds I was hearing." He squints at my face. "Were you *crying*? I thought something was dying a horrible death!"

I wipe the tears from my face. "Shut up, you big jerk. I was just . . . I was . . ." My bottom lip trembles. "Never mind."

Beckett scrutinizes something near my feet and I quickly step on the contraband to hide it, yelping out, "Fuck!" when it singes my foot.

His amused gaze comes back to me. "You know I can smell it, even if you try to hide it."

I wrap my arms around my chest protectively. "I don't know what you're talking about."

Beckett 'Man-Child' Langfield pauses momentarily before he drops the baseball bat on the lawn and takes a seat on the concrete step next to me. "Want to talk about it? I'm not good with feelings, except when it comes to my wife, but I can give you non-emotional, shut-the-fuck-up-and-stop-feeling-sorry-for-yourself kind of support."

"Gee, you make it sound so tempting," I deadpan. A beat of silence passes between us before I scrub my palms down my face. "I bet you think I'm the world's biggest crock of shit."

His brows fold as he turns toward me. "Why would I think that?"

I chuckle humorlessly. "Well, let's see . . . During the day, I put on a facade of having it all together, like I'm this regimented, perfect–"

"No one thinks you're perfect, *believe me*."

I elbow him. "Dick."

"Pipsqueak."

I chuckle. "As I was saying, I pretend I'm not a hot mess. I've almost convinced myself, in fact, by eating healthy and exercising daily. But the truth is, I'm secretly smoking in the middle of the night so I can clear my head."

"Is this every night?"

"No. Only when I'm feeling out of control or particularly shitty about myself. But does that make it any better? I tell myself it's the last time, every time, yet I can't get rid of the box of smokes, either."

"Do you bray and squawk like a donkey-hen every time you do it, too?" Beckett winces, bracing himself to be elbowed again.

I glare at him and he chuckles.

"I'm kidding, Pip. But maybe you're being too hard on

yourself. I'm not condoning incinerating your lungs by any means, but from what Liv's told me, you went through a tough time with the loss of your husband. None of that shit could have been easy to watch or accept. I imagine it changed you in ways you hadn't expected, in ways most people wouldn't understand unless they went through it themselves."

I sniffle, nodding. "It made me fearful. It took away my sense of security. And it made me feel like I had to protect whatever was left of the life I had, because everything is so damn fragile—you're here one moment, gone the next. But I hate feeling this way. I wish I could snap out of it, but I just can't seem to."

Beckett shrugs. "Then start small. Don't tackle the big mountains; start with the little hills first. Find smaller victories where you can. And if your biggest mountain is kicking this habit," he eyes the cigarette butt on the step below us, "then tackle that last."

Some of the constriction inside my chest releases. "I thought you sucked at feelings and emotional speeches?"

"Oh, believe me, I do. I was just reciting a recent TED Talk."

"I don't believe that for a second. You're a big softie, but don't worry, your secret is safe with me as long as my secret," I eye the cigarette butt, reminding myself to throw it away before anyone else sees it, "is safe with you."

Beckett snorts. "Tough chance, Pipsqueak. This one is way too juicy, and I don't keep secrets from my wife."

My mouth falls agape. "Are you serious? You're going to tell Liv?"

His jaw ticks. "As serious as a heart attack." He glances at the remains of my secret on the concrete step. "Pun intended."

Ugh, I hate how good of a husband he's turned out to be.

He's also turned out to be great with all our kids, despite the fact that the entire reason he and Liv got married was to restore his image as someone who loves children so he wouldn't lose his baseball team. A fake marriage that, in the end, turned very real.

I pinch the bridge of my nose, trying to figure out how I'm going to divulge this to Liv and Delia. They'll be so disappointed. "Okay, at least give me a chance to tell them myself."

Beckett seems to think about my request. "I'll give you until next Saturday."

I squint at him, knowing he didn't become a billionaire by sucking at negotiations. "That's . . . oddly specific. Why next Saturday?"

He purses his lips, clearly trying to fight a smile. "The Bolts have their first away game of the season at the end of next week, and Rowan really wants you to–"

"Wait a second." My mouth opens in shock. "How do you know what he wants?"

"Come on, Pip. My brother owns the damn team, and it's no secret we talk. Don't worry though, you've been cleared to go with them . . ."

I get to my feet as conflicting emotions stir inside my chest. On one hand, I feel a sense of thrill–something I haven't felt in a long time–at the prospect of being alone with the gorgeous defenseman, but on the other, I'm still saddled by my fears. "I haven't made a decision on that. Plus, Kai needs me here."

Beckett rises to his feet as well, giving me a skeptical look. "Remember the smaller hills we just talked about?"

"Leaving Kai here alone is *not* a small hill, Beckett."

"He won't be alone; he'd be in good hands with all of us. And you'd only be gone for a few nights. He'll be fine, Pipsqueak. You can leave one of those long lists of yours–"

"The health and well-being checklist," I supply. "It's a list of reminders for him, like brushing his teeth before bed with charcoal toothpaste, and taking his vitamins, and–"

"Right. That."

I squint at his forehead, wishing I could read his thoughts. "Why are you pushing this? What's your agenda?"

Beckett raises both hands. "I have no agenda. I'm just trying to do right by my brother's team. Rowan's a key player, and if it'll help him to know you're there, then I figured I'd try to convince you." I'm about to argue when he barrels past me. "And who knows, perhaps the time away will be good for both you and Kai."

I'm not convinced–the man is more calculating than a calculator–but I'm also too tired to argue. I turn back toward the side entrance to the house. "Good talk, soft-serve."

I'm just about to lock the door when I catch a glint in his eyes. "Your little secret is *safe* with me, Pipsqueak. Don't you worry your coiffed little head about a thing."

Pain in my ass . . .

Insincerity oozes off him like his barely veiled threat, and I swear, I want to drop-kick him back to his mansion in Florida.

"Is anyone else missing the mirrors inside their makeup compacts?" Delia asks, coming into the kitchen while looping an earring through her earlobe. With her custom-tailored suit and her blonde hair styled into a perfect twist at the back of her head, she looks stunning. "All of mine seem to have disappeared."

The twins, Phoebe and Colette, whisper something to each

other with their heads close together at the kitchen bar, hovering over what looks like a circuit board of some kind.

They glare at Kai and Winnie—Liv's nine-year-old, and the kid Kai feels closest to aside from Liam—who seem to be exchanging their own silent conversation.

What exactly is going on between the four of them?

"Not me," Cortney responds with a smirk, watching Dylan place the pieces of a complicated puzzle he bought her into their correct positions. The woman is a genius with puzzles. "I took stock of all the mirrors inside my makeup compacts this morning."

"Mercury is in retrograde," Dylan responds, staying focused on her task. "And I don't wear makeup during this time, so I couldn't tell you if anything is missing."

Okay, then.

I place my empty cup of lemon water on the counter, still sweating from this morning's workout. "I thought it was just me. A few of the mirrors from my vegan, cruelty-free, paraben-free, fragrance-free, non-toxic makeup kit were missing yesterday. I just thought maybe they'd fallen off somehow."

Kai clears his throat, and both Delia and I notice Winnie kick him under the bar before the twins give him another threatening glare.

"Alright, you four," Delia starts, her hands on her hips. "I don't have time for whatever it is you're up to, but I know you guys have something to do with this. So, who's going to cough up the details?"

They all look at each other, no one making a peep.

Cortney gets up, getting the kids' attention. He has an easy way of doing that, given he's their fun baseball star uncle. "Well, I was going to take everyone out for ice cream," he looks at me pointedly, "and sugar-free frozen yogurt for Kai. But I guess I won't be doing that since you guys aren't fessing up to whatever it is you're up to."

I swallow the fear of Kai eating something frozen during this time of year when the weather is getting colder. He could catch a cold, not to mention the food coloring that goes into most frozen yogurts . . .

"Well, Colette wanted to–" Winnie starts, her finger pointing to the other side of the bar where the twins are.

"It wasn't just my idea!" Colette defends herself quickly.

"Well, you did help," Kai adds accusingly. "You held the hairdryer to the back of the makeup thingy to warm up the glue behind the mirror so it would become unstuck."

"Yeah, and *you* took the mirrors out!" Phoebe adds, pointing an accusing finger at Kai.

"Girls–" Delia tries to get her twins' attention.

"But I didn't do all of them," Kai argues. "Phoebe did the most–"

"Kai?" My shock is evident on my face. Is this the same rule-abiding kid I raised all these years? "You were a part of this?"

"You're a tattletale!" Phoebe adds, giving Kai the stink-eye. "We agreed not to tell the moms!"

"I'm sorry, Mom." Kai's lip trembles with guilt. "I told them it wasn't a good idea–"

"It was a brilliant idea! We only act on brilliant ideas, not dumb ones." Colette's brows scrunch together in annoyance.

"Okay, okay," Delia tries again. "Can someone tell me what exactly was the brilliance behind heating up a bunch of our makeup compacts and ungluing the mirrors from them?"

"Phoebe and Colette wanted to make periscopes."

Delia, Dylan, and I look at each other in confusion.

"Periscopes?" I ask.

"Yes," Phoebe starts, and I can already tell this is going to be one of her sassy responses. "A periscope is an instrument that allows you to observe over, around, or through an object that prevents direct line-of-sight observation." She huffs out a breath, irritated by my raised brows and my apparent simple-mindedness. "In layman's terms—*so you understand*—periscopes let you look around walls and corners."

"Phoebe, we're all aware of what periscopes are." Delia gets on her knees and wraps her hands around her daughter's wrists gently. "What we want to know is *why* you were making them?"

"We wanted a way to look up the chimney for the times Junior leaves her babies to find more food," Colette answers. "We wanted to watch her come in and out, so we made periscopes using the mirrors we got from your makeup compacts."

As if the raccoons know we're talking about them, scratching sounds drift from inside the chimney and we all turn to look at them suspiciously.

Before anything more can be said, the twins hustle off, telling their mom they'll be back with their new gadgets. I take the time to speak with Kai. Winnie seems to be the least culpable, since she didn't take part in any of this.

"Kai-bear, can you explain why you wouldn't tell me about this plan before you decided to break my things?"

Kai's chin wobbles as he holds back his tears. "I just . . . I just wanted to make something cool with my friends. I wanted to be part of the team."

Ah.

I sigh, understanding more than he's telling me. "Does this have something to do with the skating classes and the hockey team?"

He looks up at me, hope swirling inside his irises, but stays silent.

"I was going to tell you last night when you came to my room, but you fell asleep before I could." My eyes glide over him gently. "I'm okay with enrolling you in skating classes–"

Kai lunges at me before I can finish, wrapping his arms around me. "Thank you, Mom! Thank you so much!"

I smile through the anxiety creeping up my chest. "Yes. And guess what?"

He unwraps his arms from me. "What?"

"Rowan Parker gave us tickets to come to his home game on Tuesday."

"Wha–" Kai's shocked response is muffled when Beckett's voice booms from behind us.

"And guess what else, IceMan," Beckett addresses my son. "He asked your mom to come along with him to his away games in California next weekend."

Oh, this weasley asshole. He knows letting that tidbit slip in front of my son will only put more pressure on me to say yes.

"Oh my god, Mom!" Kai grabs my shoulders urgently. "You have to go!"

I throw fire-tipped daggers at Beckett with my eyes before turning to my son. "I haven't said yes because I don't know if I'm ready to spend three nights away from you. What if . . . what if something happens to you while I'm gone?"

"Mom, nothing will happen to me. I promise."

That familiar anxious feeling twists my gut. "I don't know . . ."

"Hey, Shayla?" Beckett's voice pulls me out of my daze as he wraps his arms around Liv's waist with a sly grin on his face. "Doesn't my wife look like a *smoke show* today?"

My eyes connect with his and the message is as clear as his evil smirk. The piece of shit is blackmailing me for my consent on the away games by using that very specific and very obvious word.

Pity. I was just starting to like him, too . . .

"Doesn't she look *smoking*-hot?" He throws a wink in my direction, making sure Liv isn't watching.

Liv turns to look up at him. "What's gotten into you?"

"What?" He smiles at her innocently. "It's not like I'm blowing *smoke* up your ass, Livy. You really are the hottest woman I've ever met. Hotter than a blazing inferno. Hotter than the cherry tip of a cigarette."

"Those are really weird comparisons," Liv mumbles distractedly.

Beckett's devious grin finds my face, and my hands fist at my side. I swear, I'm two seconds from giving his smug billionaire face a high-five with my fist.

"Fine! I'll go to the away games!" I roar, reminding myself to add castor oil or a stronger laxative to his coffee.

I'm only halfway down the steps when I hear Liv ask, "What's gotten into her?"

<h1 style="text-align:center">CHAPTER 8
ROWAN</h1>

I release a short breath, willing myself to ignore the burn in my thigh. It isn't as bad as it was a few days ago, but I'll have to be careful with my strides today. I already know I won't be as fast as I usually am on the ice. I can feel that, even as I do the pre-game warmups.

But hell if I'll ride the pine on the bench. I've already been off the ice for almost two weeks, and each day that I'm not with my team, I feel like I'm letting them down. I didn't work my ass off for years trying to get here–winning not one, but three Norris trophies–only to sit out during the start of an important season.

I'm not just the player with the booming slapshots and smart passes; I'm also the player my team relies on to help set up bigger offensive plays and coordinate defensive strategies. I'm known for relying on my gut, anticipating the opposing team's plays before anyone else. It's not a skill that can be taught, but I've honed my instincts over the years–going after what feels right, even if it's risky.

I suppose I can attribute that to things off the ice as well. Like a certain spitfire physical therapist who packs one hell of a personality in that short, fit body of hers.

Though I emailed her through her work email address–because the woman refused to give me her number–I never did get a response as to whether she and her son were going to be at the game tonight.

I look up at the stadium as it fills up, trying not to feel deflated when I notice their empty seats.

We're down during the first period, Tampa taking the lead in goals and assists, but even with my thigh feeling tight, I've made some decent passes and still feel optimistic about winning this game. Why? Because while the opposing team might be up 0-1, I can already tell they're making the same mistakes–not guarding the corners and trying to make predictable plays. They're also getting sloppy, and that's great news for us.

We take an intermission, and my eyes fly back up to the stands, scanning the audience for the woman I'm looking for. At first, I don't see her behind the large man in front of her, but it's when he leaves his seat that my gaze connects with hers.

A smile forms on my face and fuck, my heart hammers for reasons that have nothing to do with the sport I'm playing.

She lifts her hand to wave at me, and I grin bigger, like a star-struck teenager. There's a boy right next to her, and even from my spot on the ice, I can see the resemblance between them. But that's not all I see. It's his bright-as-fuck smile, his glittering eyes, and the way he bounces on his seat. He wraps both arms around his mom, giddy beyond belief that I'm looking their way.

It's fucking adorable, and the only way I can show how glad I am that they're here is to turn around and do the jig I'm known for.

I twerk my hips and do the wave as the music blares through the speakers. The stadium goes wild, fans screaming from all directions, thinking I'm excited about playing in our first season game. Which, I am, of course. I'm glad to be back, but it's not why I'm dancing.

The next two periods go by in a blur, with me drawing a penalty in the third and getting us a man-advantage when the Tampa center high-sticks me. In the last minute of the game, with us tied at 1-1, I pass the puck to our center—another Langfield brother—Aiden, who bodies past the opposing defense, coming to an abrupt halt in front of the opposing goalie. He lobs the puck with everything he's got, picking the top corner with his shot, leaving the goalie with no chance at making a save. A second later, the red goal light flashes back, signaling the game-winning shot.

Thunder breaks through the arena and our fans rise to their feet, screaming and clapping. I realize that everyone had completely gone silent earlier because nerves were so high—either that, or I'd drowned out the noise.

Within seconds, I'm wrapped in hugs from the rest of the team as the guys roar into my ears, congratulating me for the assist and Aiden for his near-perfect shot that won us our first game of the season.

"Fuck yeah, baby!"

"Stanley, here we come!"

I'm only barely able to find a window between all the bodies surrounding me, and while I can't get a great visual of Shay behind the large man in front of her, I see her son jumping up and down with his hands in the air.

And for some reason, that makes this win slightly sweeter.

We're all hustling back for post-game media, but my head keeps swiveling in Shay's direction. Fuck, I want to see her. But by the time I'm done talking to the press, having a post-game huddle with the team, and showering, it'll be well after ten PM. There's no way I can expect them to stay until then.

Still, I send her a quick email, hoping she'll see it before she goes to bed.

```
Hey Doc,
Did you like the little dance I did for you?
Pretty sure I saw you crack a smile. You were
ogling my ass, weren't you? Thank you for
coming.

- The defenseman with a posterior as ripe as
peaches, Slick
```

I smile, picturing her rolling her eyes and pressing the keys with so much force with her reply, they're at risk of malfunctioning.

Grabbing a drink from the bin near the locker room, I take a quick selfie to post for my fans like I do after every game.

```
See that clinch? That's how it's done, son.
#ComingfortheStanley
```

My smile slips when my phone vibrates in my hand, and I see the name on my screen. I hadn't even bothered to reply to the last message from him, so at this point, it just looks like he's sending me message after message of rants. I don't know why it still catches me off-guard when he texts. At this point, his messages are a hell of a lot more reliable than he was as a father.

DAD

> Good assist tonight, but your form was shit.
> You were slower than the Zamboni, for crying
> out loud!

Thanks for the vote of confidence, Dad.

Oh, and fuck you!

As always, I click off the screen, trying not to let his dick-ishness put a shadow over my good mood.

I haven't spoken to my dad in six months. The last time was after his car accident, when I called him to ask if he was okay. Instead of showing remorse about driving drunk, he blabbed on about how, by this time in his career, he'd already won two Stanley Cups and that it was embarrassing his son had yet to win any.

And even though I haven't replied to a single one of his texts since, he knows I'm reading them. It's probably why he continues to message me.

I should block his ass like my sister, Piper, did years ago, but a part of me worries the man literally has no one else left, not even the woman he married after my mom. And if there's another emergency, I don't want him to have no one to count on.

That asshole voice inside my head says, maybe I'm still hoping I could count on *him* for something, too—like one genuine praise rather than the constant rants of disappointment. But if it hasn't happened in twenty-seven years, then why would I expect it to happen now?

My friend, Brooks, who's our goalie and another one of Beckett's brothers, finds me in the locker room after my shower. "Yo! The team's going out tonight for drinks. Joining?"

On most other days, I'd say yes but A.) I'm fucking beat, and my thigh is legitimately in need of icing and rest, and B.)

the idea of going out and flirting with a bunch of chicks who just want a chance to fuck an NHL player isn't appealing in the least today, and C.) there's a part of me that's still hoping Shay will reply, and honestly, I'd much rather stay home chatting with her.

Wonder if I can convince her to see me tonight?

I shake my head, throwing my towel into the used bin after having pulled on my jeans. "Nah, not tonight. I'm beat."

"Come on! We agreed we'd celebrate all the wins. Don't hold out on us now."

I put my wallet and keys into my pocket. "Next time, maybe. I need a night."

Brooks gives me a disappointed frown before offering a fist-bump. "Alright, brother. Next time, then."

I'm just getting to my car when I decide to check my email. I was sure she wouldn't reply, but my heart's already fluttering like an over-caffeinated butterfly seeing her name in my inbox. God, I sound like such a pussy.


```
Mr. Parker,
A posterior as ripe as peaches? It's no
wonder I've never been a fan of peaches. I
wasn't smiling, nor was I ogling your ass. I
was doing oral stretches—it's a part of my
regimen. Thank you for inviting us. Congratu-
lations on the win. How is your pain level
after the game?

- Dr. Shayla Kumar, PT, DPT
```


My eyes stall on the word "oral", my dick already twitch-ing. Does she even know what she's setting herself up for? I type back a quick response before unlocking my car and getting in.

Dear Doc,
I think I may have injured my shoulder and that gluteus maximus muscle you love so much. Nothing that couldn't be fixed with your hands on me again, though. Perhaps I can convince you to give me a massage? Additionally, I'd very much be interested in learning more about these *oral* stretches of yours. Any chance I could get a demonstration? And thank you for the congrats.

- The defenseman whose ass is the stuff of legends and whispered secrets, Slick

I sit in my car, looking down at my phone and refreshing my mail like it's some sort of slot machine, when another one pops up.

Mr. Parker,
I see you're back to crossing the professional boundaries we'd previously agreed to. I am a physical therapist, not a masseuse, so there will be no massaging of your glutes. I'm sorry you seem to have injured yourself further, though I will remind you, I asked you to rest.
If your new injuries continue to bother you, I can examine them at our scheduled time tomorrow evening.

- Dr. Shayla Kumar, PT, DPT

I grin down at the phone, typing out another message.

Dear Doc,
I'm not sure we *agreed* on any such professional boundaries. I believe you spewed off
some mumbo-jumbo about not breaking your
rules, and I asked you a simple question,
which you never answered: Do you want to know
what the reward for breaking the rules
would be?
I understand that we have a scheduled session
tomorrow; however, I would much rather you
examine me tonight to ensure I'm not at risk
of sudden death. If it is too much for you to
drive to my place, I'm happy to come to
yours. Or if you want to give me your number,
I can FaceTime you for a visual evaluation.

- The defenseman with a tush as rare as a
treasure in a shipwreck, Slick

I wait five minutes for her response. Maybe I pushed too hard, or maybe she's over my shenanigans and isn't interested. But the way she looks at me . . . the way she wants to smile but stifles it whenever I irritate her, says she doesn't hate my obvious flirting.

Or maybe she's just not telling me she hates it.

But from the little I know of her, she doesn't strike me as the type to hold back her opinions.

I start my car, looking at my inbox one last time, when I see her response come in.

Mr. Parker,
I can assure you, the chances of your
injuries leading to your sudden demise are
low. However, if that is something you are
legitimately concerned about, then I urge you
to seek emergency services.
Also, how are you coming up with these
ridiculous metaphors for your backside?

- Dr. Shayla Kumar, PT, DPT

I bite the inside of my cheek, trying not to chuckle while typing back.

Dear Doc,
I can see you're thinking about my backside
again. As such, I'd really appreciate your
prompt examination tonight.

- The defenseman with a booty so fine, it
should be insured, Slick

A few minutes later—time in which I'm sure she's no longer going to respond—I'm relieved to see another email come through with just her number.

I waste no time calling her on FaceTime, and she picks up on the second ring, her beautiful face coming into view. Her eyes sparkle against the dark background—I gather she's sitting outside—the longer side of her asymmetrical hair waving in the wind, and her lips look pink, plump.

"'A booty so fine, it should be insured'?" She huffs out a soft laugh, like she's trying to avoid being too loud.

I shrug, my eyes tracking down the length of her slender

neck, just a sliver of the tattooed stars visible from this angle. She's wearing a teal V-neck shirt and a K pendant hangs on the thin gold necklace above her collarbones. "It got you to give me your number, didn't it?"

"You're right. I couldn't handle one more ass metaphor." She licks her lips. "Are you in your car?"

I nod. "I just got out of the stadium."

She pauses, and I wonder if she's thinking about her next words. "So, shouldn't you be out celebrating with your teammates after that win?"

Is that vulnerability I see in that impenetrable guard of hers?

"I'm exactly where I want to be, Doc."

My response hangs in the air between us, and she clears her throat, pulling that professional mask back on. "Can you move your shoulder for me? Does it hurt when you do this?" She demonstrates by raising her shoulder up and down.

I pull my bottom lip into my mouth before releasing it slowly. I really should end this call, but I can't seem to do the right things when it comes to this woman. "I didn't injure my shoulder. And yes, my thigh still hurts, but it isn't anything I can't handle."

Her brows scrunch together. "Oh. I thought you said–"

"I just wanted to talk to you."

The soft intake of her breath is audible, even through the speaker. "Rowan, I–"

"Kai looks so much like you," I interrupt before she can find a way to end this conversation.

That seems to snap her out of her previous train of thought, and it's as if she actually looks at me for the first time. A smile forms on her lips. "Yeah . . ."

"His smile matches yours."

Her smile stretches across her face and damn, it's beautiful—a perfect set of white teeth cradled between the most luscious pink lips.

"Thanks. He was so excited when you danced. It definitely had the audience going."

"I didn't do it for the audience."

She looks down, as if our locked eyes are too much for her. "He's been begging me to put him into skating lessons." She shakes her head, looking over her shoulder, and I see a large door behind her. I imagine her sitting outside her house on some steps. "But I'm so afraid he'll hurt himself. He's smaller than most of the boys his age, and I don't want him to get trampled in a class full of kids who are also learning. I've already promised him I'd enroll him in the class, but it doesn't make me feel any less anxious, you know?"

She takes a breath. "I wish I'd learned when I was younger, then maybe I could have taught him. But it was always something Ajay was—" She halts her words, as if she's said too much. "Anyway, I don't know why I'm telling you any of this. I just meant that Kai was ecstatic that you gave us tickets to the game, so thank you."

I don't let the fact that she mentioned her late husband distract me from keeping her talking. Her past doesn't bother me in the least. All I want is to keep her talking, to hear her voice. She could talk about anything—the mysteries of the universe, the secret language of ants, or basket weaving—and I'd listen.

"I can understand why you'd be worried. People can certainly get hurt when they're first learning to skate."

Her surprise for my agreement is evident on her face. "That's exactly what I've been saying! So, you don't think I'm being crazy? I could have sworn you would have said what almost everyone I live with tells me—that I'm too overprotective of him."

Everyone she lives with? How many people does she live with, exactly?

"What if you put him in a one-on-one class with an instructor who could focus solely on him?"

She twists her mouth, her eyes drifting away while she contemplates my question. "Yeah . . . maybe."

"I know you're worried, but as a physical therapist, you know the benefits of it, too–muscle strength, balance, and coordination. Plus, it helps build confidence. You wouldn't believe it, given how sexy and strong I am now, but I used to be a scrawny kid." That pulls a smile out of her. "I know you're shocked, but I wasn't always this smooth-talking, panty-melting, Viking on skates you're secretly obsessed with."

She laughs, the sound of her soft voice hitting me in the chest like a swarm of butterflies. "You're obsessed with yourself enough for the both of us. Not sure there's any room left for me to be."

I look at her through hooded eyes. "Oh, there's definitely room for you."

A shy smile plays on her lips. "You don't give up, do you, Mr. Parker?"

"Rowan. And, admit it, you like me."

She huffs out a laugh. "It's debatable. Most of my thoughts about you are peppered with visions of strangling you."

I throw back my head, laughing. "If that's what it takes to get your hands on me again, Doc, then I'm not opposed to it."

She shakes her head before the two of us sit in silence for a moment, staring at each other. "What are you doing, Rowan?"

She's not asking me specifically about this moment, with me sitting in my car. She's asking what the hell I'm doing flirting with her. It's a question I've asked myself incessantly since I met the woman, so I'm not going to act obtuse and ask her what she means.

I run my thumb over my bottom lip, weighing my words on my tongue. "Around you, I don't seem to have a clue."

She turns away from me, before coming back to face me again, and I'm happy to see she hasn't lost that soft smile. "Goodnight, Rowan. I'll see you tomorrow."

"Good night, Doc. I'm looking forward to it."

CHAPTER 9
SHAY

"So, is there anything else besides your hamstring that's giving you trouble?"

"Well!" Mr. Howard yells, making me jump. "If I turn like this . . ." He swings one frail and wrinkled arm behind his head, looking up at it so his also-frail and wrinkled neck is in an awkward tilt. He twists his wrist so his palm faces out before trying to grab his lifted arm with his other hand, unsuccessfully. Basically, he looks like the beginnings of a human pretzel. "I feel pain in my shoulder and my neck."

A part of me wants to slam my face into my palm because I'm so exhausted, while the other wants to burst out into a fit of giggles. It's been that kind of a day.

Between overbooking myself with back-to-back patients, and managing a damn leak over my bed in the middle of the night, I'm in need of a glass of wine, a very overdue bubble bath–seeing as I haven't had access to a bathtub in quite some time–and one of those fucking cathartic screams Dylan suggests that release the bad juju into the wild.

I firmly believe the universe has a rule that all terrible and urgent things have to happen in the middle of the night, preferably while people are asleep.

One minute I was dreaming about being in a shower with an arrogant and overbearing hockey player, and the next, I was being splashed with disgusting—and probably highly toxic—water from the old pipes inside the rafters.

Needless to say, I wasn't going to wake up the whole house in the middle of the night, so all I could do was find a bucket and dry bedding to sleep on the floor. I even skipped my usual five-mile run and weight training this morning because I was so tired.

"Are you hearing me, chickadee?"

Mr. Howard's bushy gray brows reach his hairline when he shouts. The man refuses to believe he needs hearing aids. And between the fact that he practically screams his words and is somewhat of a hypochondriac, I'm on the losing side of this battle.

I clear my throat, speaking louder for his benefit. "I understand that you're experiencing pain when you twist like that," *like a damn contortionist,* "but Mr. Howard, when would you possibly be in that position during your day?"

"It's not about *when*, goddammit! It's about *if!*" Mr. Howard yells. "*If* I wanted to be in that position, I couldn't! I should be able to be if I damn well decide to be! What if I wanted to start doing gymnastics?"

Oh, boy.

I take a breath, silently asking the Lord to give me strength. "Are you thinking about starting gymnastics?"

"Well, no! Are you out of your mind?" he bellows. "I'm eighty-six years old! Why would I?"

I'm so at a loss, I just stare at him for a moment, while he stares back at me like I'm the world's biggest idiot.

"Right. Well, let me have a look at it and suggest a few

exercises," I say, trying to pacify him. "Is your hamstring feeling any better? Have you been doing the exercises we talked about last month?"

"It still feels like a bag of rocks is sitting on it, so no, it isn't feeling better. And now I'm losing flexibility in my arm, having this damn pain when I twist it the way I showed you."

Yes, the way only circus acrobats and zombies should twist their arms.

I go through some placatory checks on Mr. Howard before giving him new weekly exercises to do. Then I ask him to lay on the bench so I can examine his hamstring. I place one palm right above his raised knee, and the other on the back of his thigh, before pressing his knee toward his chest, bracing for what's to come.

As expected, Mr. Howard passes gas. *Loudly.*

Dare I say, it's louder than his normal voice, and like his voice, he doesn't hear this, either.

I clear my throat, hoping not to show any discomfort on my face, and recall one of the many reasons I keep air freshener in my drawer. "How does that feel?"

"My heel?" he yells. "My heel is fine, chickadee. It's my hamstring and my shoulder that are bothering me. Pay attention!"

"Right." Continuing my exam, I stretch the back of his thigh this way and that, using the same technique as earlier, while ignoring the trumpet-like sounds that fill the space between us.

After Mr. Howard leaves—not before telling me about brand-new ailments that seem to have surfaced in the short time he was here—and I've sufficiently sprayed the room with environment-friendly air freshener, I sit at my desk with my head in my palms. I'm so engrossed in my thoughts, I barely hear the knock on my door.

A few seconds later, my best friends huddle into my office together.

"Oh, hon." Liv gives me a sympathetic look, likely seeing the sheer exhaustion on my face. "Do we need an impromptu smutty book club night? I have your favorite organic wine and pumpkin seed Paleo bars. I'll even pretend to like them when you ask me if I want a bite."

I chuckle. "I can't. I still have one more patient today . . . the most irritating and high-maintenance of them all."

"Why do I get the feeling irritating is code for sexy or bangable?" Liv winks at me. "You know you can admit you like him, especially in front of us."

I snort. "I like him about as much as I like MSG in my food."

Liv rolls her eyes. "Look, you can keep denying it, but we see the way you smile when we mention him–"

"Or the way you pay a little more attention to hockey these days," Delia adds.

"Or the way your aura's been more orange lately. I mean, minus the fact that it's more gray today, but that's probably because you're tired–"

"I *am* tired," I confirm. I'd already given everyone the rundown about the leak in my room this morning. "I haven't slept."

"Well, Cortney and Beckett got the leak fixed," Delia chimes in. "They tried to hire some idiot plumber, but as soon as I asked him a simple question, he just bailed."

"You didn't ask him a simple question." Dylan glares at her. "You asked him why he received his one and only three-star review on Yelp, and then you embarrassed him by *reading it aloud* to him! Who does that?"

"He got that rating because he was late for a job! You know how I feel about tardiness," Delia argues.

"He had a personal emergency!" Liv jumps in. "God forbid people have emergencies! Then, you insulted his tools."

Delia waves her hand at our friends. "The guy was way too sensitive, in my opinion. If he was going to get that butt-hurt, then he really shouldn't be in the service industry."

Liv, Dylan, and I exchange outraged glances.

"Anyway, that's not why we're here," Delia says, shifting the conversation. "We saw you moping around like a rain-soaked cat earlier, and we came here to give you a hug, so," she spreads out her arms, "come on, bring it in."

I stumble over to my best friends, letting them wrap me up in a cocoon of their arms. These women–my sisters–who showed up for me today, knew exactly how much I needed them. Instantly, I feel a hell of a lot better than I did just five minutes ago.

"So what does it mean that I have an orange aura?" I mumble under their arms, remembering Dylan's earlier remark.

"That you're horny," she answers, not missing a beat.

Delia snorts. "Well, that's not news. The woman has more personal toys than a BDSM dungeon."

My shoulders shake with laughter. "Shut up. You're still upset over that plumber and his *insufficient tools.*"

"What she needs is a plumber with *sufficient* tools. The kind that'll *really* clear out that plumbing," Liv adds.

Delia pokes our friend's side, making her yelp and the rest of us giggle, with me genuinely feeling lighter than I have all day.

"But I have to ask . . ." Liv eyes me after we've all separated from our group huddle. "What's holding you back?"

I scrunch my brows together, lifting a bottle of kombucha to my lips. "Holding me back from what?"

"Fucking Rowan Parker's brains out."

I'm mid-sip when it goes down the wrong pipe, making me cough. Delia slaps my back, like she's doling out punishment, before I take another long breath and glare at her. I swear she got a twisted sense of pleasure from that.

"For starters, the fact that I'm his PT!" I look at Liv like she's lost her marbles. "And let's not forget his age, or the fact that his longest relationship was probably the same length as my longest menstrual cycle."

Liv wraps her arms around her chest, giving me a disappointed look. "That's both super judgmental and untrue."

A little thorn of guilt pricks my side.

Perhaps that was really judgy.

Admittedly, I've never looked up Rowan's dating history. Everything I ever saw about him was on TV when Ajay and Kai watched a Bolts game. So, it *is* rude of me to assume I know anything about his past.

Why am I acting like this? Granted, he's been pushing my buttons since the minute we met, and his determination rivals a cat hell-bent on catching the red dot, but he's also been sweet and gracious—and not only to me, but to Kai. Why does it feel like my mind and body are at war, and my heart is trying to find the next empty closet to hide in?

"Yeah, you're right." I nod, looking down at my feet. "That was judgy and not at all what I really think about him. I mean, he *is* young, but that doesn't mean he hasn't had a serious girlfriend." I look up at Liv and quickly add, "Not that I'm even considering a relationship with him. Not that I'm considering *anything* with him besides our current professional relationship."

"Uh huh," Delia says, hands on her hips in a way that says she isn't buying my bullshit.

"I'm telling the truth!" I urge, my eyes widening. "Whatever you guys seem to be seeing, it's not there."

"Is that why you were on FaceTime with him on the steps last night after his game?" Dylan asks, one brow rising. But before I can ask, she raises her hands. "Don't worry, I wasn't eavesdropping or anything. I just came to check on you and saw you talking to him."

"He had a shoulder injury he wanted me to see," I state matter-of-factly, knowing I'm not telling them the entire truth–that he made up the shoulder injury and how I proceeded to stay on the phone with him, anyway. Because I liked talking to him, too.

"Around you, I don't seem to have a clue."

The leak wasn't the only thing that kept me from sleeping last night. It was also his words–veiled in meaning–toward the end of our conversation that swam around my head like directionless goldfish.

My friends stay quiet, giving me their own version of skeptical looks.

"Fine, I have thought about him! Is that what you're waiting for me to admit? That I think about him all the goddamn time, and I'm attracted to him, and I want to . . . I want to jump his cocky-as-fuck hockey star bones and become his full-time puck bunny? Because I do." I lift my arms up before dropping them to my sides, but in the process, my fingertips collide with my kombucha bottle, tipping it over my desk. "Shit!"

Yeah, I could really use that damn bubble bath or glass of wine right about now.

The girls quickly come to my aid to help me clean the mess before Liv grabs my hand. "I think if that's what you want, then you should go for it. It's obvious he likes you, too."

I snort. "Go for what? And how? How do you expect me to tell him that I'd like him to fuck me all the ways to Sunday because I can't think straight around him, but that I don't want a relationship, per se?"

Liv giggles. "Maybe just like that?"

"Just remember to use birth control when you do," Dylan adds, winking at me while running a hand over her pregnant belly. She gets a faraway look on her face. "Gosh, this would make such a cute hockey romance. Remember the last one we read in book club? This one also has a forbidden doctor-patient aspect, which makes it so much hotter."

I shake my head, dismissing her gushing. "Speaking of that forbidden aspect, what about our professional relationship?"

"Fuck the professional relationship. Fuck any relationship at all," Delia answers. "You do you. Wait, you were already doing you with all those vibrators . . . What I mean is, you let *him* do you, if that's what you both want. To hell with over-thinking the consequences or putting labels on things."

My eyes widen. "*You* are telling me to get into bed with him? *You*, who wants nothing to do with men?"

Delia bristles dramatically. "Let's be clear. I'm not *telling* you to get into bed with anyone. You're a successful woman with a great head on your shoulders, and if you *choose* to fuck another consenting adult, then more power to you. Just because I find single-celled amoebas more interesting than men doesn't mean I expect my friends to feel the same way."

"Wow. That's one hell of a convincing speech," I deadpan.

"Shay, I know what you went through with Ajay," Dylan says, giving me a meaningful look. Of all my friends, she's always been the most intuitive. "And I don't mean just while he was battling cancer. Even before that, you guys were making it work, but it wasn't great. It's time for you to live for yourself. Let the universe guide you in finding your happiness."

I swallow, my bones feeling heavy inside my small frame, trying not to remember the nights well before the cancer, when I would instigate intimacy with him—asking him to touch me, to fuck me—only for him to say he was tired or maybe we would another night.

I used to excuse it, agreeing that he *was* tired, that he had a long day.

But I can't deny there were more nights spent with those toys than with him. I can't deny that was the time I felt loneliest . . .

I stare at them, scared to even consider what they're saying, but knowing I'm already doing so. "I . . . I don't want to complicate mine and Kai's lives. What if he finds out? What if someone from the media finds out?" My heart races. "I could lose my license."

Delia's eyes bore into me. "No one is going to find out until you're ready for them to, not even Kai. And, in case you've forgotten, you have the best fucking assistant district attorney in the state of Massachusetts as your best friend. Anyone will think twice before throwing even the tiniest stone in your direction."

I take a breath, picking up my things to get ready to go to Rowan's place. I give the girls a hug and just as I'm heading out, Liv slaps my ass. "Go jump his cocky-as-fuck hockey player bones," she repeats my words. "And don't you come back until you're ready to share each and every filthy detail during our next book club."

CHAPTER 10
SHAY

I bring the little bottle to my nose, taking a whiff of his cologne, imagining my nose pressed against the base of his neck. There should be no reason for me to want the man the way I do.

But, dammit, I do.

I set the bottle down, looking around at his opulent and chic bathroom, dragging my eyes over the black leathered marble floors, all glass shower with room for ten, and landing on the enormous, freestanding tub with a beautiful chandelier above it and at least a ten-foot ornate mirror behind it.

Rowan sent me a text message right as I was pulling up to his building ten minutes ago, saying he was running an hour late from practice and to make myself at home. He even asked if I wanted anything to eat since he was going to stop by his favorite Mexican restaurant. And since I'd skipped lunch and spilled most of that kombucha, I'd quickly scanned the menu and found a salad that seemed mostly healthy–minus the fried tortilla strips–so I asked him to pick that up for me.

But now I have all this time to kill.

Walking toward the beautifully decorated shelves next to the tub, I pick up another bottle, reading the label. Hibiscus and honey bubble bath, infused with Hawaiian essential oils. I flip the cap, hovering my nose over it before taking a long inhale. I swear, I've drifted all the way to heaven on a giant flower but without any of the pollen.

Jesus, I'm practically salivating over a bottle of bubble bath.

I bite my bottom lip, staring at the bottle for another minute like it'll provide me the answers I need.

He did say to make myself at home. He also said it would take him an hour to get here—technically fifty minutes now. So, if I hurry, he would never even know.

No one would blame me for using the time to my advantage and finally doing the one thing I've been dreaming about since I moved into the house of horrors with my best friends—a fucking bubble bath.

Not wasting more time overthinking it, I quickly turn on the faucet to fill the tub before undressing and leaving my clothes on the bench near the door where the towel is. Then, realizing I'd left my purse with my Kindle on the sofa in the living room, I quickly run out to grab it, hoping Rowan's neighbors don't see me running naked through the massive windows.

Another ten minutes later, and I'm enjoying the most incredible bubble bath in the history of bubble baths. Like Versace, Gucci, and Prada all mated to have a bubble bath baby kind of bubble bath. I bet even Grecian goddesses didn't bathe like this—like they were floating inside a cloud.

Over the course of the next five minutes, I shape some bubbles over my tits, pretending to be a mermaid in a bubble bikini, make some bubble mountains, and blow some bubbles off my palms like I'm making a wish on dandelion fluff.

After all that excitement, I finally settle in the bath with my head resting on the edge. I grab my Kindle off the shelf I'd left it on and open up the book my best friends and I had picked for this week's smutty book club, called Ablaze.

My thighs clench as I read the sex scene between the two protagonists, Dean and Mala.

I run my nose along the seam of Mala's thigh before taking my first swipe of her beautiful, swollen pussy. Her body quivers under my touch and satisfaction courses through my veins.

"You smell like heaven and taste like home," I murmur over her skin.

Grabbing her thighs with my palms, I lift her hips and flatten my tongue against her. I drag it from ass to clit, back to front.

I do it again and again, making her almost clamor out of my hold.

Jesus Christ. Is it hot in here?

I read the scene again—you know, just to make sure I didn't miss any key details—but about ten minutes later, my eyelids get heavy. Putting my Kindle aside, I quickly set my phone timer to wake me up, promising myself nothing but a five-minute nap so I have enough time to drain the tub and put my clothes back on before Rowan gets home.

And no one will be the wiser.

Except . . . someone is the wiser.

Because, what feels like only thirty seconds later, I hear the softest rustling, as if the hottest man in the entire world—a NHL defenseman with the number sixteen on his jersey, perhaps—has run his palm over his scruff.

Forgetting where I am, I grab hold of the edges of the tub and clamor to my feet—my mermaid bikini having long deserted me like a cheap whore. A whoosh of water pours over the sides, pooling around the tub, but it's the amount that's gliding off me–like I'm made of waterfalls–that finally has me processing what's exactly happening.

My eyes widen as they connect with the Adonis sitting on the bench next to all my clothes across the room, in a full suit no less. His ankle sits over his knee, and his fingers scratch his chin casually, without a hint of surprise in his gaze. As if he's used to seeing his doctors rising out of his tub like underwater swamp creatures.

Without thinking, my hand flies to one of my boobs and the other rushes over my eyes. "It's not what it looks like!"

His low chuckle has goosebumps smattering across my bare skin. I can even visualize the way his Adam's apple must be bobbing, the way his teeth are gleaming inside his beautiful smile. "I'm going to have to disagree with you, Doc. It's *exactly* what it looks like. And what it looks like is my goddamn fantasy just came to life, and it's a hundred times better than I could have ever imagined it."

My cheeks flame as I peek through my fingers to look at him, but the expression on his face threatens to make my knees buckle. He looks positively ravenous as he takes me in from head to toe under his hooded gaze. Sliding his tongue over his bottom lip, he pulls it into his mouth and takes a long breath.

It's then that I realize my hands could probably be positioned better, and I quickly move the one from over my eyes to between my legs, squeezing my thighs together, and covering my other boob with my forearm. Shit, why the hell didn't I bring a towel with me?

There's no telling how high my body temperature is at this point, because I feel like I'm going to overheat and pass out from mortification.

"Jesus, you're so fucking beautiful, I'm finding it hard to breathe." His voice sounds strained, like he's having trouble finding it, but his words send a flutter of butterflies soaring inside my belly.

"Thank you," I whisper, shifting from foot to foot. "Um, can I . . . Can you hand me a towel and my clothes, please?"

A sly grin crosses his face and he reaches out a large paw and picks up my navy-colored bra, dangling it in front of me. "You mean, this?" His eyes cut away from mine for a second before he picks up my matching panties. "Or do you mean this?"

I swallow. "You know exactly what I mean, but yes, those."

Rowan's eyes smolder, sparks igniting behind his irises as he brings my panties to his nose, smelling them like a tiger would his fresh kill.

"Fucking hell," he rasps. "So goddamn delicious, and I haven't even had a taste yet."

"Rowan," I urge again, my cheeks burning.

"You want your clothes, Doc?" His smirk lifts to one side. "Well, come and get 'em."

I look around, my heart thumping against my chest. How am I supposed to climb out of this huge tub without putting my arms down? And how the hell did I get myself into this stupid predicament in the first place?

This guy is not going to give me my clothes or a towel, no matter how much I beg, and I'm getting cold from just standing here, butt naked.

Taking a short breath, I decide to take matters into my own hands, and surprise him at his own game. If this asshole thinks I'm going to shy away from getting out of the tub because I'm some kind of prude, then he has another thing coming.

Dropping my hands, I grab the edge of the tub and heave myself out, splashing more water on the floor but no longer feeling guilty about it. It should also be noted that I do not look sexy doing this—no one could, not even Gal Gadot. But if this is how he wants to play it, well . . . I'm going to make sure to drench more of his pristine marble floors!

Throwing my shoulders back, despite the fact that there's a bead of sweat lining my brows and my body could burst into flames at any moment, I pad over to him, my wet feet tapping against the floor.

His eyes hood further as I come to within a foot of him, but before I can reach out for my clothes, he lifts his arm, holding them a thousand feet over my head and shifts so I can't get to the towel, either.

Ugh! I fold my arms across my chest, feeling more of the chill against my skin. "Rowan. I need my clothes back."

His jaw clenches as he looks down at me before one of his manly brows lift. "How badly?"

"You know how badly."

The fucking bastard has the gall to smirk. "Then beg."

"Beg?" My brows fold. "Beg how? I already said please."

He takes a step closer to me, the scent of his cologne wafting over my senses, and my eyes land on the exposed divot at the bottom of his neck. He clearly took off his tie before he walked in here.

With his arm still lifted above his head, he looks down at my bare chest, and my nipples harden on their own accord. "Find another way."

I huff out a breath. "Rowan, I swear to god–"

"On your knees."

I squint at him, and if my eyes could throw fire, he'd be ash by this point. "You want me to get on my knees and beg for my own clothes."

He doesn't respond, giving me his answer with nothing but his heated stare.

"No," I say, despite the fact that I can literally feel a pool of want collecting inside my folds, threatening to trickle down my legs. God, have I ever wanted—and wanted to resist—a man so badly?

"I was hoping you'd say that. I could look at you just like this all night."

"You're an asshole, Mr. Parker," I grit out, but hell if I'll admit that the idea of being on my knees in front of this man is doing all sorts of things to me that I hadn't expected.

"You don't mean that." He smirks, bringing his face closer to mine. "It's not what your beautifully hard nipples are saying. It's not what that flush over your neck and cheeks is saying." His lips trail ever-so-softly across my cheek, and a full-body shudder that has nothing to do with the fact that my body is still wet races through me. His mouth hovers over my ear. "Show me what you'll look like when you're on your knees for me, Doc."

I turn my face just slightly so my cheek comes in contact with his lips. The scruff on his chin scrapes against my skin, and I let out a soft breath.

Rowan takes the lead, pressing his mouth to my neck, kissing and licking, making me squirm. Slowly, as if time isn't even a concept, he trails back over my jaw, nipping my skin, before leaving a kiss at the corner of my mouth. I turn my head again, practically begging him to take my mouth, but with nothing but a soft, knowing chuckle, he leans back, holding my stare. "On your knees, Doc."

Giving up, I slowly get on my knees and look up at him. There's no ignoring the giant bulge in front of me, or the fact that it's so enormous because he's turned-on.

His hand wraps around the back of my neck before his thumb caresses my cheek, right over the small mole I have there. "Do you have any clue how much I want you?"

I bite my lip. "I wish you didn't. It would make both our lives easier."

He chuckles softly, looking down at me, before his thumb lands on the center of my bottom lip, pulling it down. "I don't know about you, Doc, but I've never wanted anything that was easy, and I'm not going to start now. Easy's not worth having."

And before I can respond, he drops my clothes on the bench. A soft gust of air wafts over my skin as he heads toward the door, before looking back at me kneeling in the same spot. "You're worth having, Shayla. So, get dressed and come out. We're not done discussing whatever this is between us."

CHAPTER 11
SHAY

I'm rooted in the same spot for a few moments after he leaves, wondering what the hell just happened. Wondering how I went from trying to meet him play-for-play with my own bravado to kneeling in front of him.

I gingerly dress after draining the tub and make my way out, looking for him and feeling completely out of sorts.

Rowan's plating our dinner in the kitchen when he sees me. He's no longer wearing his suit. Instead, he's changed into black sweatpants and a Boston Bolts T-shirt that fits him snugly enough that I can make out his pecs perfectly.

He gives me his signature grin, eyeing me from head to toe. "While I love the way you look in those yoga pants, I'm not going to lie, I'd rather you not wear any clothes around me."

My cheeks still feel heated, my nerves in a tangle. "I'm really sorry about . . ." I swallow, wondering where to start. "About everything. It was so inappropriate for me to use your tub, and then, uh, to act like *that* after . . ." I look down at my feet.

Rowan closes the distance between us, his finger lifting my

chin so I'm looking at him. "Please don't be sorry. Not for any of it. I finally got to see another side of you . . . a side of you I quite like. But the truth is, I have yet to find a single thing about you I don't like."

I smile. "Oh, I'm sure I'll give you a few things to dislike over time."

And just as those words come out of my mouth, the significance of them dawns on me.

Rowan's eyes glimmer. "I like the sound of that."

"Rowan–"

He puts his finger on my mouth, halting any further words. "I have a feeling you're going to ruin this moment with all your nonsense about rules and boundaries, and I'd like to have something in my stomach before you do that."

As if his talk of food has been directly heard by my stomach, it makes an embarrassing groan, and both Rowan and I laugh.

"Looks like your stomach agrees," he says, sliding his hand down my arm and grasping my fingers. "How about you sit on the couch, and I'll bring you dinner?"

I narrow my eyes at him. "Why does this feel like a date you never asked me to?"

"Did you miss the last, let's see," he puts his index finger dramatically over his chin, pretending to think, "*five times* I tried to insinuate I wanted to date you?"

I scoff. "Um, *yeah*, I must have! And how did you *insinuate* wanting to date me?"

He lifts a finger. "One, when I wanted only *you* to be my physical therapist." He lifts another finger. "Two, when I sent you that vibrator you've been using nonstop since you met me." I giggle, and he lifts another finger. "Three, when I asked you to come with me to California for the away games this weekend." He lifts his pinky. "Four, when I asked you and Kai to come to my game." He lifts his thumb. "And five, when I asked you if there was any way we could meet after the last game and compromised with a FaceTime call."

I laugh. "Oh, is that what those were? Your *attempts* at asking me on a date?"

He nods enthusiastically like I've just correctly guessed a *Wheel of Fortune* puzzle. "Yes! They were."

I giggle again, a strange warmth spreading around my chest, making me feel like I'm floating. When did this shift happen between us? When did he start chipping away at the walls I've worked so hard to build? "Mr. Rowan 'Slick' Parker, have you ever asked a girl out on a date before?"

"Yes! I just told you about the last five times, all of which you seemed cither very oblivious to or completely against. It's been hell on my ego, to say the least."

I tilt my head. "Pretty sure there isn't much that can make a dent in that ego."

He leans forward, a vulnerable smile playing on his lips, before he whispers, "Except you."

I throw my hands up in defeat. "I give up. You win."

"Does that mean you're saying yes?"

I hesitate, buying time. "I don't make good decisions on an empty stomach, and right now, I'm famished. So, you're going to have to feed me first."

He tilts his head. "I'd argue you've made better decisions today on that empty stomach than ever before. Maybe I need to keep you hungry around me." He winks. "Then you can just have me for dinner."

I lay a hand on his chest. "As tempting as that sounds, there's a salad with my name on it that I'd really like."

A few seconds later, we're both sitting with our meals on the couch–him with his massive burrito that looks like it could feed a small country for days, and me with my salad.

Rowan wipes his mouth after taking a bite, watching me pick out the tortilla strips. "You don't like tortilla strips?" He leans closer, like he's telling me a secret. "Not gonna lie, Doc, the only thing exciting in that salad are the tortilla strips."

I smile. "I don't eat anything fried or processed."

He looks appalled. "Like, *ever*?"

I nod self-consciously.

He lifts his burrito. "So, would you eat this burrito? There isn't anything fried in it." He glances at it and chuckles. "Well, except the refried beans and chicken."

I eye said burrito tucked inside the aluminum foil wrapper, and I won't lie, it smells delicious and looks like it tastes just as good. "That, and the flour tortilla, cheese, and the sour cream inside are high in saturated fat. Then, there's all that rice, which has a lot of carbs."

He smiles playfully. "And yet, you're looking at it like you'd chase it if it started running."

I make a face at him. "Leave me alone. I'm just hungry."

"Have you always been like this?"

I give him a smug look, taking a bite of my salad. "Like what? *Incredible, perfect,* the bee's knees?"

Rowan snorts. "And you call me cocky." He leans in again. "By the way, Doc, no one uses 'the bee's knees' anymore. They haven't since the turn of the century."

I poke him on the bicep with my fork and he howls, pretending to be hurt. "Well, I'm going to be the bee's knees revivalist! It's a *buzz-worthy* phrase."

He groans at my lame joke. "Good luck with that. What I meant was, have you always eaten this healthy?"

I shake my head. "I started around the time . . ." I clear my throat, not wanting to dampen the mood. "Around the time Ajay was going through chemo. After reading about cancer until I practically reached the end of the internet, I went into this health-food frenzy, eliminating everything from our fridge and pantry that had any unnatural dyes, processed sugars, and wasn't organic. Ever since, I've become really careful with what Kai and I put into our bodies."

Rowan puts his burrito down, turning to give me all his attention. It's something I notice he does every time we talk–giving me his undivided attention–and it's something I don't ever recall getting from Ajay. "Do you think it was something in his diet that caused him to get sick?"

I shrug. "No one knows for sure. It could have been anything–a genetic alteration, something environmental, who knows? But I hated that I had no control over it. I hated that feeling of having to just accept it. That feeling of . . ."

"Helplessness," Rowan adds when I trail off.

"Yeah," I whisper. "So, it's not that I control what Kai and I eat because it will keep us from becoming sick, it's just that I try to do what I can."

The memory of me smoking on the steps the other night floats into my vision, and I quickly wave it off. I'm not planning on smoking again, so I'm going to chalk it up to a stress-induced mistake and get back on the wagon.

Rowan's golden-green gaze scrolls across my face before he takes another bite, chewing pensively.

"What?" I ask, knowing he wants to say something.

He shakes his head. "No, it's just . . . fuck! It just seems like you're punishing yourself for something that could happen anyway, you know?" His eyes bounce between mine. "Let me preface this by saying this isn't a great example, nor is it the same as what you went through with your husband, but my dad left my mom when my sister and I were in our teens."

I place my hand on his forearm, my heart lurching toward him as I take in his tight jaw and the way he's white-knuckling the ball of aluminum foil he'd torn off his burrito. "I'm sorry, Rowan."

He gnaws on his bottom lip for a moment. "The thing is, Mom did everything right. She was a perfect wife, a perfect mother. She was his biggest fan and his staunchest supporter, taking on all responsibility for my sister and me so my dad could focus on his career. When Dad played home games, he could always rely on the fact that he'd get a home-cooked meal afterward.

"And you know what else?" He looks at me but doesn't wait for me to ask. "She always looked her best." He shakes his head as if immersed in the memory. "As soon as she knew he was coming home, she'd go and fix her hair and makeup, sometimes even change her clothes. But even after all that," he chuckles mirthlessly, "after nearly twenty years of being together, my dad still walked out on her—*on us*—to marry a woman half my mom's age."

I rub circles on his arm with my thumb, my eyes connected to the spot. I knew Rowan's dad was a famous hockey player, but I hadn't known about any of the other details. "How is your mom now?"

Rowan smiles, his face lighting back up like the way I'm used to seeing it. "She remarried and is living with a man who thinks the world of her, actually."

That lifts my mood. "Well, that's great. You seem close."

"We are." He nods. "My sister Piper, my mom, and me are three peas in a pod."

I don't correct him on the idiom because I get what he means.

"But the reason I told you that," he says after a pause, "is to show you that you can do everything to control a situation, but there are circumstances that will test all your efforts. I get that you want to eat healthy and do what you can to stay away from bad shit, but don't you ever just want to relax the rules? Eating an unhealthy meal from time to time isn't going to hurt you; in fact, it may actually make you feel happier. And in the end, isn't that what we all want?"

He takes another big bite of his burrito and gives me the widest, goofiest smile imaginable. "See. Look at how happy I am," he says before looking at my salad in dismay. "And look at how sad you are."

I can't even help it. I laugh. The man knows how to bring light to everything he touches. He is so fucking cute that I have to wonder how someone who projects so much power and strength—both on and off the ice—could be both so handsome and adorable at the same time.

"I'll tell you what," he starts, his beautiful eyes sparkling with another one of his mischievous ideas. "There's no pressure, but–"

"Uh huh," I deadpan, cutting him off. "Because you've never been one to pressure . . . "

He continues undeterred, "If you don't feel just a tiny, eensy-weensy bit happier after taking a bite of this delicious burrito, then we'll never discuss this topic again."

I tilt my head skeptically, trying not to find him any cuter for saying 'eensy-weensy'. "First of all, I highly doubt I'll feel any happier after eating that, because I'll just be thinking about all the bad stuff in it. And second of all, I don't see you as the type to give up after I take one, *eensy-weensy* bite."

"What are you so worried about, Doc? Scared one bite will ruin you for life?" He waggles his brows like there's another hidden meaning behind his words.

Sighing out my exhaustion, I pull his hand toward me, taking a large bite of his burrito.

At first, it feels like an explosion of tastes—spicy, salty, and even a hint of sweet—on my tongue, but the crunchy lettuce, the savory meat, and the flavorful beans have me slowing down my chewing so I can keep the taste in my mouth longer.

Holy shit! I wasn't expecting that.

I mean, I've eaten burritos in the past–I've eaten a lot of things in the past that I no longer eat–but I guess I'd sort of forced myself to forget the taste. I made myself believe I wasn't missing anything. But with just one bite, my taste buds have reawakened, as if they'd been asleep for decades.

Rowan's thunderous laugh has me safely landing back on planet Earth. "Oh, Doc. I wish I could go back in time. I'd make you promise me something in return because shit, I don't think I've ever seen a smile that big and that happy in all my life."

I lick my lips before grabbing the burrito from his hand to take another bite. Then, I pass him my salad. "You can go now," I mumble mid-bite before moaning a little louder than I'd intended. "I might need a few minutes alone with Mr. Big, Thick, and Tasty here."

Rowan's eyes flame. "Are you trying to make me jealous of a burrito, Doc? Because it's fucking working."

"Who, me?" I blink innocently at him, chewing my food.

He watches me devour almost his entire burrito until I'm in potential danger of going into a food coma–something I haven't had in years–before placing the bottom part of it in my hand back on his plate on the coffee table.

When he turns back to me, his eyes drop to my lips and there's that same hunger in them–the one no amount of saturated fat or carbs will satisfy. Raising his hand to my face, he drags his thumb along the corner of my mouth, capturing a trace of sour cream. He then brings his thumb to his lips and licks it clean.

Heat swirls in my abdomen as my heart rate kicks up, and we both stay locked in a moment neither of us want to release.

"What—" I pause, trying to find my words. "What promise would you have wanted in return?"

His gaze darkens, like a forest under twilight, before he grabs a hold of my hand and tugs me to him. In an instant, I'm straddling him on the couch—my small frame almost child-like against his. "That's easy."

I place my hands on his shoulders before I slip one around his jaw, rubbing my thumb against his short, dark scruff. "Tell me."

"I'd have asked for a kiss."

I bite back my smile, dropping my eyes to his chest, feeling completely tongue-tied. Instead, I deflect to more familiar territory, like the reason I'm here—his physical therapy and injury. "I'm probably making your pain worse."

His voice is ragged on an exhale. "Oh, you have no idea."

My eyes connect with his, my fingers trailing to the back of his neck. Have I ever felt this seen before? Like he's literally looking for any opening to squeeze through and lodge himself deep inside me. It's terrifying and thrilling at the same time.

"Rowan, I need us to have some boundaries, if—" I stutter, wondering where I'm getting the courage to even say this out loud, "if we're going to do this."

His hands rest on my ass. And though they haven't moved, it's a strangely possessive hold. "I wouldn't expect anything less. As long as the rules don't apply to my food, I'm game."

I raise a brow, feeling cheeky. "And if they do?"

"Then I'd demand you be naked around me at all times."

I laugh, watching as his eyes halt on my lips. "Deal."

"I'd really like to get through these terms and conditions in the next few minutes, Doc. A man can only wait so long."

I slide my index finger down his neck and feel him harden under me in response. "You're an impatient man, Mr. Parker."

His hands tighten on my ass. "You can't possibly imagine how much patience this is taking."

"Fine," I say after a soft giggle. "I'll start. As you know, I'm a single mom. My son's safety and well-being is the most important thing to me. So, if we do this, I don't want Kai knowing about it."

"*Ever*?" Rowan grimaces.

I'm a little taken aback by the question. What does he mean, ever? Of course, it's *ever . . .*

How long does he expect this to last? He'll fuck me out of his system and move on to one of the many women ready to throw their puck-bunny bodies at him. I can't risk telling Kai about a short, detached relationship, especially not with his favorite hockey player. He's only a little kid. We've had a brief chat about me "moving on" when the time was right, but I have no idea if he'd be ready for that now.

Plus, what if he gets his hopes up about something working out long-term between Rowan and me? He'd be devastated when it ends, and I just can't see his heart break like that again—especially not after the way it broke when Ajay died.

A small voice inside my head asks if I'm just talking about my son's heart, but I refuse to answer it.

"For as long as this lasts," I finally say.

Rowan's shoulders slump, the heat cooling inside his eyes, making me feel like I've already started us off on the wrong foot. But my son's heart isn't something I'll compromise.

"The next thing is about my job."

"Yeah, I already know," he chimes in. "I'm your patient, you're my PT, and that shit could put your career in jeopardy."

I nod. "It's the only career I have, and I support both Kai and myself with it, so I couldn't handle anyone tarnishing my reputation."

"I wouldn't fucking let them," he says vehemently.

I smile, appreciating his protectiveness, but I also need to make sure he really understands. "The media is always after you, constantly looking for stories. And this would be something that could ruin me, Rowan. Under no circumstances can we be pictured together in any way besides as two professionals."

"Yeah, I hear you," he says, lifting his hand to gently stroke my cheek. "I'm on the same page. I would never want anything to hurt you."

My heart skips a beat. When the hell did this man become so swoony? I place my forehead on his and we just breathe each other's air for a moment. "I got cleared to go to California with you this weekend, by the way."

Rowan's face brightens briefly, but quickly clouds with worry about my answer. "Does that mean you've decided to join?"

I nod, watching a relieved smile work over his lips.

"I'm looking forward to spending time with you, Doc." The mischief dancing with his brows betrays him. "In a completely *professional* way, of course."

"It has to be professional when we're in public."

"It will be." He gives me a resolute look. "But I make no promises for when we're in private."

"I would expect nothing less," I respond, and my heart does a happy somersault at the prospect of Rowan Parker doing *unprofessional* things to me.

The man is turning me into putty, making me mold and bend to his desires. I've always had a healthy sexual appetite, but around him, my libido seems to have a mind of its own, asking me–*begging me*–to jump him. And, though it frightens me, I can't help but want to explore more with him.

"Any other stipulations?" he mumbles, his hands skating down my back.

I nod, grinning mischievously. If there's one thing I already love about this man, it's his need to rise to a challenge, and I have a feeling he won't disappoint. "Well, I don't know if you can manage this one . . ."

He squints at me, already irritated that I'd question his competence. "Try me."

"I'm gonna need better orgasms than my fancy new gold-plated vibrator can give me."

CHAPTER 12
ROWAN

Before she can even process it, I've got her pinned to the couch under me. Her legs are still wrapped around my torso.

My large hands span her sides before my thumbs reach up to circle her nipples, covered by her clothes. Shay's hips jump under me as she tucks her bottom lip into her mouth, a soft moan escaping from it.

There's no end to the satisfaction I feel knowing how responsive she is with just that slight touch. "I'm not one to back down from a challenge, Doc."

Her chest rises and falls, a challenge building inside her irises. "You sure about that, Mr. Parker? Jensen is pretty hard to beat."

I freeze, my jaw clenching before I realize who—or *what*—she's talking about. I give her an incredulous look, making her giggle. "You *named* it?"

She nods, her hip thrusting up slightly against me. She's stunning in every way—large espresso-colored eyes, full lips, a square face with that adorable little mole on the top of her cheek, and perfectly styled, short hair.

She's different from the type of women I usually go for, and not just because she's older and a single mom. She's independent, tough, and as sharp as a tack. I'm not just mesmerized by her beauty, I'm in awe of her intellect and wit, too.

Apart from all that, the woman is ballsy. A ballsy little spitfire who not only took a bath in my tub—*using all my bath soaps, mind you*—like she was Goldilocks, but she also squared her shoulders and climbed out like she owned the place!

And when she got on her knees, looking up at me with those wide brown eyes, my cock practically fought through my pants to get out. Jesus, the vision of her, naked and dripping over my bathroom floor, did things to me I'd never felt in my entire life.

She was a mixture of vulnerability and courage, but for the first time since we met, she showed me a side of her that was also real and playful. A side of her that said I wasn't completely off base, that our connection wasn't just a figment of my imagination.

Because she felt it, too.

Her core rubs against me, and I urge my dick to settle the fuck down. "I name all of them."

I grind my molars. "How fucking many do you have?"

"Oh, like twelve," she says airily. "There's Brad, he's sort of my go-to—reliable and consistent. Then, there's Denzel." She wiggles, getting this ridiculous swoony look in her eyes, like she's imagining this dildo as the actor himself. "He's just long and thick. And then there's Leonardo—"

Oh, for God's sake, I need to shut this woman up.

I slam my mouth over hers, effectively doing just that. I swear, I've never wanted to throw dildos against a wall more than I do right now.

At first, she stills in my arms, but as my lips work hers, she relaxes into me. Her hands come up to my shoulders before she slips one over the back of my head, pulling me down to her. Her mouth opens and I snake my tongue inside, finding hers.

A low groan spills from my throat as my hands find the globes of her breasts and I squeeze, working over her nipples with my thumbs again. I can feel them taut against her shirt.

Shay grinds up against me, moaning as her legs tighten around me. I can smell her sweet scent as if my nose was buried in it. She's so fucking ready, so needy, and I'm having a hard time thinking straight.

My mouth works against hers, taking what I've been dying to have since the moment I saw her, tasting her and etching this moment into my memory for as long as I live. Her lips are soft and plush like pillows, and a vision of them stretched around my cock has me practically turning to stone inside my pants.

I kiss her, long and hard, soft and slow, before dragging my lips over her jaw and down her neck. My heart races like a thoroughbred sprinting toward the finish line as everything seems to disappear around me. My hands roam down her sides and under her ass, pulling her needy center toward me, letting her feel exactly what she's doing to me.

Her fingers capture the short strands of my hair and, writhing under me, she whimpers, "Rowan."

I pull back to look at her, loving the soft whisper of my name on her lips. "You want me, baby?" I ask, dipping down to run my nose along her neck, taking a long inhale of her flowery perfume.

"Yes," she hisses. "Please, yes."

I chuckle against her, nipping at her skin. As much as I want to bury my face inside her wet pussy and devour her the way we both want, I know I need to rein this in. This fever. This hunger. This goddamn maddening desire.

Because if there was one thing I realized after our little run-in inside my bathroom, besides the fact that she was the hottest woman I'd ever seen, it was that she trusted me.

She got on her knees in front of me, not because I asked her to or because she needed her clothes that badly. She did it to give me a part of her she rarely gave others–her trust.

And because I know the value of that, I want to take things slowly.

No matter how much my cock thinks otherwise.

I tuck the long side of her hair behind her ear, looking at her bee-stung lips. "There's nothing I'd like more than to throw you over my shoulder and take you to my bed–"

"Yes," she nods enthusiastically, cutting me off, "you really ought to do that."

My lips twitch. "But if we're really going to do this, then I'm going to take my time with you, Shayla."

She pouts, grasping the collar of my shirt and pulling me toward her lips again. It only takes a few seconds before I'm lost in another kiss–a mix between frenzied and slow. My hands wrap around her face, and I tilt it to change the angle and deepen our connection, making her hum contentedly against my mouth. "God, you're a good kisser."

I smile, not taking my lips off her and playing into that cocky side she loves to hate so much. "You'll find that I'm good at *everything* I do, sweetheart. That'll include *you* at some point."

"I'll believe it when I see it," she quips, clearly trying to sway my decision.

I grasp the back of her neck, my eyes boring into her. "Oh, you'll see it alright. See it, *feel* it. I plan on making it hard for you to walk for days afterward."

Her legs tighten around me, and she squirms in her seat. "Are you sure I can't get a demonstration of this grand performance you're promising tonight?"

I laugh, placing another kiss on her lips. "Soon. But I have a few conditions of my own."

She lifts her brow. "Oh, yeah?"

I trail my nose across her jaw. "First, you won't use your toys unless you're with me."

A sound between a groan and a gasp escapes her mouth. "That's not fair. I won't be able to see you every day, and Jensen gets lonely without me."

"Fuck Jensen!" I growl, pulling her closer and biting her neck gently.

"Well, that's precisely what I'm trying to do, Mr. Parker!"

"Shay, I swear to God–"

She giggles, burying her fingers in my hair. "Okay, okay, big guy. No toys unless you're there."

"Good."

"Anything else?"

I gnaw on my bottom lip as unwanted memories flood my vision, and my lighthearted mood wavers. Shadows and scars of my past burn inside my chest as I recall my humiliation and heartbreak, once plastered all over the news.

They're memories I wish I could shirk away but come unbidden when least expected.

"Hey." Shayla's hand skims down the back of my neck. "Where'd you go?"

I shake my head but make sure she sees the severity of my next condition in my expression. "I'm not sharing you with anyone, Shay. This has to be exclusive. Just you and me."

Just the thought of someone else touching her, holding her, kissing her, ignites a fire within me. And though I've dealt with the situation before–with some other asshole having the audacity to touch someone I thought was mine, with my girl-friend of three years having the audacity to tell me she allowed him to—this thing between Shayla and me feels different.

Her hands span my jaw before she leans in to drop a soft kiss on my lips. Maybe she can tell I need reassurance. "No one else. Just you and me."

"There's one more thing." I swallow, knowing this will be the make or break question. The one I've left for last because not only am I terrified of asking it, I'm terrified of her reaction. "It's about Kai."

Shay straightens in my arms like I expected. "What about Kai?"

"I want to teach him to skate."

My eyes fly to the entrance for what feels like the hundredth time in the last five minutes before I look back down at my phone to make sure she hasn't texted me.

She hasn't, but there is a text from one of the other two women in my life—my sister, Piper. I've programmed my phone so her name is what I called her when we were toddlers.

PEPPER

T-1 day until I see my baby brother. Any chance I can convince you to bring me a slice of that Boston cream pie from Oscar's? Wish they'd be willing to ship, but they won't.

I type back a response as I skate around the rink.

ME

Ah, so that's the only reason you want to see me, huh? For your favorite pie.

PEPPER

Pretty much. <kiss emoji> See you soon, baby bro. Miss you.

I put my phone away, smiling. We're only ten months apart–Irish twins–and I'm a good foot taller than her, but my sister still refers to me as her baby brother.

I suppose she's always treated me that way–putting everything on hold to take care of me if I ever needed it, being my ultimate cheerleader and protector. In fact, she pretty much vets every woman I've ever remotely been interested in, as if she's my hired PI.

My mom has often said Piper was more a momma-bear than she ever was. But hey, in a world where genuine relationships are scarce, I consider myself lucky to have a sister who'd go to bat for me, no matter what.

Even when my life blew up that first year I played for the New York Mayors, with my personal life torched on every news outlet, it was Piper who flew in from San Francisco–missing some important classes for beauty school–to gather up my pieces. It was her and my mom who kept me from drowning in my own sorrow and whiskey.

I glance at the clock on the wall, wondering if I should text Shayla. What if she changed her mind? What if her fears got the best of her, and she decided to keep her son home instead?

Truth be told, I'm surprised she even said yes to begin with, but after I answered every question she had–*Could he wear his astronaut costume from last Halloween since it had a helmet and extra padding already built in? Will his skates have an emergency brake?*—she seemed to feel more comfortable. I assured her he wouldn't need his astronaut costume, knee pads, or a mouth guard, and that he wouldn't be going fast enough to need brakes on his skates.

Still, she's been a bit of a wild card since we met, keeping me guessing with every move, so I can't say for sure that she will actually show up.

I do a couple more laps around the rink, stretching out and warming up my muscles. I wasn't able to book the Bolts' arena on such short notice, so I ended up private-booking an indoor ice skating rink for the whole day instead.

I don't foresee us spending that much time on the ice, especially since it'll be Kai's first time skating, but I just didn't want to have to rush, either. Today will be all about getting him comfortable being on the ice and finding his balance.

I massage my thigh, hoping to loosen the muscles. The injury I sustained to my groin feels better every day, but it'll take another few weeks before I'm really back in the swing of things.

Still, the exercises Shay customized for me have been a boon in my healing progress. Though, I can feel myself holding back when I'm playing a game, like the one we played and lost 3-5 against my old team, the New York Mayors, last night.

I frown, knowing I could have done better, knowing I disappointed my team, given the fact I've been out for five games already with my injury. Sure, we won our match Tuesday night against Tampa, but I was especially looking forward to gloating on a win against the Mayors. Specifically, their center, and my ex-best friend, Evan Lanthrop.

Fucking pissed me off that our plays along the boards were weak, as was our puck possession and defense. Not to mention our right wing lost his stick during the last minute in the third period. And while he was able to get a new one, it gave New York that slight advantage.

My jaw clenches, recalling the smug expression on Evan's face after the last goal horn sounded. It's a good thing he wasn't close enough to me, or I'd have likely smashed his face into the ice–and really, that wouldn't have been good for either of us.

My gaze snags on the entrance when I hear the door shut, and the two people I've been waiting for enter.

Shay is wearing some type of body-hugging athleisure-wear, her gold hoops peeking out from her short hair, while her hands rest on Kai's shoulders. They both look in my direction with tentative smiles.

Kai's bundled up in what looks like at least four layers of clothes and knee pads, his overgrown thick hair swept messily to the side.

Getting out of the rink, I quickly walk toward them in my skates, and we meet in the middle, near the boxes I'd set out earlier.

My heart gallops at the sight of the woman I haven't been able to stop thinking about. "Hi."

I want to reach out and hug her, kiss her, hold her. And though it sucks that I can't, I completely understand the reason for it.

"Hey," she responds, giving me a soft smile. I've recently become the recipient of those lately as compared to the tighter ones she used to offer me. "Sorry we got a little delayed. There was a sudden case of missing door handles, and we *literally* couldn't get out on time."

My brows furrow and I'm about to ask how the hell her door handles disappeared when she speaks again. "I saw you warming up on the ice. How's your pain level today?"

I smile. "Better! I have an amazing physical therapist."

That has Kai turning to give his mom a proud smile.

I bend so I'm at face-level with him and reach for his hand. "I'm Rowan Parker. I've been looking forward to meeting you, Kai."

Kai's smile stretches over his face, his eyes gleaming as if he can hardly believe what he's seeing.

I've been fawned over by fans since I joined professional hockey, but this might be the first time my chest feels warm because of it.

He places his small hand in mine, shaking it enthusiastically. "It's really great to meet you, Mr. Parker. I'm a huge fan."

"The feeling is mutual, Kai. Your mom has said a lot of great things about you. But you can call me Rowan or Slick."

Kai looks at his mom behind him, as if to get her permission, before he looks back at me. "I think I'll call you Rowan since we named one of our raccoon's babies Slick, and that could get confusing."

My brows bunch up again. I remember Shayla had mentioned something about this in a previous conversation, but I just thought the raccoons were a metaphor for something at the time. "Your raccoon's baby?"

Kai nods as if this should be common knowledge. "Yeah, we have a family of raccoons in our chimney, and the mom raccoon, Junior, had three babies. A few of us got to name them, so I named one of them Slick, after you. They're loud, but we can't re-home them until they're older."

"I see," I say, even though I now have a whole slew of new questions. "So, they just go in and out of your chimney as needed?"

"Yeah," he answers. "Bossman and Uncle Cortney put a metal grate around the chimney so they can't get into the house, but we can see and hear them in there all the time. Plus,

Colette, Phoebe, and I made periscopes so we can see Junior when she leaves to get them more food.

Bossman and Uncle Cortney? What the hell?

The confusion must be written over my face because Shay takes a breath, answering my unasked question, "The kids call Beckett Bossman." She eyes me, knowing that isn't explaining a whole lot. "I live with my best friends–Dylan, Liv, and Delia– and their significant others. Well, Delia hasn't had a significant other since her fourth-grade boyfriend, whom she broke up with because 'he was too entrenched in our systemic patri- archy'. But Beckett is Liv's husband, and Cortney is Dylan's fiancé." She pauses, making sure I'm following. I'm really not, but I'm trying. "And yeah, we all live together with all our children."

I blink at her. "Beckett Langfield?"

Shay nods. "And Cortney Miller."

My eyes widen. "As in, the Revs' catcher? *That* Cortney Miller?"

"Yup."

"All of you live in one house?" I ask again because, clearly, I'm still not processing.

Kai laughs, seeming to find my line of questioning funny, while Shayla lets out a puff of air. "Well, I suppose you could call it a 'house'." She air quotes around the last word. "There are parts of it that have a roof, and there are still a few walls missing."

I shake my head, not knowing what to say. Where the hell is this woman living?

I'd known she was new to Boston, having moved from Cali- fornia, but she hadn't mentioned anything about living in a house with all her friends and their families.

Was this some sort of cult?

A sister-wives situation?

"Mom and her friends made a pact last year," Kai adds. "It's why we all live together in the house Aunt Delia inherited."

"A pact?" I ask, looking back at Shayla for clarification. This definitely has cult vibes written all over it.

My mind starts buzzing with more questions, like how much am I willing to do for this woman? *Am I willing to join a cult?*

I've never been interested in doing any sort of wife swapping . . .

And how does that work with Delia, since she doesn't seem to like men? In any case, I don't want any other woman except Shay, so what would this all entail if we started getting serious? I certainly don't want to share her; I'd fucking break Beckett's pretty-boy face if he touched her. And Cortney Miller? Yeah, he can forget about catching anything ever again when I break his hand for doing the same.

Shit, this all seems really complicated.

Shayla nods, as if what she was about to share was just another run-of-the-mill sort of life story. "After college, my best friends and I remained close. So, when Delia inherited a humongous, dilapidated brownstone here in Boston, and we all ended up being single moms, we decided to move in and raise our kids together. We've been struggling to repair the house ever since, mainly due to unreliable contractors, but also Delia's unattainable standards." She pauses, taking a breath. "Anyway, that's how Kai and I ended up here."

I reel back, taking it all in. "Wow. That's . . ."

"It's really fun!" Kai exclaims as I trail off, trying to find the right word! "Thirteen-and-a-half of us and our raccoons!"

I feel like I keep hearing the wrong things and asking dumb questions. "Thirteen-and-a-half?"

"Yeah, Dylan and Cortney are pregnant," Shay answers for him.

I blow out a breath before looking at Kai. "Seems like you live quite an exciting life, kid. Thanks for naming one of the raccoon kits after me."

He gleams. "Well, you're my favorite player. Plus, I think he's getting pretty big with all Mom's food we've been–"

His mouth falls agape suddenly, his eyes going wide, like he's just seen a ghost. A flush takes over the tops of his cheeks, and he turns around to face his mom, who's giving him a look a lot like my own mother did when I'd majorly fucked up.

"Mom–"

"Kai Kumar!" Shayla chides, making me feel bad for the poor kid. And though her tone is sharp, there's a gentleness to it, too–that perfect gentle-firm tone only moms somehow know how to get right. "Have you been giving your protein bars to the raccoons? Do you know how much time I put into making those?"

Kai looks down at his feet. "I'm sorry, Mom. I saw Aunt Dylan give the high fiber bread you made to Uncle Cortney. Usually, he's the one who eats most of the food you make her, but then I saw him sneak it to the raccoons. So, I . . . I did it, too."

Shayla wraps her arms around her chest. "We're going to have a chat about this later."

Kai nods, accepting his fate, and I take that as my cue to cheer him up a little. Picking up one of the boxes, I open the top. "Hey! So, I didn't know your size, but I figured you could try on a few and see what fits best."

Kai's eyes light up again. "You got me new skates?!"

Shay eyes all the boxes next to me. "Rowan, did you purchase an entire store? You really didn't have to do all this.

You're already doing so much by giving him private lessons that I could never afford."

I shrug sheepishly. "Perks of being my–" I stop myself right before I accidentally say the word, 'girlfriend,' flicking my gaze to ensure Kai hasn't heard anything, "physical therapist."

Our gazes stay locked while Kai busies himself opening up more boxes, before she whispers, "Thank you," tucking her hair behind her ear shyly.

God, I want to kiss her so fucking bad, I'm physically having to restrain myself.

Wrenching my gaze away from hers, I pick up another box, opening it to show Kai the helmet I bought. We put it on his head, but it's too large, so I open up a smaller size that works better.

I help Kai into his new skates, tucking them under what seems to be three pairs of pants, and letting him open up the last box on his own.

When he peeks inside, his mouth drops again. "A special edition number sixteen jersey!" He looks at his mom, surprise in his eyes. "Mom! Rowan signed it!"

Shay's shiny eyes collide with mine before she looks at Kai. "What do you say, sweetheart?"

Kai wraps his arms around my neck, and I instinctively hold him to me, wondering if I've ever met a sweeter kid in my life. "Thank you, Rowan. I love it."

My chest tightens and I rub his back. "You ready to get on the ice, bud?"

He nods, his face still squished to my neck, making my throat go dry. "So ready."

CHAPTER 13
SHAY

My eyes track Kai closely as Rowan teaches him the basics of how to fall properly and finding his balance.

He towers over him, but for as big and burly as he looks next to my little boy, he's just as gentle and patient.

They've been at it for well over an hour, taking needed breaks to warm up off the ice. And though I was sure Kai–or Rowan–would call it quits after the first half hour, they're continuing as if they could go on for days.

Rowan skates backward, bent down, firmly holding Kai's hands and pulling him forward. I can see Kai's knees wobble, but he's got a steel grip on Rowan's hands. Or is it the other way around?

Kai says something I can't hear, but a moment later, Rowan throws back his head, his thunderous laugh echoing against the empty seats. He scoops Kai up in his arms and zooms around the ice, as if he weighs nothing. And even though my heart hammers inside my chest–not just from concerns of Kai's safety–I grip my phone tighter, reminding myself to breathe.

He's in good hands—the best hands on the ice, at least—so I have nothing to fear. But above all that, I'd promised myself that I wasn't going to let my fears control my son any longer. Sure, I obviously can't just tuck them all away inside a box and get rid of them for good in the matter of a few days, but I promised myself to work on it, and I plan on doing just that.

I refuse to let "ball of nevers" be my lifelong nickname.

I take another breath, allowing myself to smile, as I watch Rowan set Kai down and they practice marching on the ice.

Is it crazy that I find a man who can get down to a child's level—letting go of his own inhibitions—so sexy? My ovaries sure do, based on their twerking and gyrating inside me like the little tramps they are, catcalling and yelling, *"Ooh, pick me! Pick me!"*

It doesn't hurt that said man is a certified jaw-dropper from head to toe with a derriere carved from marble. But even so, at this very moment, that's not what makes him sexy. It's the sheer joy on his face as he looks at my son, the encouragement he provides as Kai struggles.

Warmth spreads through my chest, intense enough that if Rowan was to make eye contact with me right now, he'd see my thoughts written all over my face. Pushing them aside, I get off my seat. Bringing up my phone's camera, I zoom in on the two of them.

Rowan is still teaching Kai to march, but now he's also doing some sort of goofy dance, making my son laugh. They both have their arms out, but Rowan bounces with each step, trying to get Kai to loosen up and enjoy being on the ice.

I snap a picture of them laughing at whatever the other has said.

Sliding back into my seat, I tuck my hair behind my ear and look down at the picture I just took. My mouth curves up into a smile, knowing this is one I'll have to frame for Kai to keep on his dresser.

I flip to the one I took before Rowan and Kai walked into the rink. This one might be my personal favorite–with Kai standing next to Rowan, his head tilted as far up as it can go, looking at his hero with the biggest smile on his face.

It both pinches my heartstrings and sets an ache inside my chest. It's as if through those two pictures–spontaneous moments captured inside a frame–I finally see what Kai's been missing all this time.

And that scares the hell out of me while also filling me up with hope.

Because, for the first time in longer than I can remember, he's acting like a kid–silly and happy. For the first time in a long time, he's not worried about looking at me for permission, gauging my expression to see if I'm happy; he's solely thinking of his own happiness. And for the first time in a long time, he isn't being saddled with my fears.

And Rowan's smile? It's brighter than the lights reflecting off the ice. This man, who doesn't know either of us well, who doesn't owe us anything, but who's put his all in from the get-go.

With Rowan, what you see is what you get. He's an open book, honest and direct, where most people–including myself– wear a mask, pretending to be someone else. Rowan is authentic to a fault.

And damn if that's not the most refreshing surprise in all this.

My phone buzzes in my hands from an incoming text.

JEENA

Did you bone him yet?

I chuckle to myself, shaking my head. Between my best friends and Jeena, I swear all the women in my life have banded together to get me laid.

Jeena was ecstatic when I told her about Rowan. Aside from Liv, Delia, and Dylan, she's the only one I've acknowledged my attraction to my gorgeous patient and, as expected, she's been messaging me nonstop for updates.

ME

It's only been two days since he and I talked about it.

I'm not surprised to see her reply within seconds.

JEENA

So?

I sigh.

ME

So, we discussed some rules since neither of us is looking for anything serious. And he said he wants to take it slow.

I look up and spot Rowan and Kai heading out of the rink for a drink. Rowan hands Kai a sports drink, and though I'm tempted to check the ingredients, I consider it a personal victory in restraint that I don't.

Kai looks up to meet my gaze, clearly asking for my permission, and even though there's an anxious swirl in my stomach, I nod, getting a bright smile from him.

Jeena's response helps distract me from my anxiety acrobatics about potential Carmine dyes in Kai's drink.

JEENA

Interesting. Did he specifically say he's not
looking for anything serious?

My brows furrow while I string together a response.

ME

No, not specifically, but it was implied. Why?

And while I wait for her response, I question my conversation with Rowan. I'm sure he picked up on my reluctance to get into anything serious, given that I'm a single mom and his PT, but he showed that same reluctance, too . . . didn't he? Now I'm not entirely sure . . .

JEENA

Well, he said he wants to take it slow. If he
didn't have hopes for anything serious, then
why take it slow?

Shit. I hadn't really thought about that.

Does that mean I need to make things more clear before anything happens between us? Is this another stipulation in this relationship, like they put in the romance novels I read? Something like the 'No falling in love' or 'No dreaming about happily-ever-afters' clause?

I almost snort-laugh because everyone knows that's not happening. One attempt at a happily-ever-after was plenty for me.

ME

I'm not worried about it. This is a strictly fuck-
each-other-out-of-our-systems sort of
arrangement. But if feelings start to blur
whatever this is, I'll amend our agreement or
get out.

A little annoying voice in my head chimes in with a, *Sure, honey, whatever you say*, but I give it a mental eye roll.

Jeena's response comes in a minute later.

JEENA

If he's as gorgeous, persistent, and sweet as you've described him, it's not going to be easy for you to avoid feelings. Sometimes feelings develop before you even realize that your heart's been in play the whole time. I can tell you this from my own experience with Wayland. He was simply supposed to be my fake date for a party . . . and now, I've popped out two of his demon-spawns.

This time I outright laugh. The thought of this thing between Rowan and me being anything more than what is, is hilarious. I'm about to respond when another message from Jeena vibrates in my hand.

JEENA

I can hear you laughing.

ME

Yes, I almost gave myself a stomach cramp. Believe me, this is NOT the same situation as you and Wayland. I'm feeling'd out for the rest of my life, so I have none to spare.

JEENA

If you say so, but how about we chat after you've boinked him at least three times this weekend? My bet is, by the time I see you, you'll be singing a different tune.

I roll my eyes, exasperated with how much she wants to romanticize this, but also giddy about the prospect of seeing one of my closest friends this weekend.

ME

Why three times?

JEENA

It's the way of the universe. It's why they say
the third time's the charm. Anyway, I bet the
first and second time you guys fuck will be to
get it out of your systems, like you said, but
I'm willing to bet that third time will change
things.

I shake my head, knowing there's no point in arguing.

ME

You sound like Dylan with your talk about the
ways of the universe, but I'll keep you posted.
Excited to see you in a couple of days!

JEENA

Prepare to be squeezed to death, woman! See
you soon.

I'm still thinking about Jeena's text twenty minutes later, when Kai and Rowan make it back out of the rink, seeming to be done for the day. I rise to help Kai get his skates off, but Rowan beats me to it, crouching in front of him.

"Are your toes cold, buddy?" he asks, placing one skate to the side before taking Kai's foot in his large palm and rubbing his toes.

Kai's eyes bounce from the hockey star to his foot. He's hardly able to believe any of this is real. "A little."

Rowan continues to rub Kai's feet for a few more minutes until he's satisfied they're warm. He wiggles them back into Kai's shoes. "Cool velcros!"

A shallow groan escapes my son's lips. "They're embarrassing, but my mom thinks shoelaces are dangerous."

"Well, these are the slickest velcros I've ever seen," Rowan responds. "So, whether laces are dangerous or not, I'm going to get myself a pair of shoes just like these."

I clear my throat as I approach them, feeling all sorts of combobulated. "You guys looked like you were having fun."

Kai turns to smile at me, his hair mussed from being under his helmet. "Did you see me, Mom? I didn't even fall without meaning to!" He and Rowan exchange a meaningful look before Kai amends his words. "Rowan said it's important that I know *how* to fall, though, and that it's only natural to fall when you're learning. So, we practiced that, too."

I sweep some of his hair off his forehead before giving Rowan a grateful look. "You were picking it up really quickly from what I saw. Did you say thank you to Rowan, again?"

"At least a hundred times," Rowan answers for Kai, his eyes gleaming at my son. "You've got one hell of a polite kid, Doc."

Kai beams. "Good thing Phoebe and Collette aren't here; you'd have to put a thousand dollars into the swear jar for saying a bad word."

Rowan's head reels back. "A thousand dollars for saying 'hell'? That seems like highway robbery! Are these the twins you told me about on the ice?"

Kai nods, and I take in the ease in their conversation. Within just a few hours, they've become so comfortable with each other, you wouldn't know they hadn't met before. "Mom calls them the 'Destructive Demons' sometimes."

My mouth falls in shock. Firstly, I've never heard this kid have so much to say—not even in front of people he feels close to, like Liam or Winnie—but secondly, what the heck! I'd only called Delia's twins that name under my breath, when I didn't think anyone was listening.

They deserved it, too, after the last prank they pulled on me when they downloaded audio files that sounded like yawns, farts, and burps, replacing all my computer system sounds with them. I couldn't figure out how to undo them for weeks, and it made for awkward moments while I was with my patients if I didn't have my computer volume off.

"You were not supposed to have heard that, and you were definitely not supposed to have repeated it!" I scold Kai, who gives me a half-apologetic smile. I turn to Rowan. "Delia's twins are incredibly sweet in their own way, but let's just say . . . I wouldn't put it past them to become tyrannical dictators one day."

"Yeah, Bossman calls them the Shining Twins!" Kai adds, making Rowan laugh.

The rumble of his voice bounces around the empty seats, and I notice, not for the first time, just how ruggedly beautiful he is—a square jaw, a slightly crooked nose that may have been broken at some point, and a small faded scar in between his brows. His teeth are pristine white, nestled between plush lips, and the tops of his cheeks always seem flushed.

"I'm looking forward to meeting them someday." He gives me a meaningful look before smiling down at Kai.

"What about today?" Kai asks before turning to me. "Mom, can Rowan come over to say hi to everyone at the house today?"

I'm just about to respond that today won't work, given that I don't want Rowan over without giving my best friends a heads up, when he speaks. "Actually, I'd love to do that another day. How about I make you lunch at my house instead today? I bet you're both hungry."

Again, I'm about to decline when my son practically squeals in delight, nodding. "Yes!"

I give Kai a raised brow. "You promised you'd do the homework Aunt Dylan assigned you after hockey." I see Rowan's brows furrow, and I rush to explain before he even has a chance to ask, "Kai is homeschooled by my friend Dylan."

Kai's downturned eyes plead with me. "I can still get it done afterward, Mom. I promise."

Jesus. The kid could charm a genie into giving him an extra wish. Still, I try once more.

"Kai-bear, you promised not to beg, remember? Plus, I'm sure Rowan has other things to do than have us over for lunch. We have an early flight out tomorrow."

Plus, I can't have another meal of excess saturated fats and sugar. Not to mention that Kai's already had what I'm sure is more sugar than liquid inside that sports drink he chugged.

"Oh, I have nothing going on until practice tonight, and I'm already packed for the trip." Rowan winks at me, and I gather he knows I'm trying to dodge his invitation. "Anyway, you wouldn't want to miss what I have planned for lunch today."

Yeah, monster-sized burritos that could cause all sorts of terrible things, like near-orgasmic moans and gastrointestinal hibernation.

Both Rowan and Kai wait for my answer.

Ugh, this is not what I wanted! It's one thing for Rowan to teach Kai to skate, but it's another for my son to be around Rowan and me in his home. He's an observant kid. What if he can tell there's something going on between us?

Not that anything has even happened besides that kiss.

But Jesus, that kiss . . .

Let's talk about that fucking kiss. A kiss to obliterate the memory of all other kisses. A kiss that, even when Rowan and I eventually fizzle out, will be fodder for my nights alone with Jensen, Denzel, Leonardo, George—

"Mom?" Kai's voice pulls me out of my musings about my battery-operated lovers.

I sigh. "Fine, but—"

"Thanks, Mom!" Kai throws his arms around my legs before he marches up the stairs, calling to us over his shoulder, "Let's go!"

And I wonder, yet again, who this bright-faced and confident kid even is.

CHAPTER 14
ROWAN

"Whoa!" Kai gasps as soon as I open the door to my penthouse, going straight to my floor-to-ceiling windows to look at the panoramic view of the Boston Harbor, focusing on the ships and boats that glide over the glistening water. He turns his wide eyes to his mom. "Look at this view, Mom!"

She smiles at him, taking off her jacket. "It's pretty cool, right?"

Our eyes connect behind Kai's back and, taking a chance, I quickly run the tips of my fingers down the exposed skin under her forearm, getting a subdued shudder from her. My eyes drop to the goosebumps sprinkled across her neck, and it's only when Kai shuffles to the other side of the windows that I break away from her to wash my hands in the kitchen before getting things out of the fridge.

Shay follows me in as I'm retrieving the turkey meat, the tray of sliced vegetables, and the spices. Her eyes scan each ingredient carefully before she picks up one of the spice bottles. "These haven't been opened." She winks. "You sure they're not just for decoration?"

I smirk before opening up two full-length drawers filled with all my used spice bottles, perfectly laid out in alphabetical order—I don't like to search for things when I'm in the kitchen— making her eyes go wide.

"Positive. Rest assured, you and Kai will be well-fed. These new spice jars are from an organic store I found recently. They come with a non-GMO, no pesticides guarantee."

Shay fixes me with a bewildered look, still holding the bottle of paprika, but turns away before I can decipher her expression.

I watch Kai admire the trophies on my living room shelf with dazed adoration, and a renewed sense of pride runs through me. Never would I have thought that one kid's admiration was what I'd aspire for, but the look in his eyes makes me want that even more.

I clear my throat before mixing breadcrumbs and spices into the turkey. Balling a handful into my palm, I flatten it into a patty with my other while Shay watches me intently. I tilt my head toward the fridge again. "Want something to drink? You might like what I got for you."

She eyes me curiously before heading to the fridge. Her eyes find the bottles of wine I'd bought. "These are organic, too," she states, but I don't miss the little fold between her brows. "And my favorite kind."

I nod. "So was that drink I gave to Kai earlier." I smirk, taking in the confusion swirling on her face. "I don't know if you were wondering at the time, but I figured I'd let you know. It had all natural ingredients without the dyes and sugars."

Her mouth drops open, and for a second, she doesn't say anything, looking down at the wine bottle in her hand like she doesn't know how it got there. Meeting my eyes, she asks, "You got that for Kai? Why?"

I shrug, going back to my task. "Pour me a glass, too, and then come help me with this."

She does as I ask, placing my wineglass near me before washing her hands and coming to stand next to me, closer than I would have expected. The heat of her body and the sweet scent of her flowery perfume has me clenching my jaw. "What can I do?"

I nod toward the pantry. "Mind slicing some potatoes for me? I figured we could airfry some French fries along with the turkey burgers."

She comes back with a few potatoes before finding a peeler in one of my drawers and getting started.

"Do you cook much?" I ask, too intrigued with the way her delicate hand wraps around the large russet potato—while shoving off the thought of her grasping the half-hard erection inside my pants with that same hand.

She chuckles. "If you consider blending or tossing ingredients together, boiling pasta, or making soup in the slow cooker 'cooking', then yes. Some nights I'm in charge of cooking for everyone at the house. I can also make a mean ham and cheese omelet, bake sweet potato brownies, and roll some delicious protein bars. "

I side-eye her playfully. "You mean the 'delicious protein bars' the raccoons have been getting hefty on?"

"Hey!" She elbows me, catching my sarcasm. "They have tons of nuts, seeds, and good oils! Almost everyone I know loves them."

Kai coughs dramatically in the living room, and Shayla squints at him before he goes on pretending to be busy with the puzzle I have laying out on the coffee table.

"When did you learn to cook?" Shay asks, grabbing a knife from my knife block.

I think back to helping my mom with nightly dinners when we all lived together in the same house with Dad. She'd always make the most extravagant meals–even on weeknights–when Dad played a home game. She'd say shit like, *"A man needs a clean home, a good wife, and a hot meal to come home to. Otherwise, what's the point?"*

I still remember rolling my eyes at the statement, but I never argued. If it made her happy to cook and clean for him, well then, that was her prerogative. I just knew it wasn't something that gave a woman more worth in my eyes, and it wasn't something I'd ever look for. And in the end, look where it got Mom.

"When I was eight or nine. I loved helping my mom out in the kitchen." I glance at her, placing the last of the turkey burgers on the plate next to me. "My sister, Piper, not so much."

Shayla laughs at that. "She sounds like me. Don't get me wrong, I'd love to be able to cook more, but I just never have the time or energy." She pauses after slicing up the first potato to take a sip of wine. "Are you and your sister close?"

"She's one of my best friends, but acts more like a mom than even our own mother. I'm actually meeting up with her for dinner after the game tomorrow. She lives a half hour from San Jose but she'll be at the game, and then I thought you and I could grab dinner and drinks with her after my media wrap up." I scan her face, trying to gauge her reaction.

She puts the knife down. "You want me to come with you? I mean . . . we just started this." She picks up the knife, waving it around. "Whatever this is. Is it a good idea to involve more family? Plus, what if someone photographs us together or something? I'm fine just hanging out in the hotel room."

I give her a resolute look, gathering that her fears are starting to ensnare her. "I'm not letting you hang out in the hotel room. Piper is looking forward to meeting you, and I have a feeling you guys will really get along. As for getting photographed, we're going to a really low-key place that Piper and I have met up at before. The owner of the restaurant is one of my friends, so he takes extra measures to make sure I'm not seen."

After a moment of consideration, she nods. "Okay." She looks at the potato on the cutting board. "How big do you want the slices?"

I wash my hands and come back to stand next to her. "Here, let me cut a couple of strips and you can use that as a guide."

Shayla scoots over a bit, handing me the knife, and when our hands brush, a ripple of goosebumps climbs over her arm. Our eyes connect before mine drop back to those damn lips I'm dying for.

"You're so fucking beautiful," I whisper only for her to hear. "I can't wait to spend time with you this weekend."

Her shy smile makes an appearance, and she murmurs just as softly, "Thank you. You're not so bad yourself."

I lift a brow, my cocky smile on full display. "Dare I say, was that a compliment, Dr. Kumar?"

She rolls her eyes, trying but failing to erase her smile. "Don't get used to it." She takes a breath, looking at Kai with concern. "And I'm looking forward to it, too."

I follow her gaze. "You're worried about him."

"I haven't left him for this long in a while. I know he'll be in great hands with my friends, but there's still that little worry, you know?"

"It's understandable," I agree. "If at any point you want to leave, I'll get you on the first flight out. No questions asked, okay?"

By all accounts, I've seen what an incredible mom Shay is. She has this way of being both loving and firm, and I see how much Kai respects her. Despite what they've gone through, she's doing the best she can to work through her fears and give him a good life, so I don't blame her for being cautious. Instead, I commend her for stepping out of her comfort zone when she knows it's holding them both back.

Her brown eyes bounce around my face. "Has anyone ever told you how sweet you are?"

I cut the potato in half before cutting a few thick slices, a smile still stretched over my face. "You can feel free to tell me that anytime you want, sweetheart."

She huffs out a soft laugh.

"What about you? Any siblings?" I ask, handing her the potato.

She shakes her head. "Just me. Both my parents passed away when I was younger, so neither Kai nor I have much of a family, save for my stepmom, who lives in Arizona." She smiles as if thinking about her. "She raised me from the age of fifteen after Dad died. She's really sweet, but very *interesting*."

"How so?"

"Well, for one," Kai steps into the kitchen, joining our conversation, as if he'd been in it the whole time, "my *nani* changes her entire outfit daily."

I don't understand what the big deal is. Isn't that what most people do—change their entire outfit daily?

Shay clarifies, "*Nani* means grandma in Hindi by the way, in case you were wondering, and Kai's grandma, Merna, changes *every* part of herself as much as she can, every day. As in, her entire outfit, her nail color, eyeglasses–"

"Don't forget her hair color, too, Mom," Kai chimes in excitedly.

"She changes her hair color every day?" I ask, surprised. "How is that possible?"

Kai nods. "Yup, sometimes she wears a wig. The only reason I know she's actually blonde is because I've seen her take the wig off."

Shayla shakes her head. "Actually, I think her natural hair color is red."

"Wow," I say, not knowing how to respond, and finding everything about Shay—from how she lost her parents at a young age, to how she was raised by her eccentric stepmom, to how she moved across the country to fulfill a pact with her best friends—simply fascinating.

Despite the fact that she's had to deal with so much loss in her life—her parents and her husband—she's fiercely loyal to those who are still a part of it.

And a lack of loyalty is one thing I know too much about. One thing I wish I knew nothing about.

Once Shayla is done with slicing the potatoes, I add them to the air fryer. We chat more about family and their life in California before I put the turkey patties in too for a few minutes while I heat up the whole grain buns.

Twenty minutes later, we're sitting down to eat at my dining table with our assembled burgers in hand.

It's crazy what one can learn about people by the way they assemble their burgers. For example, I learned that Shay hates ketchup. And it has nothing to do with the amount of sugar in the ketchup—because I got unsweetened ketchup for her—but because she doesn't like the taste of it. I also learned that Kai likes all his toppings on the side and only cheese with his burger. Then he likes to eat around the bun before he eats all the vegetables.

"This is delicious!" he mumbles around his bite.

Shayla eyes him wearily. "Kai, don't talk with food in your mouth, sweetheart. You could choke."

Kai's shoulders deflate a little, but he perks back up, finishing his bite. "Okay, Mom."

I get the feeling he's used to Shayla hovering over him, but I love that he seems to take it in stride. He still lets his mom know what he wants, but he lets her win some of the battles, too.

Shayla smiles at him before addressing me, "This really is good, Rowan. I'm seriously impressed. I don't know how long it's been since I've had French fries."

"I guess I'll have to continue to press your limits." I wink at her. "Maybe I can get you to break a few more of your self-imposed rules."

She tucks her bottom lip into her mouth, looking down at her food, but it's clear she got my gist.

At one point during our conversation, Kai takes a break to go to the bathroom, leaving me and Shay alone.

I've just heard the bathroom door shut when I pull her toward me. She leans in easily as I take her mouth with mine. Fuck, I'd already missed it, and it's only been two days.

She braces her hand on my shoulder, falling into our kiss, and I swirl my tongue inside, tasting her thoroughly. Shay wiggles in her seat like she's rubbing her thighs together, trying to ease the want starting there. I bet if I was to place a finger in between her folds, she'd be dripping for me, too.

I curl my hand around her neck, my thumb fluttering over the tattoos behind her ear, deepening our connection. My breaths come out ragged. "Fuck, baby, I can't wait to devour you from head to toe. I can't wait until tomorrow . . . come back over later."

I swallow the moan that leaves her lips, kissing her as thoroughly as I can before we break our connection.

"I can't," she whispers against my lips. "I've got smutty book club with my friends tonight."

I give her a lopsided grin. "I don't really know what that means, but I'm assuming it has to do with the *very* graphic book you were reading on your Kindle."

She leans back, her chest still heaving. "How do you know?"

"You left your Kindle in my bathroom the same night you climbed out of my bathtub in all your naked glory like a water nymph."

"So that's where it's been. I've been looking for it, actually." She pauses, realizing what I'd previously said. "Wait. You read my book?"

"Hell, yeah, I read it! *Ablaze?* I read it from cover to cover." I blow out a dramatic breath. "Talk about angst and pining. It gave me a stomachache. But fuck, when they go at it like–"

"I like your bathroom, Rowan."

Both Shayla and I practically jump out of our seats at the sound of Kai's voice. Thank God, we had the wherewithal to break away from each other when we did, or . . .

I don't want to think about the *or*. I don't want to think about what would have happened if he had walked in on us kissing. Not only would it have put Shayla in an awkward situation, but it could have had the potential to ruin whatever this is between us before we even started.

She'd specifically made that one of her conditions–for her son not to find out. And though I'm still not happy about the prospect of never revealing it to him, I respect her wishes. I'm well aware that her stipulation means she's already put an end date for us, but what other choice did I have?

But if she thinks she can be half-in and half-out of this

because she's sure it's going to end, well, she obviously doesn't know me very well. I don't give up easily, and I definitely don't give up without a fair shot.

The scent of lavender and citrus hits my nose, and I bite back the smile when I see Kai's arms freshly lathered in the sweet-scented lotion I keep in my bathroom. Clearly, he and his mom have a thing for my toiletries. "Thanks, buddy."

"Can I go do the puzzle on the coffee table?" he asks, directing his question first to me and then to his mom. "I don't get a chance to at home since Aunt Dylan finishes them so quickly."

"Sure," I respond, watching Kai skip back into the living room.

With him out of earshot, I direct my next statement to Shay. "So, that one scene in the book, though, where Dean and Mala are stuck in a snowstorm and have to share a bed in that motel? That whole scene in the shower had me hot and bothered. And the dude is *pierced*?!" I cringe, my dick shriveling in on itself at the thought of having something sharp . . .

I'm about to speak again when Shay slaps her palm against my mouth. "Rowan, I swear to God. If you give me any more spoilers, I will re-injure that groin of yours and make sure it's more painful this time around."

My shoulders shake as I chuckle under her hand. God, the woman is so easy to rile up, and it's driving me a little crazy that I can't just sit her down on the table and bury my head between her legs like the best dessert after a filling lunch. Fuck, she'd be worth the food coma.

My dick strains inside my pants with the prospect of doing exactly that, hopefully tomorrow. "Is that a promise, Doc?"

CHAPTER 15
SHAY

"I swear, Kai was so hopped up on sugar and adrenaline today, he was shaking," I say, pouring wine into my glass that Dylan got us all that says, *Fueled by wine and smut.*

I mentally scold myself for having another glass tonight after the one and a half glasses I had at Rowan's place this afternoon. Just because it's organic doesn't mean it's good for my liver.

"Give the kid a break. He was excited to meet his hockey hero today," Liv says, taking a seat in the breakfast nook, ready to start our book club meeting. She wags her brows at me. "And how about you? Were *you* excited to see your hockey hero today? Have you banged him yet?"

I roll my eyes, leaning my hip against the kitchen counter. "When would I have time to bang him?"

"True," she says agreeably before she winks at me. "But I'm sure there will be time for it this weekend."

"Sometimes I wonder if you guys and Jeena have a separate

group chat discussing my love life, because you all seem to be saying the same things."

"Not me," Delia adds quickly. "I'm not encouraging you to bang anyone. Most men don't deserve us." She looks at Liv and Dylan pointedly. "And though they've grown on me, my assessment includes the cranky billionaire and the piece of man candy in the room next door taking care of our kids."

"I heard that," Beckett hollers from the hallway. He must have come out from the restroom.

"Go do your job for once, billionaire," Delia teases. "This is a pretentious-free zone."

Taking a couple of steps toward us, Beckett looks at Liv, like *'see what I have to deal with'* before addressing Delia again, "Well, then, I'm surprised you're included."

"Beckett . . ." Liv warns, taking a breath.

Delia's about to retort when the sound of Kai's voice has Beckett turning over his shoulder. "Bossman, can you come back? Adeline seems to have woken up."

Liv's about to jump out of her seat when Dylan lays a hand on her, shaking her head subtly, making us realize it was her.

Our best friend is not only a universe-loving, aura-reading, laid back momma, but she's also a world-class ventriloquist. And oftentimes, she uses her talent to throw her voice into another room, mimicking any one of us to confuse the billion-aire grump we're living with.

Like now.

There's no end to the joy it brings us to see Beckett Lang-field confused and rushing toward what he assumes is some disaster awaiting him in the room, when in fact, Dyl just pretended to be Kai and made up an emergency.

The four of us giggle, knowing he'll figure it out soon enough.

Liv turns back to me after we've all wiped the tears from

our eyes. "You were over at his place the other night. You never told us about what happened."

My face flushes as I think about the whole bathtub incident. "Right. Well, something *did* happen, but it's not what you guys might think."

"No wonder you have this strange mix of pinks and purples around you," Dylan chimes in, scrutinizing the space around me as if she's following a fly, before taking a sip of something from her metal straw-cup. "That's the color when you're enamored with someone."

"I'm not *enamored* with him," I press before my eyes zero-in on her cup. "What are you drinking?"

Dylan hides her cup under the cardigan she's wearing. "Nothing . . . water. Actually, it's organic kale juice with protein powder and avocado oil mixed in."

Even *my* nose wrinkles, trying to picture that. She's lying through her teeth, the gorgeous little pregnant weasel. "Show me."

She hides it even further back, practically pushing the cup behind her. "No, I . . . it'll reduce the freshness if I open the lid. You wouldn't want me to consume anything with reduced freshness, would you, Shay?"

Delia and Liv snort, laughing as they watch us.

"Dyl." I place my wine on the counter and cross my arms over my chest. "Is that a cherry Slurpee in there?"

"No!" she huffs, but then deflates. "Okay, fine, yes. The baby was craving it, and I just couldn't say no."

I shake my head, disappointed. I'm not clueless; I know Slurpees have been her craving during this pregnancy, and Cortney gets them for her whenever she wants them, but that doesn't change the way I feel about my best friend filling her body with red dye 40.

But then I see the plea in her eyes.

Dylan doesn't need my approval; she wants it. And the fact that my best friend feels she has to hide things from me, when she's seen me secretly smoking toxins into my lungs and has kept her judgment at bay? That just doesn't sit well with me. This isn't who I want to be.

I recall the conversation I had with Rowan the other night, and it's as if what he said–what I've sort of known inside my bones but have been too stubborn to acknowledge–has an alarm bell ringing inside my head.

"Don't you ever just want to relax the rules? Eating an unhealthy meal from time to time isn't going to hurt you; in fact, it may actually make you feel happier. And in the end, isn't that what we all want?"

He was right. Food shouldn't be a source of stress for anyone–not for my friends or my son, and certainly not for me. And as much as I preach about healthy eating and living, I've allowed it to become a stress factor in my life and the lives of the people I love.

Because, for all the control I show over myself and my loved ones, I'm actually the one letting my regiment and restraint control me to the point that I've lost my sense of fun. I've lost my inner peace.

I've lost myself.

I've been so focused on living for the future that I've forgotten to live in the present. I've forgotten the needs and wants of the people closest to me–my son and my incredible friends.

And that can't be the way forward. That can't be the way I live.

Not anymore.

I smile, letting a rejuvenated sense of duty flow through me. "I get it. You should have seen the number of doughnuts and candy bars I ate when I was pregnant with Kai. I remember telling Ajay one night that I was going to die if I didn't have a doughnut for dinner."

Dylan smiles back at me, but strangely, she's not surprised by my change in attitude. In fact, none of my friends seem to be.

"Did he go out and get it for you?" Liv asks.

My smile wavers and I shake my head. "He was busy . . ." I look down and wiggle my toes on our yellow kitchen floors. "I never wanted to be a disruption to him, you know? I adjusted my life and my needs around his. He always had so much on his plate, from his startup, to his travels, and I didn't want to add to the stress–"

"He was a selfish bastard," Delia states, her eyes shooting fire. She raises her hands and drops them to her sides in her seat next to Liv and Dyl while they stare at her in horror. "There, I said it. I said it, and I won't take it back, Shay. The man treated you like a used accessory. He wasn't there for you when you needed him the most, even though you were there for him time and time again. Remember the day Kai was born? Remember how you asked him to take you to the hospital because your water broke, and he was on some huge video conference with Russia or some shit–"

"Canada," I correct.

"Canada!" Her voice rises before Liv tells her to quiet down because who knows where our kids are. They're known to listen to all things we don't want them to. "Fucking *Canada*!" she hisses. "The easiest-going people in the world! He couldn't get off the phone with them because he didn't want to lose some deal, so he let his wife drive *herself* to the hospital!" She whisper-screams the last few words. "I'm sorry, honey. As much as I hate that he died so fucking young–God rest his soul–none of us were happy that you were with him. Me even more so because he reinforced my reasons to hate men."

Liv and Dylan keep their faces glued to Delia, and I get the sense they're scared to even look at me while the sob that had been rising inside my chest throughout the time Delia was speaking finally emits with tears streaming down my face.

My friends hustle toward me with Delia apologizing profusely for her words. "I'm so sorry, honey. You know how I am. My loyalty to you . . ." I hear her choke up as her arms secure me to her.

It's a rare moment of emotion from my best friend, but it has nothing to do with how much or how little she feels. She feels deeply, *fiercely*, when it comes to the people she cares about, and when she feels like they've been hurt, all that anger bubbles out with screams and tears.

I shake my head inside her arms and the arms of my other two friends. "No, it's not your fault. I'm not even crying because of what you said. I'm . . . I guess I'm sad for the person I used to be before I met Ajay. I'm sad that she didn't thrive; she didn't survive. I'm sad that Kai didn't get to meet that fun-loving girl–"

"Who smoked pot with a homeless guy on her way to a fucking biology test, and then aced the damn thing!" Delia chimes in, blubbering.

"The girl who took part in a fried chicken eating contest at the local fast-food restaurant and won!" Dylan adds, tucking my hair behind my ear.

"The girl who danced in a damn cage over a full dance floor at a club for an entire night because she was low on cash and had to pay a late parking ticket."

I sniffle and laugh, shaking my head. "I made so much money that night."

My friends hug me again and I get a sense of déjà vu. We were huddled together almost exactly like this, not even three or four days ago. God, I'm a mess, aren't I? And as much as I'm glad to have these ladies here to pick me up, I vow right here and now to figure out my shit. To forgive the woman I became while I was with Ajay and to become the woman—*the mother*—I want to be for the little boy I'm raising.

Giving my friends one more hug and wiping my tears, I look them in the eyes. "You guys might be surprised to hear, but I'm reverting back to some of my old spontaneous and crazy ways."

"How so?" Liv asks, taking a seat at the table again.

"Well, for one, I'm now also the woman who got on my knees, completely naked, to beg a particular hockey player to give me back my clothes. For two, I asked said hockey player to give me better orgasms than my new fancy toy that he purchased for me. And for three . . ." I give Liv and Delia a guilty look. I'd promised Beckett I'd tell Liv and I have to honor that. "I've been secretly smoking again."

"What?!" Delia practically yells. "You got on your knees for a man? Have I taught you *nothing*?"

"Since when?" Liv asks over her, a frown pulling down her lips. "And I'm not talking about the naked begging or the orgasms—I'm all for that. I mean the cigarettes."

"I don't do it often, but I'm going to quit. It's just been a way for me to . . . cope some days."

Liv doesn't look pleased with my response, but I know she's just worried. "Tell us everything."

I take in a deep breath, connecting my eyes with Dylan.

She gives me a calming nod, rolling her rose quartz in between her fingers. "I have a feeling book club is going to last a while. Why don't I pour you a bigger glass of wine?"

And right as she brings me more wine, we hear Beckett holler from the other room, "Real funny, Dippy Doo." He uses his nickname for Dylan. "I know it was you doing that thing with your voice again!"

I get back to my room three hours later, after tucking Kai into bed and giving him a million kisses, and reminding him for the hundredth time that he could call me if he needed to talk to me at any time and that if he told me to, I'd catch the next flight back.

As usual, my son visibly refrained from rolling his eyes at me, but mumbled, "Yes, Mom," in a drone-like voice.

I then went back to my best friends to go through the health and well-being checklist again. It only took an hour, and I did have to shake Dylan awake a couple of times, but thankfully, we got through the seventy-two items on the list. Thankfully, she was awake for the most important items—aside from what to do in major emergencies, which all my friends were well-capable of handling—like the fact that Kai needed to be reminded to apply shea butter to his knees every day because otherwise, his skin got dry and flaky, and that I really preferred if he got thirty-five grams of protein a day and at least two hours of sun.

But, of course, I didn't want him running around too much in the sun either, because what if he tripped and I wasn't here, so I specified that as well. Along with the fact that I really preferred he wore his velcro shoes, though he'd probably insist on wearing the ones with shoelaces.

Anyway, it really wasn't all that much information, so I'm not sure why Delia kept repeating, "Oh, for the love of God!"

Honestly, I felt good about myself for not going through

the *additional* twenty-item checklist I'd recently made that was still sitting on my work desk.

See? *Progress.*

After taking a shower and putting last-minute toiletries inside my suitcase, I get into bed. I look up at the exposed rafters, thinking about the cathartic conversation I had with my best friends.

They'd been keeping their feelings about Ajay behind a barricade for so long–out of respect for him being my husband at the time–that once the floodgates opened, it was like everything came spilling out. Even Dylan, the most laid back of us all, got a little worked up talking about how she didn't like the way he treated me at times.

I don't think anyone would call Ajay a bad guy, because he wasn't. He was loving and charming in his own way. But, like everyone else, he was flawed. He had some good qualities, but he had ones he needed to work on, if life had given him a chance. Except, the ones he still had to work on ended up affecting me the most. And for that, I'm disappointed in myself for not speaking up sooner.

Because for a woman who doesn't shy away from speaking her mind, I sure didn't do right by myself when I was with him. I allowed him to put me in second place, and that was just as much on me as it was on him.

But I'm slowly finding myself again.

I'm slowly realizing that I want more.

And with the vow I made to myself tonight to forgive myself–and my late husband–for the hurt I've kept pent-up inside, the hurt that has manifested in strange ways in my life, I decide to let my past life go and live in the present.

I know that all of it–from the hurt I've carried for years, to the grief of watching my husband lose a horrendous battle– contributed to my need for control. It contributed to my obsession with food, my debilitating fears, and my random intrusive thoughts.

But it needs to end now!

My mind takes me back to an hour ago, when I told my friends to make sure Kai wore his velcros outdoors ...

Okay, so it has to end *soon*. Fears and habits aren't things most people can break in a day, but at least I'm trying. I'm working on trying not to be a "ball of nevers".

I squint up at the rafters above me.

I really should have a celebration for this newfound thinking. I turn toward my nightstand, pulling the drawer open to get Trick out. That's the name I've given my new gold vibrator, honoring the rapper with gold teeth. I'm just about to push the button to turn him on when I remember the promise I made to Rowan.

"Ugh!" I groan, throwing my shiny new toy back into the drawer. "Fucking Rowan!"

Tossing and turning once more, I decide to get out of bed. I hate the idea of not getting enough sleep, especially since I have to be up early tomorrow to catch the flight, but I also can't just lay here with all my thoughts.

I've just placed the vibrator inside my nightstand when my eyes catch the pack of cigarettes I keep toward the back. I open the box, noticing only one left in there.

"Okay, good. Just one." I nod to myself. "One last smoke to celebrate new beginnings. Not buying another pack, ever."

I was going to quit anyway, but I'm also not a proponent of waste. I mean, there are people going hungry out there! Okay, so my last remaining cigarette doesn't apply to the hunger crisis, but I'm sure it applies to something. Maybe the drug crisis ...

That doesn't really make sense, either.

I'm just going to quit applying this moment to any crisis but my own!

Grabbing a shawl from my chair, I step outside through the door to my room and find the step I've become quite familiar with in all the months I've lived here.

Only a handful of winking stars grace the dusty Boston night sky, but the breeze definitely lets me know we're in the middle of October. It skitters down my spine under my shawl, and I shudder, wrapping the fabric closer to my body.

Lighting up my cigarette, I take a long drag, reminding myself this is it. This is the last time I'll do this.

Because the guilt of doing so isn't worth the few moments of reprieve. Because even though I'm going to relax some of my rules, my diet, and my regimen on both myself and my son, I'm not going to straight up put toxins into my body, either.

I look at the bright bud at the end of the cancer stick in my hand. "This is the last time. Do you understand me? The last time I let you fill me up and take me. The last time I'll let you fuck me the way you've been fucking–"

"What the fuck?" The familiar, charming voice I'd heard this afternoon has transformed into a venomous growl as Rowan's massive form dominates the dimly-lit space in front of me, his tense jawline the only visible feature. "Let me make it real clear, Doc. If you let any other motherfucker touch you, you'll be the reason I break every goddamn bone in his body. No amount of physical therapy will ever fix him again."

CHAPTER 16
SHAY

"Rowan? What are you doing here?" My mind whirls, and for a moment, I wonder if I've just conjured him up simply of my own volition. He has been on my mind a lot lately, and I did drink a decent amount of wine . . .

"I should ask you the same thing." He glares at me, his features set like stone, before he glances at the cigarette in my hand. "What are you doing out here? And who the fuck were you talking to?"

My shoulders deflate. I should be embarrassed; I should be apologizing for being the fraud I am.

Instead, I feel a strange sense of relief. Relief from not having to hide this from one more person. Relief that another piece of my mask has been ripped off, even if I wasn't intending for it to happen.

Maybe this will be reason enough for him to walk away, like he probably should.

I lift my cigarette, flaunting my truth. "This guy right here. I was just saying goodbye to him because I won't be smoking again."

Rowan shifts from foot to foot, probably reconsidering everything between us, given I sound like a crazy person.

I wouldn't blame him.

Our arms touch when he sits next to me, before he removes the cigarette from my fingers. I'm about to object when he places it to his lips and takes a long drag.

"You smoke?" That sounds . . . unbelievable, but who am I to pass judgment?

He shakes his head, a chuckle vibrating in his chest, before he hands the cigarette back to me. "Nah. But now when I kiss you, we'll both have tobacco on our breath."

I gaze at him, struggling to form complete thoughts. Does he realize how fucking swoony he is? That might have been the strangest thing a man has said to me, but is it crazy that I find it so endearing?

He leans into me, nudging me softly with his shoulder. "I know I got to kiss those lips of yours today, but it wasn't enough, and well . . . I couldn't fall asleep without another one."

I let out a huff of air, shaking my head as I break my gaze from him to look at the house across the street. This man. What the fuck am I going to do about this man? "How do you manage to surprise me at every step, Rowan Parker?"

He doesn't answer, and instead, we sit in silence for a few minutes, passing the cigarette back and forth until there's nothing left.

"Thank you for teaching Kai how to skate today. He had a lot of fun," I say, breaking the silence between us.

"I probably had more fun than he did, to be honest. He's a really good kid, and in just one session, he made so much progress." His perfectly white teeth sparkle from between his lips. "Did you see him march on the ice? That's not easy to do when you're just learning!"

My chest feels warm. That same warmth I felt earlier this morning when I saw my son laugh and come out of his shell with the man sitting next to me, like they were old friends.

Swallowing the lump in my throat, I work up the question I've been wondering about. "So, what are you really doing here?" Surely, he wouldn't have come from downtown Boston for a kiss . . .

"What do you think I'm doing here, Shay?" His golden green eyes hold mine. "I wanted to see you."

I look down at my feet, feeling his intense gaze to be all too much. "Why?" I let the question hang for a moment before adding, "What I mean is, are you sure you want this, Rowan? Do you not see the hot mess in front of you? I'm a thirty-five-year-old woman with a kid and baggage that could fill up an entire seven-fifty-seven. I'm at least ten years older than you–"

"Eight years," he corrects.

I chuckle. "I secretly smoke–"

"You're quitting, and it's no longer a secret," he argues.

"I constantly live in fear and don't take risks–"

"I disagree."

That has me turning in his direction.

"I disagree." His voice is soft as he tucks a wayward strand of my hair behind my ear. "You might have fears, like anyone else, but you're working to overcome them. You've already come so far in just a few days."

My eyes bounce between his, contemplating. Yeah, I have made a lot of changes in the past few days. I've stepped out of my comfort zone and pushed myself, even when I wanted to quit and go back to what felt normal for me.

And I can attribute a lot of that to him.

He's given me a glimpse of the woman I used to be. And while she hasn't fully emerged, she's gathering her nerves, curious about all that she missed while she was in the shadows.

His thumb brushes over my cheek, bringing me out of my thoughts. "How long have you smoked?"

There's no judgment in his question; no shade thrown my way. Just curiosity.

"On and off for three years–"

"After your husband died," he states knowingly.

I take a breath of the cold breeze. "I did it a few times in college, but yeah, after he died, it became a secret way to cope from time to time."

Rowan's lips quirk. "How are you going to cope now that you're quitting?"

I admire the curve of his luscious mouth, the scruff around his jaw. "I have a few coping mechanisms inside my nightstand."

The air around us thickens with insinuation and his voice deepens. "Pretty sure we agreed you wouldn't use those unless–"

"Unless you're there," I finish for him while my heart speeds up at the thought of him being there while I use my toy.

An electric current buzzes around us as Rowan's gaze drops to my lips, and it's as if he's reading my lustful thoughts. "I'm here now, baby."

"That you are."

His eyes darken. "Do you think about me when you do it?"

I lick my lips. "I haven't thought about anyone else since you."

Rowan's hand curves around my neck and his lips crash against mine. Apparently, he liked my answer. His tongue trails along the seam of my lips, and I open my mouth for him, inviting him in.

He pulls me onto his lap so I'm straddling him, my shawl

falling from my shoulders. His tongue glides into my mouth as he tilts my head to get a better angle.

God, I love this side of him—dominant and hungry, taking what he wants, unapologetically. I've never had this with a lover; never felt so desired or treasured.

Our kiss turns frantic, our bodies heating up as we rub against each other. A groan rumbles in Rowan's chest and my hands tighten in his hair. My nipples feel like shards of glass against my shirt while my pussy begs for relief.

I moan into his mouth. "Rowan, please. Please, do something. *Anything.*" I'm practically sobbing. "Please make me come. I'm begging you."

I swear, the man makes me ravenous, like a beggar for his touch.

With his hands palming my ass, he drags me over his erection, over and over until I feel practically possessed. When his thumb finds my center, I hiss against his mouth, my pussy pulsing and swollen.

He rubs a few circles against my clit, and I feel my juices penetrate the thin material of my pajamas.

Rowan's mouth finds my ear. "I love when you beg, baby."

I grind against what I know is the thickest cock I will ever see, shamelessly. *Is he packing a steel pipe or a baseball bat in there?*

His lips take mine again, sucking, teasing. "Beg for my cock."

"Please."

"Please what, Shayla?" His voice is stern as he thumbs my nipple over my shirt before pinching it and making me jump.

I slide my lips down his neck, loving the rough feel of his scruff against my swollen lips. "Please give me your cock."

Rowan picks me up easily, my legs around his hips, and walks us toward the doors behind us, while I give him mumbled directions with my lips pressed to his neck, like "through that door" and "my bedroom's in there."

Once inside, he puts me on my bed before examining my bedroom door. If he notices the exposed rafters or the missing parts of the crown molding, he doesn't seem to care.

"Is your door locked?" he whispers.

I nod, my chest heaving against his. My hands are still locked around his neck, our breaths colliding.

Rowan's lips find mine and his thumb circles that same spot between my legs. I whimper into his mouth, digging my nails into his shoulders.

He tugs on the waistband of my pajama bottoms, and I help him pull them down, lifting my hips. His hungry gaze roams over my wet center before he slides his fingers between my wet folds.

"Look at this beautiful pussy." He licks his lips and I mewl under his touch. "And that sweet little clit, so needy for me."

Taking my mouth with his again, he circles my clit with his fingers before he inserts his middle finger, testing and teasing.

I buck up at the feel of him before he puts one more digit in, making me moan. My body thrums with anticipation, goose-bumps breaking out over my arms as he swivels his fingers inside me. "Rowan!"

He pumps his fingers into me, never releasing my mouth from his, and I can feel the clench of my pussy around him. A flush rises over my skin and my thighs quiver.

I'm close. So fucking close–

But right as I'm about to shatter, Rowan pulls his fingers out of me, breaking away from my mouth, and leaving me completely dazed.

"Wh-what are you . . .?" I breathe heavily.

"Where are your toys?"

Is he for real right now? "What do you– But I thought–"

Rising to his feet, he keeps his eyes pinned on me before putting both his fingers, covered with my juices, into his mouth, licking them clean. "Jesus Christ, sweetheart. I can't decide which taste I like better–your lips or your pussy."

He opens up my nightstand, and I get on my elbows to watch, irritation strumming through my veins, as he pulls out my gold vibrator, dropping it on the bed next to me.

His darkened eyes roam over my body once again, snagging on my exposed and needy center before a smirk lifts his lips and he takes in my bewildered expression.

Before I can debate further, he casually strolls to the chair across the room, taking a seat. His arms drape over the armrests before he leans back, his foot over his knee, like the sexy bastard he is.

And if I didn't know better, based on the tightness in his jaw, the fever burning in his eyes, and the way his fingers squeeze the fronts of the armrests, I'd think he wasn't the least bit affected by the past ten minutes.

His eyes flick to the shiny toy next to me. "Show me how you think about me, Doc."

My nostrils flare, my eyes blazing. What is the matter with this guy? Who the fuck ramps a woman up to the point she's going to explode, only to stroll across the room and leave her like a sack of potatoes? "Rowan, I swear to–"

"I want to see you fuck yourself to *my* name, sweetheart." He lifts a brow. "Follow directions, and I might just reward you with something more."

Gritting my teeth, I take the vibrator in my hand, fisting it and pretending it's his dick. I swear, if it really was his cock inside my fist right now . . . God have mercy on him.

And on his dick.

Locking my fevered eyes with his, I switch the vibrator on,

the hum familiar to my ears. My wet and heavy center, still pulsing with need, begs for a reprieve.

If the flames I'm throwing at him with my eyes could do their job, he'd be incinerated by now.

I might just reward you with something more?

Bullshit! I'll reward myself!

I'm just about to place my vibrator against my hardened clit when Rowan's low and rough voice finds my ears. "You stop when I tell you to stop."

"No." I shake my head defiantly, knowing he probably won't let me finish. "You listen to me, asshole–"

"Shay, I swear to God, if you defy me, I will not let you come for a month."

My mouth falls open. The audacity of this guy. But fuck, how those words make my center throb even more. It's like my pussy is dick-whipped for him, and she hasn't even seen his dick yet!

Rowan's lips twitch; the bastard's holding back his laughter because he knows he's won. He knows that even though I'm *verbally* refusing, I'll do exactly what he tells me to.

I work my center with the vibrating tool, covering it with my juices and circling it around my clit. My stomach tightens, my eyes wanting to roll back in my head, but I dare not break my connection with my gorgeous and cocky hockey player.

If I've never seen a sexier man, he's sitting mere feet from me, grinding his molars so hard, he might need dental surgery if he doesn't let up. He pulls his bottom lip in between his teeth as I slowly push the bulbous end of my toy inside me.

"Ahh!" I moan a little louder for his benefit, realizing that I have just as much power over him as he has over me, and if this asshole wants to play . . . well, he better join the big leagues. "Oh, Trick!"

Rowan's eyes catch fire, his hands white-knuckling the

armrests, before his warning resounds inside my room. "Shayla."

I grab my breast with my other hand, squeezing as my chest rises and falls, my orgasm not far from the horizon as I push the toy deeper inside me before taking it out again. "Fuck me, Trick. God, you feel so good."

Before I can even get another thrust in, Rowan is hovering over me on one elbow while his other hand has managed to grab both my wrists above my head. I hear the *thunk* of my vibrator as it rolls off my bed, and Rowan's nostrils flare. "I'm not a violent man, Shay, but I swear to God, I'll break every one of your precious toys right this second if any other name but mine leaves your lips again."

I lick my lips before reaching up to try to kiss him, but Rowan pulls back before I can. I lay back down, frustrated. "Then make me come to your name."

Rowan slips down my body, stopping only to take my breast into his mouth from over my thin shirt. He sucks so hard, my back arches off the bed, and right when I'm about to scream, his hand finds my mouth. He presses his thumb in between my lips, silently asking for me to suck.

And as I suck the pad of his thumb, swirling my tongue around it, he moves to my other nipple. He teases and sucks, making a new pool of wetness drip out of my center and onto my bed.

Leaving the wet fabric against my rock-hard nipples, Rowan slowly moves down my body, kissing around my navel. But as soon as he gets to my center, he pushes open my legs with his hands behind my knees and dives in.

I feel his tongue on my clit, and I writhe underneath him like a wild animal. His scruff grazes against my thighs deliciously while his tongue explores my pussy. My hands move from fisting my comforter to the back of his head as I try to hold back my scream. "Oh . . . oh my God!"

Rowan flattens his tongue against my entrance, lapping and sucking, before he inserts his fingers back inside me, finger-fucking me until my thighs start to shake around him. And though he's working his magic between my legs, I feel him everywhere. My toes curl and my body feels like it's about to go up in flames.

"Ahh!" I cry against the back of my hand as softly as possible, knowing the walls in this house are thin, if even fully erect.

But right when I'm seconds from detonating like a fucking atom bomb around him, he rises to his feet again.

No.

No, no, no!

My chest heaves with a barely held sob, and if I wasn't so stunned, I'd launch myself at him like a wild ape.

The bastard licks his lips, glistening with my juices, before giving me a completely unapologetic smirk. "That's for not following the rules."

He starts to turn toward the exit for my room, and I'm ready to scream. "Rowan *fucking* Parker!" I snap my mouth shut, taking a breath to steady my racing heart. "You better finish what you started right the fuck now!"

The asshole looks over his shoulder at me lustfully before smiling. "Sweetheart, I never intend to finish anything with you, but I do intend to give you all the reasons to scream my name tomorrow."

My mouth drops open and strangely, my arousal heightens with his punishing words. "Ro–"

"See you tomorrow, baby. Oh, and Shay?" He reaches for the door handle before he changes his mind and saunters back toward me. My heart skips at the sight of his hungry prowl. Leaning down to my ear, he caresses my face with his hot breath. "Don't even *think* about finishing." He dips a finger between my brazenly open legs, coating it with my juices and making me whimper before sucking it clean. He walks back toward the door, turning over his shoulder again. "The only one who gets to make that sweet pussy of yours come, is me."

And with that, he heads out of my room into the darkened night, like some sort of blue-vagina-inducing phantom.

I hear the soft hum of an engine starting down the street as I lay there in shock; pissed beyond belief, completely frustrated, and . . . so fucking impatient to see him tomorrow.

CHAPTER 17
ROWAN

My blood's boiling.

It's the fourth fucking time in the past hour the new flight attendant on our team plane–a clean-cut Clark Kent looking dude with black-rimmed glasses–has stopped to chat with Shayla.

He's one of those discreetly good-looking guys. The kind who looks buttoned-up on the outside, but is really just a douchebag when you peel back the layers. Yes, I'm making assumptions, but I have a right to when some asshole is leering at my girl.

My nostrils flare. I bet he plays sudoku or some shit in his spare time, too. He seems like the type.

And that fucking smarmy smile of his? With those fluorescent white teeth? Oh, yeah. Definitely a sudoku-playing douchebag.

I'm ready to fucking pound down the aisle to him and smack that shit right off his face.

My molars grind as I regard his casual stance–his weasley

elbow laying on the seat in front of her, one foot crossed over the other, like he's posing for some nerd-man magazine.

It pisses me the fuck off. And if I didn't have a deal to uphold with Shay, I'd throw him out the emergency exit.

I can't see her face from here—just the back of her arm displaying her butterfly tattoo—since she's turned the other way, but I know it's her he's talking to. What the hell is he going on about, anyway?

An inkling of satisfaction runs through me, recalling the quick exchange she and I had when I passed her seat to get to mine.

"Doc." I'd nodded, keeping up appearances for everyone else, but knowing she could see the lust floating in my irises as I took her in. Knowing she was drinking in my suit-clad form the same way I was drinking her in, in her tight white dress that hugged all her curves and fell off one shoulder. Knowing she remembered last night as keenly as I did, when I left her begging for my cock with a promise to make it up to her this weekend.

"Mr. Parker," she'd responded, playing her part to perfection. "Are you ready for the game? I hope your pain is manageable."

"It's not," I'd answered, not giving a shit I was holding up the line. "I'm going to need your help in releasing some additional tension today." Yeah, so there was an added innuendo there.

I saw the flush that crawled up her neck before she cleared her throat and tucked her hair behind her ear like she did whenever she was nervous. "I'll see you after warmups, then."

"Oh, you're so screwed." Brooks, our team's goalie and one of my closest friends, follows my gaze, looking over the seats in front of us before bursting into laughter and taking me out of my thoughts.

I purse my lips, tamping down my irritation, before turning toward the guy who also happens to be our team owner and

Beckett Langfield's brother. "Shut the fuck up. It's not like that."

Brooks chuckles, flitting through his phone as if he even has enough brain cells to read. He does. Honestly, he's one of the sharpest guys I've ever met. He's also one of the most polite and down-to-earth, but I don't need to compliment him in my inner monologue.

I catch him shaking his head right as I tip my head back to close my eyes. "It all makes sense now."

I exhale a sharp breath through my nose, forcing myself to keep my eyes closed and count to ten, hoping the douchebag at the front of the plane finds something better to do with his time by then. Otherwise, he risks incurring my wrath.

I roll my shoulders, addressing Brooks, "What all makes sense?"

If it wasn't for holding up this ruse and not getting anyone's suspicions up, I'd be sitting next to Shay. Bet *Smarmy-Sam* wouldn't be able to find his balls to leer at her then.

Brooks snorts. "I'm just surprised it took me this long to put it together."

I give him a sharp look, but it doesn't do much to shut him up. Thankfully, the hum of the flight engine drowns out his voice as he continues, so I don't have to worry about the rest of my team jumping in to listen to the gossip like teenage girls. I swear, they might be worse.

"I should have known the second you insisted she be your full time PT, instead of going to Greg like the rest of us." He refers to our athletic trainer. "Don't think I don't know that you had your agent call Gavin to figure out a way to pressure her to come with us to our away games, too. He told me, and I had a suspicion it was because you had a hidden agenda, but I hadn't confirmed it until now."

"You're an idiot; I've got no hidden agenda." This is true.

I've pretty *openly* stated my agenda to the woman in question, and that is, I want her. I want her badly; I want her now, and I want her all the goddamn time. "My leg is fucked up and she's helping me fix it. End of story."

"Uh huh," he says, flipping through the photos on his phone. "And that's why you're sitting here with smoke coming out of your ears? You're going to cause a fire, bro."

I take another breath, trying to relax back in my seat and close my eyes. It's the only hope I have of not losing my shit. Clearly, I need to do a better job of reining in my temper because if it doesn't let up, the whole team's going to find out why I'm pissed.

They haven't seen me be crazy about a woman. Hell, *I* haven't even seen me be *this* crazy about a woman. Not even Audrey, not by a long shot.

The feelings I've developed in this short amount of time for the knockout sitting at the head of the plane are unrivaled with anything I've ever felt about anyone in my past. And that's both unexpected and obvious.

Unexpected because, for so long, I've been keeping my head down, focused only on my career. I definitely didn't have any notions of getting into a relationship with a single mom. Not that I disliked kids or anything; I just never thought about them. But ever since I spent time with her son yesterday, the thought of having kids of my own someday doesn't seem so foreign.

And obvious, because from the moment I saw her, I've been enamored. Enamored with her wit, her charm, and her disarming beauty. Enamored with her perfection and her flaws. Enamored with the truths she tells, and the facade she sometimes hides behind.

Hell, I might even be enamored with her fears.

It sounds strange, but I like the idea of being by her side as she works through them. I like the idea of being there when she leaves them behind—like the cigarette I caught her smoking last night—and takes a step forward.

It's not surprising that, from the moment I saw her, I had no chance. No chance of surviving whatever this was going to become without getting my heart involved.

I open my eyes a few moments later to see if Smarmy is still there, but my view is blocked by Fedir Rudenko, our right wing, doing his yoga exercises in the middle of the damn aisle.

He does this on every flight as part of his ritual—a full warrior one and warrior two pose before doing a few sun salutations—while the rest of us let him do his thing. Even the flight crew works around him.

The man is a giant—there's no other way to describe him. If you think I'm large, you haven't seen Fedir. And though his size makes him slightly slower on the ice, I wouldn't want to be on the receiving end of the impact if he ran into me.

So, to watch a virtual giant doing yoga on each flight, because he says he's scared of flying and it helps him calm his nerves, is somewhat comical. And he does it so nonchalantly, too, not giving a shit if he's inconveniencing anyone trying to get around him.

"Hastauttanasana," he chants, bending his body backward, stretching out his abdomen and chest. Oh, right, he also talks through each pose, as if he's instructing a class. "Focus on your core. Let your navel be a direct line to the heavens. Let your soul transform into butterflies you release into the sky."

I lean to my left and then to my right to see if I can see Smarmy-Sam still chatting it up with my girl, but no matter how I try, I can't get a clear view over the enormous right winger in front of me.

"Fedir," I call, trying to get his attention to no avail. I'll have to wait until he gets to the pose where he's folded over, touching the ground.

"Beautiful, colorful butterflies. Lovely butterflies. Watch them float."

I wait, tapping my fingers on the armrest before turning to watch Brooks' shoulders shake with laughter. I don't know what the fuck is so funny. Asshole.

"Parvatasana," Fedir says as he folds down to the ground a few moments later. "Feel the stretch behind your thighs. Release the tension when you're upside down. Viewing an upside-down world will allow you to appreciate the right-side up. Don't let the need to vomit deter you."

Finally, I'm able to peek behind Fedir to see that Smarmy is still talking to her! Does the guy not have a job to do?

That's it. That's fucking it!

I look behind me, noticing the other flight attendant handing out drinks, before I press the attendant button above me, making Smarmy excuse himself from the spot he's gotten way too comfortable in.

A minute later, he's tripping to get past Fedir in some sort of reptilian pose on the ground–"Bones are just constructs holding us back. Allow your bones to melt. Find comfort in melting."–before he's standing next to me.

Smarmy turns off the attendant light above me. "Can I help you?" he says with a flat tone, completely devoid of the smile he was giving my girl.

I steeple my fingers over my abdomen, letting my shoulders go slack. "Yeah, but I'm going to need you to come closer since it's a private matter."

Brooks pinches the bridge of his nose, but I don't miss the smile on his face.

Smarmy-Sam bends, bringing his ear closer to me.

"I'm going to make this clear, once and only once," I say

without a hint of humor. "That woman you've been gabbing with in seat 3B? She's *mine*."

His brows lift, but he keeps his ear near my mouth, likely knowing I have more to say.

"So, I don't give a fuck how you manage it, because I know I wouldn't be able to in your position, given how fucking beautiful she is. But, if you want to keep your job, I'd suggest you stop talking to her from this moment forward. You're not going to look at her, smile at her, or even fucking breathe in her direction. Nod if I've made myself clear?"

Smarmy's face blanches, but he manages a small nod.

"Oh, and Smarmy?" I add before he can rush off, because I know that's what he wants to do. "Let's keep this little chat between us, shall we?"

He nods again before running to the front galley like his ass has suddenly caught fire.

And right when I'm feeling pretty fucking satisfied with the way I handled things, I catch Shayla's confused eyes. I shrug, giving her a sheepish grin, but it only makes her narrow her eyes at me like she knows I've done something that'll piss her off.

She throws daggers of irritation my way before I wiggle my fingers at her, saying hi from afar, but she abruptly turns back to the front, unamused.

"Shit," I say, under my breath, knowing I might have to explain this shit to her later.

Brooks laughs outright before bringing his pillow around his neck and closing his eyes. "No hidden agenda, huh?"

CHAPTER 18
ROWAN

I twist my mouth, looking down at my phone, before I lift my head to see if Shayla is reading the text I sent her.

We're on the bus to our hotel, sitting in almost the same order we did on the flight, and I still haven't had a chance to talk to her all day. It's driving me crazy.

A message vibrates my phone.

Oh, right. She probably saw that Smarmy was talking to me and put two and two together.

Still, irritation and jealousy climbs over my skin like a rash at the fact that she is on a first-name basis with the asshole on our flight.

ME

> I just told him, in a very polite way, that I don't like to share. That's all. Also, he totally doesn't look like an Oscar. Based on his douchey looks and personality, I'd personally peg him for a Gaston or a Caledon. Maybe even a Benji.

I stifle a chuckle, watching her fingers fly rapid fire over her screen. God, I will never get tired of irritating this woman.

SHAY

> You're unbelievable, you know that? He was just telling me how his sister is a physical therapist, too. And what you said to him could come back to bite me in the ass. You won't lose anything, but I could, Rowan.

My brows furrow as I type back. I'll readily admit my reaction was uncalled for, and I'll take accountability for it, but she has to know that I would never let her reputation take a hit. The Bolts have an incredible PR team that would handle any such situation if it arose. Still, she deserves my apology.

ME

> I'm sorry. Truly, I am. I let you down, and I feel like an asshole. Not that it's an excuse, but I have no idea why I lose my shit at even the thought of anyone but me looking at you . . . touching you.

I watch Shayla type her response. Thank God she's not icing me out like some women would at the shit I just pulled. I suppose that has something to do with the fact that she's more mature, more experienced, as compared to most women I date.

178

SHAY

Well, I guess you're really not going to like
what I have to tell you, then.

My heart stutters. What the fuck is she going to tell me that I won't like? Is she calling quits on this? We've barely begun. Oh, hell no, I'm not letting her give up on us this quickly.

Or wait, is she still referring to Smarmy-Sam? Did he . . . did he touch her?

I can feel my ears turning red. Just like my vision seems to be doing.

ME

??

I watch as she puts her phone away in her purse, starting a conversation with the team doctor sitting next to her. She moves her hands around animatedly, like she didn't just give me a heart attack, while my stomach rolls.

What the fuck?! Is she serious right now? She's going to ghost me after saying that?

I call her phone, hoping she'll pick it up and we can have a discreet conversation, but she slides her hand into her purse, sees that I'm calling, and turns around to give me a perfectly arched brow.

"Pick up your phone," I mouth while my stomach continues to flip-flop around like a fish out of water.

But she just turns around, paying me no mind.

The woman gives as good as she gets, that's for fucking sure, and I have never met anyone as confident and bold as she is. She knows exactly what she's doing. She knows she's driving me to the brink of insanity, and she doesn't give a single fuck.

I love it and I fucking hate it at the same time.

I message her again, seconds away from getting off my seat and going over there to demand an answer in person.

ME

Shay, I swear to God. I won't fucking have a heart attack on this bus before I get an answer, so tell me what you were going to say or I'm coming over there.

Maybe she senses my nerves, maybe she can hear the thumping of my heart. Whatever the case, she finally responds.

SHAY

Oh, it was only that I brought Trick with me, and I intend to let him touch me any way he likes.

My hand fists my phone, my eyes blazing, but it's the little smile on her face that I can see even from her profile, that has me falling.

Looking to make sure the hall is empty, I knock on her hotel room door.

We only have an hour before we have to meet everyone downstairs to catch the bus for warmups, but like an addict, I'm at my dealer's door, needing my fix.

She opens the door, still wearing that same white dress

from the flight, before inviting me in. Her brows lift in a silent question as I step inside—*did anyone see you?* I shake my head, letting her know I made sure to be discreet.

But before her door can even shut, I have her lifted up and pinned against the wall, my lips covering hers. She smells amazing, the hint of her perfume lingering around us.

Her legs wrap around my hips as I palm her ass, grinding my erection into her center, while her dress rides up her thighs.

She whimpers, biting my bottom lip before sucking and teasing it. Her arms wrap around my shoulders while she lets me explore her mouth. Her fingers dig inside my hair as her hips thrust involuntarily against me.

I've had a permanent hard-on since the moment I saw her this morning, and now I'm seconds from embarrassing myself all too quickly.

"I need you like I need my next breath," I groan, digging my erection between her legs. Our bodies are a heated mix of desire and need, and I honestly don't know how slow I can go at this point.

She moans into my mouth, her hands curling around my shoulders, her eyes hooded. "Then take me; we can't have you asphyxiating."

I chuckle as I drop my lips to her jaw, kissing and nibbling, before I let them slide to her neck, tasting her delicious warm skin. She's so intoxicating, she should be lethal.

I come back to her lips again, and our kiss turns ravenous and messy. Our mouths move with urgency, like we're each other's lifelines. My hands work up her dress, sliding over her velvety skin, before my thumb brushes the crease between her thigh and center.

My brows pucker as my thumb slips further to her center, realizing she doesn't have any underwear on. I glare at her, ready to take her over my knee if she answers incorrectly. "Tell me you had panties on during the flight?"

"And if I didn't?" She bats her eyelashes.

My jaw ticks, and in an instant, I'm carrying her over my shoulder, making her yelp. I drag her dress over her bare ass before my palm connects with one cheek, making her shriek and moan.

"You've been testing me all damn morning," I groan before throwing her down on the bed. I get down on my knees, pulling her glistening, bare center toward me. "Put your feet on the edge and hold on to something. I need to fuck your pussy with my tongue."

She does as she's told and I note her beautiful toes, painted red. Yeah, with this woman, I notice everything. Her knees frame my face while she squeezes the comforter between her fists. She's writhing and heaving before I've even taken the first swipe. "Please."

I drag my tongue over her slit, tasting her from bottom to top and making her mewl. I do it again, slower this time, and she bucks against me. Lapping at her entrance, I let her juices cover my tongue. She's so fucking sweet, I wouldn't be lying if I said I could eat her all damn day.

I slide up to her clit, flicking it with the tip of my tongue before pressing two fingers inside her. She's tight, but I feel her walls release to accommodate my digits.

"Fuck, Rowan." She writhes and rolls under my lips, asking for more.

I give her more, sucking on her clit while my fingers thrust into her heat, in and out, until she's a mess of gasps and wails.

She grabs the back of my head tightly as she rocks under me, taking what she wants. Widening her knees, she opens up for me and I don't disappoint, laving her needy center thoroughly, groaning with satisfaction as I do.

"Oh my God, Rowan! I'm going to come. Please don't stop."

I glide my tongue over her, driving my fingers into her and feeling the warmth of her walls pulse against them, before I suck on each of her folds.

Her breath hitches, her walls tightening around me, when she clamors to pull a pillow over her face and screams into it. Her thighs quiver around my head as her orgasm rolls through her, gifting me with the taste of her release on my tongue.

Seconds later, my shirt and gym shorts lie on the ground. Shayla's hooded gaze works over my body, taking me in from head to toe, snagging on my erection. I take the condom I took out of my wallet in between my teeth.

"Take that dress off," I mumble around the foil.

She does, throwing her dress and bra over the bed before laying back on the pillow.

I rip the foil with my teeth while my eyes roam over her bare, tan skin. There's a horizontal scar right under her panty line–likely from a C-section–a row of tiny moles under one breast, and some stretch marks on the sides of her hips. She's nothing short of stunning, an absolute beauty with her flushed cheeks and the beads of sweat lining her brows.

She pulls her bottom lip into her mouth while her eyes blaze, watching me roll the condom over my thick shaft.

This isn't exactly how I intended our first time to go. I'd intended for us to take things slow and to have more time, but my craving for her had come to a head–no pun intended. Even the thought of holding off until later this evening feels too painful.

I lift the back of her knee as I angle the tip of my cock at her entrance, arching my brow at her to ask for permission. "Yes?"

She nods enthusiastically. "Fuck, yes! Absolutely, yes."

My soft chuckle dies on my lips as I press myself inside her. We both groan as she expands around me, sheathing me from root to tip. Keeping my weight from crushing her, I look down at our connection. It's so hot, so fucking beautiful, I have to physically hold myself back from coming just from the sight of it.

I'm fully seated inside her, my tattooed forearm next to her head, when I take a moment to just stare into her espresso-colored eyes. They look up at me with a rare vulnerability she keeps hidden. I know she can feel this, too–this connection between us, far from the physical one we have now.

Perhaps it was the spontaneous and combustible chemistry we felt the moment we met. Perhaps it's the easiness I feel around her, same as what I know she feels around me. Perhaps it's neither of those, and it's just that our souls seem to want to intertwine.

I want to know everything about her, from her favorite color to her favorite season. I want to play connect-the-dots with the moles on her body and trace every tattoo with my tongue. I want to fall asleep looking at her and be the person she wakes up to. And fuck, I can't wait to have her at all my games, wearing my jersey, so I can show the entire world she's mine.

I want all that, knowing I have to take this one step at a time. Knowing that while she hasn't stated it explicitly, she thinks this is just a temporary thing between us.

I rock into her and she releases a soft gasp, cupping my ass with her palms. She pulls me further into her, opening up to give me room. She's so tight, she's choking my dick in a vice-grip, but I'm not complaining. It feels like fucking heaven.

"Jesus Christ, Shay, you feel so fucking good. All those nights I fucked my palm to your name . . . nothing compares to the real thing."

She lifts to catch my lips and I skate my tongue inside her mouth, slowly dragging it against hers. We kiss without the urgency of the first time as I fuck her, deep and slow, making her hiss and mewl.

Our pace gets faster, our bodies slick and crashing against each other. My balls feel heavy and my eyes beg to roll back into my head as she matches me, thrust for thrust. I brush the tips of my fingers over her forehead before leaning down to kiss the little mole on the top of her cheek. I might be obsessed with it.

I might be obsessed with *her*.

I drop my hand under her ass, lifting it and thrusting into her at a slightly different angle, and feeling a tingle build at the base of my spine. "I can't hold on much longer, baby. Are you close?"

"I'm right there with you," she breathes, never breaking away from my eyes. "I'm so close."

I dip to take her nipple into my mouth, teasing it around my tongue before sucking deep. Her hips jump under me, her nails dragging over my back as I continue my unrelenting pace. Our bodies move in sync as I delve deeper, knowing I'm hitting the spot inside her that'll have her seeing stars.

I feel her tighten around me and, seconds later, she sucks in a sharp breath as her release rolls through her. "Yes! Oh God, yes!"

She throbs around my cock, sucking it deeper into her while my release sends currents rippling down my spine.

Our rhythm slows, along with the aftershocks of the biggest fucking orgasm I've ever experienced. My lips find hers again, pulling them into a soft kiss. "Do you have any idea how crazy you make me?"

A soft laugh leaves her lips. "I'm starting to get the message, given that caveman-like pissing contest on the flight."

I nuzzle my face into the crook of her neck, breathing her

in. My heart still hammers inside my chest. "Given the fact that my cock is still buried inside you, I'm pretty sure there was no contest. Smarmy-Sam had nothing on me."

She pokes my side. "Always so sure of yourself, Mr. Parker." I can hear the smile on her lips as she wiggles under me, instantly making me hard again. "But I suppose Keanu really did come through today."

I lift up, glaring at her, my blood boiling inside my veins. "Who the fuck is *Keanu*?"

She giggles. "It's what I've named *your* cock."

I shake my head, appalled. "You most certainly have not! No way is my cock going to be called *Keanu*. I could possibly entertain *Rowan's Magical Hockey Stick* or *Emperor of Vaginas* as potential names, but that's where I draw the line."

She snorts. "Yeah, that last one is definitely not happening. Your big head does not need more inflating."

I roll my hips, letting her feel my 'big head' again before I slink down to capture her nipple in my mouth. "Admit it, you're obsessed with both my big heads."

She moans, her body betraying her words, as she buries her fingers in my hair. "You wish."

I bite her nipple, making her squirm. "I'm not one to make wishes, Doc. I'm the one to make things happen." I lift back up and stare into her eyes so she can see what I'm saying as clearly as the way I feel about her. "But with you, I find myself searching the sky for shooting stars."

CHAPTER 19
ROWAN

Our head coach is pissed.

"What the fuck was that out there?" Coach yells at the top of his lungs in the locker room during our first intermission against San Jose. "We're sitting at a two-goal deficit and playing shitty defense."

He paces for a few seconds, fuming.

It's been a brutal first period with San Jose feeding us heavy hits, keeping their defense tight, and winning the last two face-offs. Every one of their players has thrown in everything they have on the ice so far, ready to win this game, come hell or high water. They're relentless and calculated, and it shows with every play.

Meanwhile, my head's not in it, despite the fact that I spent the most incredible hour in bed with Shay earlier today—a mere drop in the bucket of hours I plan to spend with her. My good mood was shot to hell as soon as I left her hotel room and made the mistake of reading the text from my dad.

I've told myself time and time again to not open his

messages, especially before a game, but of course, I didn't follow through with my own advice.

DAD

> Get your head in the game today, son, and act like you actually want the Cup. It was embarrassing enough to lose to your old team because you guys played like shit, worse that Evan played better each period. And now he's one-upped you again. Audrey messaged me saying he proposed to her afterward.

I don't give a flying fuck that my ex-girlfriend and my former best friend are engaged. They could get married or divorced. They could have a cat farm or move to Mars. None of it makes a difference to me.

But the fact that my dad still thinks he can get inside my head by reminding me what a poster boy Evan is and that he still communicates with my ex–a woman who not only cheated on me with my then-best friend, but the same one I found in bed with him mere hours after I'd proposed to her–makes me want to punch the fucking wall.

Apart from that, he continuously berates me, giving me unsolicited coaching from the sidelines–*via text messages*–regardless of the fact that I still have yet to respond to him.

Enough is fucking enough.

I'm done being the punching bag for a useless piece of shit who has never spared a single word of genuine kindness toward me.

"This is not what this team is made of!" Coach roars, snapping me out of my aggravating thoughts. "We are better than what you showed that team out there today. You understand me?" His hands ball into fists and his face turns the color of an overly ripened tomato. "Now, if you guys are here to throw in the towel, well, someone fucking tell me right now. Otherwise, you're going out there, taking possession of that puck, and winning the next shift! Am I clear?"

"Yes, Coach!" we all roar together.

"Next time you get out there, you make this team proud." He raises a brow in my direction as the rest of the team busies themselves. "You hear me, Parker? We need you to help us win this; you can't be missing easy cues like you did last period."

I nod sternly, knowing I have no defense for myself. I played like shit the first period and I'll own it. But he'll get my all from here on out. "We're leaving here on a win, Coach. No questions about it."

He tilts his head toward my leg. "How's that bum leg?"

I flex my foot, stretching out my thigh. "Better. A little tight, but nothing I can't handle."

"Go see that PT of yours in the medical room. You've still got ten minutes."

He heads out and I follow him, making my way to the medical room where Shay's been watching the game on the TV.

I knock on the door, making her and our team doctor turn to look at me. I've been a ball of irritation for the past hour and half since I got the text from my dad, but seeing Shay has all the tension releasing from my shoulders.

"Dr. Kumar, mind helping me loosen up my thigh?" My mouth quivers with a held back smile, not having anything to do with what I've said. I just simply can't help smiling when I'm around the woman.

I might also be picturing her naked and writhing under me. And now that I know exactly what she looks like in that position, it's hard not to conjure up the image.

She gets off her chair, tucking the long end of her hair behind her ear. She's wearing our team shirt, tucked into a pair of jeans that mold around her ass like a glove, and I'm instantly hard watching her walk toward me.

She waves her hand to the spot next to her on a mat. "Since we don't have much time, why don't we do a few sumo squats and lunges, just to get that stretch in?"

For the next couple of minutes, she leads me in the stretches and evaluates my movements. I give her my normal shameless grin when she finds me ogling her ass.

Another minute or two later, the other doctor excuses himself to grab something to eat, leaving me and Shay alone. But as soon as the door closes, I'm on her like white on rice. She doesn't resist when I drop my lips to cover hers; instead, she melts into me, her fingers tightening around my jersey.

Breaking away a minute or two later, she eyes me curiously. "Is everything okay? I don't know much about hockey, but it seems like you were off your game based on what the announcers were saying." She flicks a concerned glance at my thigh. "Is it really your thigh that's bothering you?"

I take a breath before shaking my head. "It's my dad. He's just a dick, but I can't get into it right now. I'll tell you tonight."

She gives me an understanding smile. "I'm looking forward to meeting your sister."

"She's excited to see you, too."

I'm just headed out when she whacks my ass with her palm. "Go after that puck, Slick. I have dessert planned for after dinner tonight," her eyes gleam with mischief, "but only for a winner."

"That last period had my heart racing!" Piper says excitedly, scooting into the private booth Zach reserved for us on the other side of Shayla and me. "That pass you made to Aiden Langfield, and the way he slid it past the San Jose goalie, with literally two seconds left in the game? Not kidding, I was holding my chest."

"It was a fucking close win, but," I look over at the beautiful raven-haired woman sitting next to me, "I had an extra incentive to win. Dessert tonight."

Piper's gaze bounces between the two of us before she seems to glean the meaning and wrinkles her nose. "I have a feeling I wouldn't want to know about this specific *dessert*." She smiles at Shay. "I've heard a lot about you, Shayla, and while I'm not at liberty to divulge anything my brother tells me, out of respect for the sister's oath and all, I can say . . . you seem to make him very happy."

I can feel the heat emanating from Shayla's body, and I don't need to look at her to know her cheeks are flushed. I clasp her hand with mine, letting her know it's okay.

"He makes me happy, too," she says, meeting my gaze before breaking away to address Piper. "So, Piper, what do you do?"

The three of us—my sister, Shay, and I—drove here after the game, but during that short drive, I swear I haven't gotten a word in since.

Between my sister firing off a machine gun of questions at

Shay, and Shay desperately trying to squeeze in her own, it was as if I didn't exist. Not that I minded.

I'd hoped for their meeting to turn out this way, and I can already tell Piper's taken a liking to Shay–not an easy feat considering how protective my sister is of me. What's been surprising is how fast Shay let her guard down, though Piper's always had a way of getting even the most guarded people to loosen up.

"My three best friends and I own a luxury men's salon in the East Bay," my sister declares, leaning in with her boundless enthusiasm. She's the most energetic and tireless person I know, and that's saying something given my high-energy career. Mom and I used to joke that she must have been born with additional batteries. "It's a lot of work, but I wouldn't trade it for the world."

Shay's eyes widen. "I don't think I've ever heard of a luxury men's salon. That's really cool. What makes it different from a normal salon, aside from the fact that it's tailored for men?"

Piper pulls out her phone, showing Shay pictures of the salon. "Well, anyone is welcome–men or women–but we provide specific services for men, like facial grooming, back and chest waxing, shoe polishing, so on and so forth. We always have sports playing on the TVs, offer beer or soft drinks to every customer, and just generally make it more of an experience rather than a place where someone comes for a haircut."

Shay looks at her with awe. "That's incredible, Piper. I'd love to see it one day."

"You're welcome anytime!" Piper turns to me. "I tell Rowan the same thing. I mean, he's the reason I was even able to make the investment and become a true partner. He paid for–"

"Piper," I warn, trying to shut her up. "No one needs to know how the financials worked out. Stop giving unnecessary information."

Piper crosses her arms over her chest. "Yes, they do, and it's not unnecessary information. You're the reason I have a business." She ignores my glare, speaking to Shay, "The man sitting next to you? He'd literally give the shirt off his back to help his friends and family. In fact, our friend Zach, who's the owner of this restaurant, was about to shut this place down a few years ago because he had some unexpected expenses come up and couldn't afford his lease–"

"Jesus, Piper." I pinch the bridge of my nose. "Can we just figure out what to order–"

"You hush and stop interrupting me," my sister snaps, before rolling her eyes exasperatedly and continuing her unnecessary account of shit no one is asking about. "Well, Rowan paid for all those expenses so Zach could keep the restaurant open."

"It's true." To my horror and embarrassment, my buddy Zach materializes from nowhere at our table, placing our drinks in front of us. He already knew what my sister and I would order—our regular drinks when we're here, their Mexican mule—but he places the special drink I'd asked for in front of Shay. "There's no way I would have been able to keep this place open if it wasn't for Slick." He looks at me with complete sincerity. "I owe you big time, brother."

"You don't owe me shit." I quickly change the subject, introducing him to Shay. But since I don't really know how to label our relationship in front of Zach, I end up calling her my "friend" but hating the word on my tongue. "How's the family doing?"

Zach's face lights up. "Macie just turned fifteen, but she acts like she's twenty-five; Braxton is nine and as sweet as can be. He still uses those skates you sent him for his birthday."

"Shay has a nine-year-old son, too," I tell him, feeling

Shay's hands tighten on mine. I look at her when I speak. "He's cool as shit, just like his mom."

Zach points to the drink in front of Shay. "That right there is a handcrafted cranberry vodka and club soda with a hint of lime, ginger, and mint. You'll be happy to know that all the ingredients in it are organic, with only natural sugars and no artificial flavoring."

Shay looks at me for an explanation since she hadn't ordered a drink. "Did you put him up to this?"

I shrug. "You don't have to drink it. I just figured I'd have Zach modify one of his popular bar drinks with ingredients you wouldn't have to worry about."

A soft look transforms her features, and she brings the drink to her lips. "Thank you. That was . . ." her brows pinch together, "really thoughtful, Rowan."

"You see my point?" Piper says to Shay as soon as Zach leaves. "My brother is a caretaker through and through."

"As if you aren't?" I punt back. "How many times have you dropped everything to come to my games? And when all that shit happened five years ago . . .?"

My sister and I exchange a silent look with Shayla's gaze bouncing between us, trying to glean more meaning from my cryptic statement.

I have nothing to hide and I'm not one to prolong mysteries or drama, so I turn toward her, unveiling what I always intended to tell her. Clearly, she hasn't looked me up online because she'd have found most of it in a simple search. And since I don't have much to hide, I've never really asked our PR team to bury the news.

"Five years ago, I was playing for the New York Mayors and dating a woman named Audrey. We'd been together for three years, and I thought I loved her enough to marry her."

As if Shay can tell she's not going to like what I'm about to say, she rubs circles over my thumb with hers.

"But the night we got engaged, I found her in bed with one of my closest friends." My jaw tightens as the memories flood back. "He played center for our team."

"Rowan . . ." Shay's breath hitches, an unmistakable frown on her face. "I'm so sorry."

"Girl was a total back-stabbing bitch! And Evan Lanthrop was a snake in disguise," Piper chimes in as she gets out of the booth. "Excuse me a moment. I need to use the ladies' room."

"Is that why you moved to Boston to play for the Bolts?" Shay asks after watching my sister's back retreat.

I place my index under her chin and turn Shay's gaze toward me. I have a feeling she needs to hear this, even if she doesn't show it. She's a master of masking her vulnerability at times. "I want you to know something. I don't give two shits about my ex; I haven't in a very long time. But yes, at the time that I asked to be traded, my life was imploding publicly and I couldn't work with Evan, knowing what he'd done."

Rage flashes in her eyes. "I hate that they did that to you. And I wouldn't wish this on even my enemies, but I hope they both develop high-fructose corn syrup addictions!"

I throw back my head, laughing before I capture her lips with mine. "God, you're so fucking perfect."

CHAPTER 20

SHAY

My chest burns, even as I ogle his upturned full lips and the way his cheeks lift when he laughs. Even his sheer beauty can't quell the ire I feel for the two people he thought he could trust, but hurt him in such a deep way.

It boggles my mind that anyone could ever hurt him. For all his cocky and overconfident displays, the man I am *really* starting to like is just a huge teddy bear with a heart made of soft wool.

An incredibly thoughtful, generous, and kind teddy bear who could be hurt, despite how strong and virile he looks on the outside.

His smile dwindles when he sees the look on my face, his eyes bouncing between mine in silent question.

I shake my head, pulling him closer by the collar and pressing my lips to his.

He doesn't hesitate to follow suit, wrapping his large hand around my cheek and neck, kissing me like we're not in a public restaurant. But I know we're well-hidden, given the large partition Zach placed around our booth to keep us from being visible to the rest of the patrons.

"Oh, Jesus," Piper huffs without a hint of the disgust she's trying to go for. "Maybe send me a text before you guys decide to get into a lewd tongue duel next time. I'll find ways to entertain myself in the bathroom a little longer."

"Sorry." I break away from Rowan, though he tries to keep me from moving too far, as heat ripples over my skin. In fact, I physically have to force my toes to uncurl, given that's exactly what they'd done in the time his lips were on mine.

"Don't apologize," Rowan says, giving his sister a squinted look. "My sister is the *queen* of grossing me out every chance she gets. And she's determined to make me turn one of her boy-toys into a pretzel."

I raise my brows. "Boy-*toys*? As in, the plural form?"

Piper rolls her eyes. "My brother may be younger than me, but he's always acted like a protective jackass when it comes to the men I choose to spend my time with."

"Yeah, because they aren't men," Rowan retorts, his jaw ticking. "Not one of them has been good enough for you, which is why you always have multiple assholes you're keeping around."

She winks. "Hey, don't knock it til you try it." She turns to me with a hand around her mouth like she's letting me in on a secret. "I don't remember their names sometimes, so I give them nicknames related to hot dogs. Like, I'm currently dating Oscar Mayer and Frank's Uncle."

My brows pinch. "Why do you give them hot dog names?"

"Why else?" Piper waggles her brows. "Because they're packing well-endowed sausages, of course!"

She doesn't even get the last word out when Rowan spits some of the water he'd just sipped, spraying his sister across the table and making me burst out laughing.

He looks like he's going to be sick. "Jesus Christ, Piper! You just made me lose my appetite."

"Oh, get over it. You know I am the way I am because I have deep-seated daddy issues." She laughs, but it sounds hollow.

Rowan groans. "Yeah, no shortage of daddy issues here, either."

He's about to say something else when Zach comes back to take our orders.

As soon as we've all ordered–two cheeseburgers and a Caesar salad–Piper aims her frown at Rowan. "Did Dad text you before today's game, too?"

Rowan's nostrils flare. "Right before the first period. It's partly why I played so shitty."

Rowan mentioned his dad when he came to see me in the medical room. And from what he told me a while ago about how his dad left them all for someone a lot younger, it seems there's a lot of harbored resentment there.

"Why won't you just cut him off, Row?" she asks, sitting back in her seat with her arms folded over her chest. "That's what I did, and I'm happier for it."

Rowan tilts his head. "Are you?"

"I'm happier than when he was in my life and I was just the butt of his jokes. I know you have this inherent need to be there for him, but Dad hasn't ever done the same for you. For either of us. He's not going to change, and you know that. So, why hold on to hope for a real relationship with him?"

Rowan seems to be pondering her question when our food arrives. He slides his burger and fries toward me, looking from me to the burger in a silent question to see if I want a bite.

I smile, swiping my bottom lip with my tongue. Any drool that might have slipped out has nothing to do with the delicious smelling burger in front of me and everything to do with the delicious, incredibly sweet man sitting next to me.

I ask the others if they want to cleanse their hands with the natural and homemade hand sanitizer I always carry in my purse, and I feel better when they both agree. Then, lifting the burger to my mouth, I take a big bite.

It's so fucking good, I almost break out in a dance. Rowan throws back his head in laughter, watching my eyes roll back in my head. I'm reaching for my napkin to wipe the corner of my mouth when his fingers pinch my chin and his lips drop over mine.

"You guys need me to go?" Piper asks, finishing up a bite of her burger. "I can go back to the bathroom, in case you need a minute to hump inside this booth."

I giggle, saying, "No, we're good," while Rowan retorts with, "That'd be nice."

I elbow him, still laughing, when he turns back to Piper. Some of his good mood seems slightly diminished. "If I do decide to cut Dad off, I'm going to look him in the face and do it."

Piper sighs in defeat. "Just don't be surprised if he turns it all around on you to make you feel like you're the one who owes him something. Dad's a master at playing the victim card."

We're almost done eating when Dylan responds to the text I sent her, asking how Kai was doing. I saw him on FaceTime earlier when he and Winnie were playing baseball outside with Cortney. Neither Kai nor Winnie wore enough layers for my comfort, but they seemed to be having fun, so I bit my tongue. I also resisted in asking Kai which shoes he was wearing, which I thought was a small personal victory.

DYLAN

All good, but Cortney says he's going to have to work with Kai on his swing.

My brows pucker, and I'm just about to type in a response when a picture comes through of our house—one of our windows clearly shattered with a baseball-sized hole in it.

I gasp, showing Rowan the picture. His face transforms from a wince to a laugh, his shoulders shaking. "Hey, it's not a fun day unless a window gets broken."

I shake my head. "We just had the windows replaced, too."

Rowan rubs my back, knowing I'm tense. "He's a kid. These things happen."

His phone buzzes on the table right as I'm sending my response to Dylan, a frown replacing his grin.

"What?" Piper and I ask at the same time.

"The team wants me to meet them at a bar nearby to celebrate our win." He starts typing out a message. "I'm telling them I won't be there."

"What? Why?" I ask, placing a hand on his forearm, loving the way his tattoos peek out from under his long sleeve.

He turns to me, his eyes dropping to my lips. "Because I'm going back to the hotel to enjoy my dessert."

"Gross," Piper grunts.

"Rowan, it's tradition. It's important for you to be there."

He sighs, thinking momentarily. "Then come with me. I have no desire to go without you."

I shake my head. "That's not a good idea. I have no business being there tonight, and people could catch on. You know I can't risk any rumors flying."

Piper chimes in, getting our attention, "What if you come with me? The guys don't really know I'm Rowan's sister, and I could use another drink." She winks. "Who knows, maybe I'll find another *hot dog*."

Rowan points at her. "No fucking hot dogs! But the rest isn't a bad idea."

I twist my mouth, thinking. I haven't been to a bar in ages, and I can't deny that a part of me wants to remember what it was like to be out without any real responsibilities waiting for me at home.

I still remember the times Jeena asked me to go out with her and her friends. I always refused, knowing Ajay wouldn't approve or he wouldn't be home to take care of Kai. But maybe this time I could be the one to ask her to join us.

We'd intended to meet tomorrow while Rowan was at practice, but it might be fun to change the plan a little, if she can join, too.

I look at both Piper and Rowan. "Would it be okay for me to invite my friend Jeena? She's a little crazy, but I think you guys would really like her."

"Did you say she's crazy?" Piper gets a mischievous glint in her eyes. "Because crazy is my kind of people."

Jeena scans the Bolts players across the bar, sipping her pink, sugary concoction. "Good God. Are all hockey players this hot and beefy?"

She flags down the bartender for the third time. "Hello again, kind sir. Thank you for this magnificent drink, but could I get a dash more sweetener? Simple syrup, agave, maple syrup, honey, molasses, aspartame, or good ol' granulated sugar, perhaps?"

The bartender deadpans, "Should I get a glucose IV going for you?"

She shakes her head, taking him seriously. "That's very kind of you, but the items I previously listed will do perfectly fine."

The bartender mumbles something under his breath before he takes out every type of sweetener he has and slides it toward her. "Have at it."

Jeena's eyes sparkle with delight. "You're a saint." She turns back toward Piper and me, beaming. "The service here is just impeccable!"

I don't suppress my smile. I wouldn't trade my kooky, sugar-fiend of a best friend for the world. She's one of the only people I know who is unabashedly herself, unintentionally funny, and unapologetically sincere. Not to mention, she's a complete knockout.

"I don't think you have anything to complain about, given you're married to one of the hottest men I've ever seen," I quip, answering her previous question.

"Oh, believe me, I'm not complaining. Wayland is the only man I have eyes for. Plus, have I told you about his potatoes?"

Piper leans forward, as if she may have heard incorrectly. "His *potatoes*?"

I squeeze my eyes shut. "Yes, I have heard about his potatoes in *great* detail." I turn to Piper. "Please don't encourage her. You will never be able to meet her husband without blushing."

"I'm so confused right now, but I'm going to take your word for it," Piper says, taking another sip from her bottle.

Jeena and I giggle before she looks over her glass at the gorgeous and incredibly loud men still standing across the bar. "Speaking of hot beefcakes and their large *potatoes*, yours hasn't been able to take his eyes off you."

"It's been like this all evening," Piper adds, tipping her beer back again. "I've never seen my brother so smitten."

"It's nothing like that," I state, chancing a glance at the man in question, sitting on a barstool across the bar. Rowan's teammates holler and take shots around him while his eyes blaze even under the dim lighting, glued to me.

"I mean, just the way they're looking at each other . . ." Jeena gestures between Rowan and me. "It reminds me of the porcupine documentary I watched on Animal Planet where the female sprays her . . . you know, *eau de vag* on her chosen suitor–"

"Ew." My nose crinkles.

"With the way he's staring down anyone who even dares to look at you, I wouldn't be surprised if he walks over here with a face full of needles, having fought the other porcupines, and pees on you to claim you as his."

Piper's brows come together. "I think my beer's going to come back up."

Jeena clutches her chest, batting her eyes dramatically. "Wouldn't it be all so romantic?"

"No, it would be gross."

"I don't mean the peeing part. I meant the face-needles part. And the vag pheromones, maybe–"

Piper blinks at me. "Please make her stop."

I laugh. "I wish I could, but once she gets started on animal facts, there's little that can be done."

Jeena lifts her drink toward Piper in a toast, as if I've just given her the biggest compliment, and my attention gets snagged back in Rowan's direction.

Thankfully, we had a chance to go back to the hotel after dinner so I could get out of the clothes I was wearing all day. But what was supposed to take fifteen minutes turned out to be thirty–with Piper waiting at the hotel bar for us–because Mr. Rowan Slick Parker decided he wanted his dessert, and he wasn't going anywhere without it.

My body feels warm as I recall our quick but productive use of those thirty minutes.

"Goddamn," he rasped as I widened my mouth around his length. And though his hand was wrapped around the back of my head, he gave me all the control, letting me take the reins on how I wanted to pleasure him.

I worked my mouth down his shaft, taking him in deeper before lifting back up to tease his tip with my tongue. The taste of his pre-cum had ripples of desire drumming inside my wet center.

Drifting down his cock again, I took him as far back as I could until his tip hit the back of my throat, and I almost gagged.

Rowan exhaled before his head fell back and he mumbled words of encouragement, like, "Pure perfection," and "Want to be here all night."

I slid my hand over his thick and veiny cock, pumping him while sucking on his tip, siphoning out more pre-cum, along with his gruff moans of pleasure.

His lazy gaze landed on mine as my other hand lifted to play with his balls, and he released a slow breath while I relished in the knowledge that I was driving him to the brink of insanity.

"Get on the bed, knees apart, face on the pillow."

His command sent shivers zipping down my spine. My clothes had already been discarded, so I did as he asked.

I looked at him over my shoulder and the sight of him strolling toward me—all six-feet-something and golden-tan perfection. His hand wrapped around his thick shaft, stroking while readying it for me, had my pussy throbbing with need.

I pulled my bottom lip into my mouth, and he gave me a slow smile. "You want to see me jack off, baby?"

I nodded. "Yes, please."

He chuckled. "Such impeccable manners, Doc, but not this time."

He dipped to his knees, and I saw his face disappear in between my lifted ass. I felt his tongue on my pussy before I felt it drag over my crack. I rocked back against him when he did it again, before he rose to his feet.

Gliding the tip of his dick in between my folds, he covered himself with my juices before he drove into me without further preamble.

He slapped my ass, and I bit down on my lip. And when he did it again, I groaned a sound I'd never heard from myself. After making sure he was buried inside to the hilt, he pulled halfway out before he slid back in. He repeated the gesture over and over, pounding me relentlessly until I was seconds from stars exploding behind my eyelids.

But as usual, he knew. He knew I was close and wouldn't let me find my release that quickly. The man was all about delayed gratification.

He leaned down and grabbed me around my waist, drawing me up so my back met his chest. Panting, I let my head lay back on his shoulder as he continued to fuck me like he was on a mission. Like it was his job, and he had to do it with all the seriousness in the world.

My chest heaved, and I could feel his heart blitzing against my back when he bit down on my neck. His fingers trailed up my stomach before he rolled my nipple between them, making me hiss. And when I started to beg and plead, he slid his fingers down to my clit, teasing it, all the while his cock continued to pummel me like a machine.

And as soon as he could feel the pulsing of my walls around him, he pushed me back down to my hands and knees on the bed and fucked me through my release.

My muffled cries inside the pillow spurred on his orgasm before we were nothing but a heaving, panting, sweaty heap against each other.

Our breaths intermingled as we lay there, staring at each other like we'd both experienced a life-altering event, before he tenderly lifted my wrist and kissed the blue ribbon tattooed there. It was then that I realized it wasn't the sex that made me feel like I was floating in space; it was that little gesture that sealed his fate.

"Oh my God." Jeena's voice has me tumbling out of my recent memories, and I realize my eyes have been fastened to the defenseman on the other side this entire time.

I turn to Jeena, breaking my gaze from Rowan, noticing her eyeing me. "What?"

"You like him!" She exchanges an excited look with Piper. "Holy shit, you really like him!"

I bring a glass of ice water to my lips, hoping the cool liquid tempers the warmth I suddenly feel. "He's alright. Don't make it weird."

"You do!" she presses. "I can see it in your entire demeanor. Even in this lighting, I can see your post-orgasmic glow."

"This is the worst form of torture," Piper groans, squeezing her eyes shut.

"Talk to me," Jeena says, ignoring her. They've become rapidly familiar with each other over the past hour and a half, and the likeness of their boisterous personalities has me wondering if I did the right thing by introducing them. I can already tell they're going to use their combined effort to be a pain in my ass. "Have *we* had at least three orgasms yet?"

Piper puts her beer down, placing her hands over her ears dramatically while singing, "La la la la."

I give Jeena an exasperated look, though I can't hold back the smile that's determined to escape. "Fine, yes, *we* have. Are you happy?"

Jeena squeals, bouncing on her toes, and I wonder how much of this energy is coming from all the sugar in her drink. "I knew it! Go ahead, feel free to dole out your adulation for my insight and wisdom." She places her hands on my shoulders and turns me to face her. There's a more serious look on her face this time. "All I need is a yes or no. Yes, if I was right or no, if I was wrong."

I swallow before flicking my gaze back to the man who's managed to seep under my skin and into my bones, despite all my efforts for the opposite. When did that even happen?

As much as I want to brainwash myself out of that admission, I can't. Somewhere between the first time we met to now, everything has changed.

And while I still don't know what our future holds, I can admit one thing: I have feelings for the gorgeous, cocky-ass defenseman smoldering at me like he's imagining all the ways he'll devour me later.

Turning to my best friend, I say the only answer that's true, "Yes."

CHAPTER 21

ROWAN

I pull up to the four-story Boston brownstone, viewing it for the first time in the light of day versus the last time I saw it, almost in the middle of the night.

Would it be wrong for me to say it actually looked more appealing at night?

I mean, it's big enough for multiple families, but it's clearly in desperate need of repairs, least of which are the criss-crossed boards over one of the front windows, hiding what I assume is the baseball-sized hole Kai had made last weekend.

There's a tree in the front, displaying the vibrant colors of the season, though many of its yellow and orange leaves lay like a colorful blanket on the ground.

I amble up the worn steps to the blue front door adorned with a Christmas wreath, a large rectangular box in my hand, noting the stack of pumpkins on the bottom and—*is that an Easter bunny?*—a statue holding a carrot at the entrance?

I hadn't planned to be here today, but when Shay told me her car wouldn't start and she would need to cancel Kai's skating session with me, I decided I'd just come by and pick them up.

She hemmed and hawed about it for a bit, *because of course she did*, counting off every worry, from if I was a good driver, given I drive a sports car, to if somehow Kai would start suspecting there was more going on between us. The woman was a serial overthinker.

But after I gave her what I thought were good rebuttals to each of her concerns, she was more amenable to me coming over.

I've just barely lifted my hand to knock on the door when it suddenly flies open, and two very serious-looking replicas of a little blonde girl peer back at me, as if they're viewing me through X-ray vision.

Clone A whispers to Clone B with a hand over her mouth, "That box doesn't look like the portable external hard drive we ordered."

Let me point out that Clone A doesn't know how to whisper.

"No. And he looks . . . *primitive*."

"Like a science experiment gone wrong."

What the hell? I reel back before dropping my head to examine myself. *Primitive?! A science experiment gone wrong?* That's not what the "Hottest Men of Boston" list I was featured in would say. Man, these girls are mean! They've gotta be the Destructive Demons Shay talks about.

Before I can defend myself—or string any two words together—they slam the door in my face.

I look up and then behind me, wondering if there's a hidden camera somewhere and if the past two minutes have been a practical joke. I lift my arm to knock on the door again when it once again swings open. *Is this place haunted?*

But this time it's Beckett Langfield on the other side.

"What have we talked about with slamming doors in peoples' faces?" he says over his shoulder to the Destructive Demons, I'm assuming. "Or not opening the front door, period?"

He grumbles something like, "Worse than The Shining twins," under his breath before looking at me. He's holding an adorable, chubby-cheeked little girl in his arms, who puts her head into the crook of his neck, looking like she's trying to find an escape through it. Her eyes peek through, watching me cautiously. "Slick! Sorry about," he throws a thumb over his shoulder, indicating the twins, "those two. Shay told me you were coming by to pick her and Kai up. She's finishing up with a patient downstairs, so why don't you come on in?"

I follow him inside and immediately wonder if I've accidentally walked into a rundown set for the *Addams Family*.

"Wow," I say, turning my head from right to left, trying to keep my face from giving away my thoughts.

Beckett must notice, anyway. "Yeah, it's a bit of a fixer-upper."

A fixer-upper? To say this house is a fixer-upper is akin to calling a car that's been propelled into a tornado and catapulted to the ground with full-force 'malfunctioning'. You'd have to blatantly ignore the gaping hole in the ceiling, the interesting paint job, and parts of the flooring that are either mismatched or missing entirely to call this place a *fixer-upper*.

I have to wonder if living in a tree house would be safer. And the fact that both Shay and Kai live here makes me uneasy.

I don't have a chance to comment because, as soon as we turn into the family room, Kai comes running toward me. "Rowan! You're here!"

Bending down to put the box I brought with me on the ground, I pound his fist. "Hey, Kai! Dude, did you grow a few inches in the last week?"

He shakes his head, giggling. "No. I think it's because you're bent down."

"That must be it."

"Mom and I watched all your games on TV this week. You were amazing in that last period against Chicago!"

"Thanks, bud," I respond, feeling like a million bucks. "So, your mom watched the games, too, huh?"

I catch Beckett's smirk behind Kai before he pretends to hide it, ambling over to switch on a humidifier in the corner of the room.

Even though both Shay and I have been good about keeping things on the down-low with the rest of the world, I haven't been able to hide much from Brooks. To be honest, it's been nice to have someone, aside from Shay, I can acknowledge our *relationship* with. But, though Brooks knows we want to keep things private, I can't exactly tell him not to tell his brothers. I can only hope he doesn't. But by the sheer fact that our team owner and Brooks' brother, Gavin, hasn't approached me or my agent about Shay being anything more than my PT, I can only assume he and the other Langfield brothers don't know.

"Yeah. She doesn't know the rules as well as I do, but she's getting the hang of it," he boasts.

"Well, I'm glad you're there to teach her."

With the number of games this past week—two of which were overnight trips to other cities—I've only been able to see my girl twice, for just a few hours. The other few nights, we talked on FaceTime, and I was sure to get my daily kiss, even if it was on the phone.

She came over both evenings I was home, walking me through more of my PT exercises and assessing my thigh with extreme professionalism. She insists on doing that, regardless of the fact that we've slept together multiple times, saying we need to keep our professional and personal relationship separate as much as possible.

But once those exercises were done, I was able to entice her into other, *more pleasurable,* exercises. The kind that involved my bed, my sofa, the shower, and the kitchen counter.

But it hasn't been enough. No amount of time spent with her ever seems to be, and I'm already dying to hold her, touch her, and taste her again.

Luckily, we were able to get a decent number of hours together while we were in California, with me being able to sneak away into her room for the night, but it's been hard to get that kind of time ever since, and I'm dying to be with her again.

I hand the box to Kai and his mouth hangs open even before he's seen what's inside.

"Thanks, Rowan!"

A laugh rumbles in my chest. "You haven't even opened it. What if it's just a cardboard box?"

"He'd probably still thank you," Beckett says, laying a kiss on the little girl's forehead in his arms. "Out of all the little monsters we have running around here, he has the best manners."

Kai opens the box with minimal help from me, taking out the new hockey stick I bought him. "No way!" His eyes practically pop out of their sockets. "My own hockey stick?!"

"I wrapped it with black tape, too. And look here." I turn the stick in his hands so he can read the back of it.

"You got it engraved with my name?" He peers up at me, his eyes misty.

A lump forms in my throat. "It's nothing, little man. But remember, you can't use it unless your mom is okay with it, and only when you're better at skating."

Kai wraps his arms around my neck. "Thank you, Rowan."

I clear my throat. "So, are you going to show me the raccoons you've been telling me all about?"

I follow Kai toward the fireplace, kneeling with him in front of the meshed wire fence.

"That's their mom, Junior." He indicates with a pointed index finger. "And that there, with the brownish patch on his back is Shadow, there's Newton, and that one in the back is Slick."

The mother raccoon eyes me wearily, while her kits chirp, nestling under her and ducking away for safety.

I'm just about to ask what the plan is for these raccoons when Beckett's voice resounds behind us. "What the duck is that smell?"

I turn to watch a woman with fiery red hair walk into the room alongside Cortney Miller.

Rising to my feet, I introduce myself to both of them and learn that the woman's name is Dylan—as in one of Shay's best friends, who is now pregnant with Cortney Miller's baby.

"Yeah, what the heck is that smell?" Dylan repeats Beckett's question, sniffing the air.

Our faces contort in various ways as the stench of ammonia and something familiarly unpleasant hits our senses. If someone was to watch a silent footage of us with our heads in the air and grimaces over our faces, they'd think we were enacting hyenas in the grasslands, sniffing for prey.

"What in the world are you guys doing?" This from a red-headed teenager, shuffling in lazily while looking at us like we've all lost our marbles. We probably have. His eyes widen a bit in recognition when his gaze settles on me, and I notice the striking resemblance between him and Dylan. I have to assume he must be Liam, the kid Kai told me he felt close to.

The stench gets worse as Beckett and Cortney start to search for the source.

A clicking of heels that stops abruptly at the entrance of the family room has us looking over to where a tall, well-dressed blonde glowers at us, her expression mimicked by the two clones on either side of her. "What in the–" she gasps. "Oh dear God, what the hell is that smell?!"

"Mommy, you owe us a thousand dollars," says one of the spawns, pinching her nose.

I'm just starting to wonder who else will follow their nose and join us to the epicenter of this stink bomb explosion when a boy with a buzzed haircut and an orange-and-black tutu–showing his early Halloween spirit–dashes into the room, holding a Nerf gun aimed toward me, like some sort of avenging angel.

A dark-haired woman I recognize as Liv, Beckett's wife, and another girl of about eight or nine, rush in behind him and also come to a stop. Liv glances at me before looking at her husband. "What is going– Jesus Christ, *what is that smell?*"

"It's coming from the humidifier," Cortney says, visibly wincing as he turns it off. "It smells like . . . like–"

"He did it!" The boy in the tutu points at me like he's ready to put me on a stake after an unjust witch trial. He shoots a few Nerf balls in my direction. They bounce off my chest and thighs, but I'm too stunned to even understand what the fuck is happening right now. Oh, and it still smells like ass in this room. "He did it! I sawed him!"

The raccoons inside the chimney scurry and chirp as if concurring with his accusation, and I lift my hands. I don't know what the hell this kid is accusing me of, but holy crap, this is madness!

"Hey! Sorry I ran late, but Kai and I are ready to go. I wasn't expecting the appointment to take so long, but–" Shay is the last one to join everyone in the family room, wearing a cropped white shirt and yoga pants, looking like my wet dream. Her concerned gaze finds me before she enters the room, and if we weren't under cover—*or in the middle of the strangest meet-and-greet I've ever experienced*—I'd kiss those lips of hers until she told me to stop. "What's happening here?"

The blonde bends down in front of boy G.I. Joe. "Finn, what did he do?" She aims a perfectly arched, accusatory brow in my direction. "What did you see him do?"

Finn looks at his toes and mumbles, "Peed."

A hurried snort-laugh leaves Liam and Dylan while the rest of us try to put together what Finn just said.

Liv puts a hand on her son's shoulder. "Finn, I'm pretty sure you know the rules about lying. Now, tell us the truth. What happened here?"

Finn's face twists with guilt. "I wanted to sees what it would be like."

"What are you talking about, Huck?" Beckett addresses Finn in what I'm gathering is the kid's nickname.

Finn's voice is barely audible. "Fine. I peed inside the humidifier."

There's a collective gasp in the room, along with all the little girls and some of the women saying their own versions of, "Ew!" while Dylan, Liam, and Kai crack up.

"You peed inside the humidifier?!" Liv looks positively horrified while Beckett pinches the bridge of his nose.

Shayla and the blonde exchange a look, their lips twitching, before they're laughing, too.

And, fuck it, so am I. If this isn't the craziest welcome I've ever gotten, then I don't know what is.

<h1 style="text-align:center">CHAPTER 22
ROWAN</h1>

She tucks her legs under her, her smile practically taking over her entire face. Her golden hoops twinkle from her ears. "Try it."

We're sitting on my living room couch after having done some strengthening exercises. I really don't need them anymore since my thigh seems to have healed considerably, but Shay insists it's important. Plus, I like having an excuse for her to come over.

A part of me doesn't know what the status of our situation would be if I no longer required the physical therapy sessions. And since both she and I know that time is coming to an end, I'm too afraid to ask.

I inspect the green slush in my hand, both with my eyes and my nose, taking a tentative whiff. I'm no newbie to smoothies and protein shakes, but this? I'm feeling about as green as this looks. "What's in it?"

Her shoulders slump as if I've already said no. "Will you just taste it? I got groceries and stocked up your fridge and pantry with all sorts of healthy ingredients, so you can make these smoothies yourself when I'm not around."

Oh goodie!

When I continue to examine what can be described as green goop, Shayla huffs, "Fine. There's kale, blueberries, banana, matcha, kiwi, and almond milk. Oh, and I also added walnuts and peanut butter for protein."

Hmm. Those don't sound terrible, though, this smoothie is the ugliest looking thing I've ever seen. I hesitantly touch my tongue to the rim, making Shay roll her eyes.

"Will you just take a sip! Everyone at the house loves it!" She amends her statement at my squint, "Okay, so Cortney really loves it. And it's so good for you."

"Babe, just because things are good for you, doesn't mean they should be blended together and shoved down your throat. Most people like to enjoy their food."

Shay sighs as her only response, and I know I have to bite the bullet. In all honesty, I'm wondering if biting an *actual* bullet might be less painful.

Praying to Jesus internally, I take a bigger sip, rolling the mixture around my tongue like a wine sommelier. Except, this tastes nothing like wine . . .

"There's this," I wave my hand, all while trying not to gag. "This meaty flavor coming through that wasn't on your list."

"Oh right, I must have forgotten to mention it." *Uh huh. We know for damn sure she didn't forget.* "It's bone broth and lima beans–"

"Ah, yup." I nod, placing the glass on the coffee table and hoping the one sip I had doesn't have the rest of today's meals coming back up. "That'll do it."

Shay crosses her arms over her chest. "You didn't even give it a real try! Do you know how good lima beans are for you?

That smoothie has an entire serving of all the things you need daily."

I pull her onto my lap and she comes easily, despite her rigid stance. "I'll tell you what, you take the lima beans–or any beans, for that matter–and the," I shudder, "bone broth out of the next smoothie you make me, and I'll drink it."

That seems to placate her. "Fine, I'll just start making it without those things. I bet Kai will like it better that way, too."

Over the past couple of weeks, we've made it a habit of cooking together in my kitchen. While I'm happy to just cook for her or get a healthy takeout, she's insisted on learning and getting more comfortable in the kitchen.

Last week, we made fish curry and rice one day, and chicken parmesan the next time we hung out. We made lemon chicken a couple of days ago, and today Shay wanted to make her "famous" smoothies. Clearly, we have different definitions of the word famous, and I'll need to order from a *non-famous* menu later.

"Oh, and guess what?" She wiggles her ass on my lap, making my dick go from half-hard to rock solid in an instant. "I made the chicken parmesan you taught me for everyone at home last night."

My brows rise. "What did they think?"

"Delia and Dylan poked it with their forks for a few seconds, as if they thought it would come alive, but after they tried it, they couldn't believe I'd made it. Everyone loved it!" She lays kisses on my jaw before finding my mouth. "In fact, I thought I could thank you properly for teaching me."

I nod. "It's only fair that you do."

I rise to my feet with her wrapped around me, while she kisses down my neck, and take her to my bedroom.

I swing my arm around her waist before she can get out of bed and put her clothes back on. This is the part of our time spent together I hate the most—when she has to leave.

It's like I've become a lovesick puppy, whining and crying after his owner leaves to get on with her life.

I hover over her, thinking she's going to tell me she needs to get going. Instead, she trails her fingers over my bare back, lifting up to press her lips on mine.

"Did your dad text you after the past few games, too?" She brushes her nose along the stubble on my jaw, sending currents down my spine.

Why does every touch feel electric with her? Why does every moment, every conversation, every kiss feel unprecedented and exhilarating, like I'm either walking into oncoming traffic or falling off a skyscraper?

Is this all one-sided? Am I going to be left stuffing the empty cavity inside my chest with random bullshit once she walks away? With all the conditions she placed on us, isn't that what she's planning to do?

I glide my thumb over her nipple, making her arch her back and thrust her hips into me. "I don't want to talk about my dad when I'm five seconds from fucking you again."

"Rowan." She cups my face and I turn my face to place a kiss on one palm. "I think you should talk to him; tell him how much he's hurt you."

My lips quirk up at the corners. "Nah, I don't get hurt. I'm

Rowan Slick Parker, baby. I let his words glide off me like water."

She arches a brow, unimpressed with my macho act. "I see you through your facade, Rowan *Slick* Parker. You might have everyone convinced you're ironclad, but not me." She rests her hand on my chest. "I know that under this tough exterior is a guy with a huge, vulnerable heart. A guy who'd move mountains for those he cares about. But those huge, soft hearts are also vulnerable to pain. And whether you acknowledge it or not, you've been deeply hurt by your dad, your ex-best friend, and your ex.

"You may have moved on from the pain your ex and your old best friend caused you, but I'm pretty sure you're still carrying the heartache your dad caused you. So, do yourself a favor and find the closure you need. I think you and your dad both deserve it."

I gently run a knuckle over her cheek, thinking about her words. How is it that this woman has figured out more than I ever intended for her to when this was all just supposed to be about sex. *Well, for her, anyway.* "Okay, I will. Thank you for . . . for what you said."

She shrugs. "What are friends for?"

I swallow and she watches my Adam's apple bob. "Is that what we are? *Friends*?"

She grabs my ass. "Aren't we? Friends with benefits."

I try to keep my expression neutral, despite the fact that her response felt like a jab to my heart. Clearing my throat, I change the subject. "Beckett asked me to come over for a traditional Halloween barbecue in a few days."

Her hand loosens on my rear end. "A *traditional* Halloween barbecue? How can we have traditions when we haven't lived together long enough?"

"I don't know. I was talking to his brothers after practice, and Beckett was in the arena. He came over and asked me to come over. He said we'd be grilling and then taking the kids trick-or-treating."

Shayla squints. "He's up to something."

"What would he be up to?"

She gets a faraway look, twisting her lips to the side. "I'm not entirely sure yet, but if I know Beckett Langfield, he's never done anything without a reason. Well, he loves Liv and her children without reason, but apart from that . . ." She looks at the clock on my nightstand. "Shit, I need to get going. I want to make sure I get a chance to spend some time with Kai before he goes to bed."

She's just getting her clothes back on, and I'm ogling her backside in her spandex leggings, when my phone rings with a call from my agent. Huh. He's usually not one to call unless it's important.

"Hey, Bradley," I say, picking up the phone, my eyes still glued to the woman pulling up her jeans.

"Slick, we've got a problem."

My spine straightens and I shift to a sitting position on my bed. "What is it?"

"There are multiple pictures of you coming out of a restaurant in California with a woman you looked particularly friendly with."

My heart starts a gallop as Shayla's concerned gaze finds me. She mouths, *what's wrong?* "What do you mean *particularly friendly with*?"

Bradley makes an indiscernible sound on the phone. "In one of the pictures, you're holding her hand, and the two of you are looking at each other in anything but a platonic way. Like, it's clear she's not your sister—who is also in the picture, by the way. We're working to get them all down, but I wanted to make sure you knew." He pauses. "The good thing is only a fraction of the woman's face is visible since part of her is blocked by a passing vehicle, so it's unclear who it really is."

I swipe my tongue over my lips, my mouth suddenly feeling dry. "What else?"

"There are a couple of reports that speculate it's your physical therapist. One report even revealed her by name."

"Shit." I run my hand through my hair, feeling Shayla's weight press down on the mattress next to me. "Shit, shit! How quickly can the team get it down?"

"They're doing the best they can, and if need be, we're going to spin this as something related to your treatment, but Slick, I need to know the truth right now. Are you seeing your PT?"

My previously galloping heart is now in full sprint mode. I look at Shay's worried face. "Can I get back to you in a few minutes, Bradley? I'm not in the best . . . uh, location. You're cutting out. Let me call you when I get a better signal."

"Rowan—" Bradley says right as I hang up. Right now isn't the time to answer him, and I don't really know how to answer his question, anyway. What's important now is to update Shay, since this concerns her. She should have a say in how we proceed.

"What's going on?" she asks as soon as I click off my phone screen.

I wrap my hands over her biceps. "Someone took pictures of us holding hands and looking at each other a certain way in front of Zach's restaurant in California. The pictures don't show your face completely, but some sources are speculating it's my PT."

"What!" She jumps off the bed, the blood draining from her face.

I get up as well, disregarding the fact that I'm completely naked. Taking a step toward her, I pull her to me again. "My agent is handling it. The Langfield PR team is top-notch, so I don't think we have to worry–"

"Don't have to worry?" Shay rubs her face with her palms. "Shit! Rowan, this is exactly what I was worried about. This is *exactly* what I told you from the beginning. What do you mean, we don't have to *worry*?"

I cup her face in my hands. "I know, sweetheart. But you have to trust me. I will work all day and night if I have to, to make sure the pictures are taken down and any speculation that it was you gets removed from online."

She breaks away from my grasp and paces the room. "This could cost me my career, Rowan." Her lips tremble. "This could ruin my reputation as a reliable or trustworthy PT."

I cover the distance between us, holding her by her hips. "Shay, look at me." I wait for her to look up, and when she does, I continue, "This is all just specula–"

"Don't you see? It may be speculation *right now*, but what about next time? What happens when they see me enter or leave your apartment from now on? Will they suspect we have more than just a professional relationship? Gossip travels like wildfire on the internet. How do I know I won't have people following me the next time we meet?"

I stare at her silently. She's freaking out, and I don't blame her. It's exactly what she was worried about, and now it's happening. So, I want to hear her out. I need her to know I'm right here, listening.

"God, this is such a mess." She puts a hand on her forehead. "I knew this would be a bad idea. I knew *we* were a bad idea. I should have listened to my gut and stayed away."

Ouch.

Her eyes widen as if she just realized she said those last sentences out loud. "I'm sorry, Rowan. I didn't mean that . . ."

She drops her face into her trembling hands. "I don't know what I'm saying or doing. I'm just scared–"

"I know, and it's okay." I tug her toward me, and she presses her face into the middle of my chest. We're both quiet for a few long moments, reeling in light of the situation.

My stomach feels tight, my arms heavy around her, as I think about the consequences of this going south, if the PR team can't get those reports down and clear her name. This could be catastrophic for her, as she rightly said.

Fuck! What was I thinking, holding her hand outdoors? Why wasn't I more careful? This is all my fucking fault. I have to accept accountability for all of it, just as I have to accept that she holds the fate of our relationship in her hands.

I lift her face so I'm looking down at her again, my heart thumping against my chest. I weigh the words I'm about to ask on my tongue, wondering how a perfectly great evening turned into this. "Do you want to stay away from me now?"

She hesitates, blinking the mist from her eyes. My heart drops when her hands wrap around my wrists. "I need to think about everything." *About us.* Those are the words she leaves out. "This is just . . ." She takes in a trembling breath, breaking away from me. My arms feel weightless without her. "I just need time, Rowan."

I nod, watching her hang her purse over her shoulder. "My agent wanted to know if the nature of our relationship was anything but professional." My words feel heavy on my tongue. "Is that what you want me to tell him? That we're nothing but professional? He needs the truth."

Her hands hang by her sides, but she closes her eyes as if trying to process it all. "I . . . I don't know, Rowan." She presses her lips together, shaking her head, and I don't miss the heave of her chest. "Yes? No?" She shrugs. "I don't know right now."

It's like a fucking thousand-ton block dropped into my

stomach. *She doesn't know . . .* She doesn't know where we stand.

I watch her leave my room, my heart a fucking pretzel inside my chest, before I grab a fistful of my hair. My mind buzzes, warring between letting her leave and pulling her back and talking this out.

And though I know I can't force her to talk to me right this second, I do need to tell her something that changes the terms and conditions of how we started. It isn't the time or the way I intended to tell her, but it's now or later, and later doesn't seem like it bodes well for me.

Getting my boxer-briefs on, I rush after her, opening my front door and finding her right as she's getting into the elevator. Lifting my arms to keep the doors open, I hold her surprised gaze.

"I know you have to think, and I respect that. But I need you to think about one more thing, sweetheart." I swallow, hoping to tamper the drumming inside my chest. "This was never a *friends with benefits* situation for me; it's always been more. So, when you take your time to think, just know there's one more decision you'll have to make—whether you want to go the distance with this because I'm ready to conquer every fucking mile and obstacle, if it means I get to do it with you."

CHAPTER 23
SHAY

My friends exchange looks as I heave myself out to the back patio. I'm never late to our morning stretches, given I'm the one who insists on everyone being here bright and early so we can kick-start the day, but today has been the opposite. The day has already kicked my ass, and it's not even seven AM.

"Did you not sleep again? Was it that leaky pipe over your bed again?" Liv asks, probably seeing the runs of my mascara under my eyes and over my cheeks.

I didn't even have the energy to take off my makeup last night. The only thing I managed to do was to keep myself together in front of Kai for the few minutes I cuddled him, but as soon as he went to bed, I ran into my room and cried myself to sleep.

I roll my yoga mat on the ground, letting the cold breeze prick my skin. After the night I've had, it feels like a reprieve. My chest still hurts from the memories of a wonderful night with Rowan that went sideways.

One moment I was nestled against him, wondering about

the next time I'd see him, and the next, I was walking into his elevator with barely held back sobs.

I don't blame him for any of it. None of this was any more his fault than mine. I went to the restaurant with him, knowing the risks, and I enjoyed every moment of it. And while I have no regrets about going and meeting his sister, I just wish I was more prepared for the consequences of being captured on camera.

I wish they didn't matter; that I could just be with him without having to worry about who photographed us together. I wish I could go to his games, don his jersey, and cheer for him, regardless of who was watching.

But how can I do that and still manage a reputable business?

Even if we were to terminate our professional relationship today, what would happen if the gossip channels discredited me based on our past, as doctor and patient? Could I handle the blowback from that?

"Yeah, I don't even think our daily gratitude chants to the universe are going to help today," Dylan adds with a frown. "Your usual pink and purple aura is more like a drab gray. Do we need another bonfire night to release all our troubles into?"

I sigh, lowering myself onto the mat, keeping my legs stretched out in front of me, knowing the others will follow my lead. "I left Rowan's place last night with our relationship in a strange place."

Liv and Dylan gasp. "Why?!"

"I knew her mood had to do with him," Delia claims tightly, flames rising in her irises. "What did he do? Tell me if I need to go over there and chop his balls off. You know I will."

"No, it's nothing he did—" I start.

"I will take those ice skates of his and shove them up his ass!"

"Delia—" Liv tries.

"Does the fucker think he can just get away with whatever he wants because he's rich and famous?" Delia jabs a finger into the air. "Well, I've got news for him!"

"Delia—" I attempt again.

"I don't care what he did; I will bring the wrath of a mountain of lawsuits down upon him! I will—"

"Mom? Our computer is smoking, and we think it might catch on fire."

Delia's head snaps toward the house at the sound of one of her daughters, and she jumps to her feet, rushing in to check it out.

Liv, Dylan, and I all watch her leave before Dylan's face morphs into a smile as big as the Cheshire Cat's. The lightbulbs flick on in mine and Liv's heads, and our mouths drop to the ground.

We all start giggling guiltily, knowing Dylan threw her voice to sound like Phoebe or Collette, effectively snapping Delia out of her man-hating tirade.

"You know, I've gotten pretty good at figuring out when you're doing that, but I feel like you keep getting better," Liv says to Dylan, wiping the moisture from under her eyes. "God, I'd love to see her face when she realizes it was you."

I laugh, already feeling lighter than I have all night. "I don't know if I want to be here by the time she gets back."

"Now," Dylan says, bending at the waist and reaching for her toes, the same as me. "What happened last night?"

I groan. "Someone took a picture of Rowan and me holding hands and looking at each other in a flirty way when we were in California and put it online. I saw the picture on my way home last night, and unless you knew who I was, it's hard to tell it's me since I'm mostly behind this moving van, but there were some rumors calling me out by name."

My friends mutter curses under their breaths, knowing how important this stipulation was for me–that my reputation as a physical therapist was never compromised.

Liv straightens up, putting her hands on her thighs. A couple of strands of her hair have come loose from her messy bun and fly in the breeze. "You know the Langfield PR team will be on this. Dealing with situations like this is literally what they do."

"Yeah, but I'm not going to lie, I'm freaking out. I mean, what if there are more pictures than the ones they've caught online, or what if they pop up again? What if Kai finds out because he's watching some sports channel, and they bring this up? This isn't the way I would ever want him finding out, you know?"

"Are you planning on telling him about you and Rowan?" Dylan asks.

"Eventually, yes, but as it stands now, I don't even know where this leaves me and Rowan." My chest tightens as I replay my words to him last night, knowing I hurt him. "I sort of just left his apartment in a state. I told him I didn't know where we stood or how I wanted to proceed." I wince, remembering our conversation. "I even told him at one point that we were just friends with benefits."

Dylan and Liv make separate, but equally uneasy, noises.

"Yeah, that must have hurt." Liv states what I already know; what I've beat myself up over practically all night.

The look on his face–defeat mixed with a hope that I would choose the correct answer–when he told me he was ready to go all-in with us. He didn't have to say it; I know he was hoping I would feel the same way.

I left with a roller coaster of emotion inside my stomach.

He wanted more.

A commitment. A promise for something real and long-term.

Something I hadn't given to anyone since Ajay.

My second chance at love . . .

And while my heart gave me a shove to follow its lead and jump into his arms, even in that moment, while leaving behind my doubts to the wind, my brain kept me on a short leash.

What if you and Kai get attached and he breaks your hearts?

What if something happens to him and you have to face loss again?

What if it doesn't work out for the sheer fact that you can be a loonie-bin sometimes and not everyone can handle you?

"Is that how you really feel?" Dylan asks, following my lead as I straddle my legs out into a wide V and bend forward in the middle. "Like you're still just friends with benefits?"

I shake my head vehemently. "No. I haven't for a while."

"Then he deserves to know that, Shay." Liv removes a dry autumn leaf that blew onto her mat. "As for this whole PR thing, I know it's stressful, but it'll get sorted out soon, if it hasn't already."

I nod, mulling everything over in my head, and hoping she's right. I bend to my right with my arm over my head, feeling the stretch along my side. "Did you know Beckett invited Rowan to our *traditional* Halloween barbecue in a couple of days? When did we start having traditions? And, of course, he told Kai that his favorite hockey player was taking him trick-or-treating. Kai was so ecstatic, he couldn't breathe properly when he told me earlier."

Even if I was thinking about messaging Rowan to hold off on coming to Halloween, I couldn't, knowing it would break Kai's heart.

I look at Liv, who seems to be overly interested in our dead grass. "Liv, do you know anything about it?"

She places a hand on her chest. "Who? Me?"

"No, Beckett Langfield's *other* wife," I sass back. "Of course, you!"

She rubs her nose. "Nope. I have no idea."

Dylan and I exchange a look before she says what I'm thinking, "Yup, the nose rubbing was a dead giveaway. She's lying."

I'm just about to start another round of interrogation on my secret-keeping friend when Delia stomps over, waving her finger at all of us. "You bitches!"

My phone buzzes inside my pocket, and I turn my wrist to scan the message that came through my watch. I make it a habit to not check my phone when I'm working, but I've been waiting for an update all morning.

ROWAN

> Hey. All incriminating pictures and reports have been removed, so I think we're in the clear. I had to tell my agent the truth about us, but the team has made a firm public statement holding the line on our strictly professional relationship.

I exhale out a relieved breath before sending him an automated, Thanks ! back since I can't type out much more. Once I get a moment, I'll send him another message, wishing him good luck on the game he'll play against New Jersey tonight.

I'm just about to walk over to where my patient is folding himself down to the gym mat lying in the corner of my room when another message lights up my watch.

ROWAN

I know I said I'd give you time, and that's exactly what I'll do for as long as you need, but I reserve the right to tell you I miss you every single day until you tell me to stop. Because I do. I fucking miss you. It's only been one night, but I miss you.

My throat tightens as I keep my tears at bay. I'm just about to type back a message when Mr. Howard's loud bark has my head snapping back up.

"You know, I see you tapping on that fancy spyware around your wrist, chickadee! I might be old, but my eyes work just fine!"

I take a breath, keeping my professional face intact. "I apologize, Mr. Howard. How can I help you today?"

The man makes more trips to my office than he does to the grocery store.

"Well, that's why I made the appointment—for you to help me. Not like I like hanging out here for no reason! I need you to help me do the splits. I tried 'em myself yesterday, and it started hurting when I went any further than half-way."

I control the urge to suck in my breath and close my eyes as Mr. Howard proceeds to show me said splits by spreading his legs.

I want to ask if, perhaps, he's thinking about getting a job on a local cheerleading team or the circus, but I hold back the urge.

"Doing the splits can be a pretty intense flexibility challenge for your body, especially your hips and hamstrings. And it can take time to get there. Why are you suddenly interested in doing splits when it hasn't been something you've done in the past?"

"Well, that's none of your concern, now is it, chickadee? Maybe I have a lady friend I'm trying to impress, or maybe it's for my own satisfaction. Your job is simply to help me."

Dear God, give me strength.

For the next ten minutes until my next appointment, I help assess Mr. Howard's flexibility, during which he passes gas no less than four times–loudly, I should add–makes a rip along the middle seam of his pants, and yells at me for not showing him proper techniques at least twice.

I'm just taking a short, much-needed lunch break in my office while finishing up some paperwork when there's a knock on my door, and Beckett peeks his head in.

"You got a minute?"

I wave him inside. "What's up?"

"I heard about the pictures and reports that the PR team handled last night. I talked to Gavin, and it looks like everything has been taken down."

I nod, pricking the cucumber slices on my plate with my fork. If Beckett knows about the pictures, I'm sure he also knows about the admission Rowan made to his agent about us. "Yeah, Rowan messaged me to tell me earlier. I'm sorry your team had to deal with that kind of mess."

"It's what they're paid to do," he says, studying me for a moment before leaning back on his heels. "So, you and Rowan Parker, huh?"

I sigh. "Me and Rowan Parker. Although . . . it's a little up in the air right now. I'm glad the pictures were taken down this time, but what about the next?"

"Well, as I see it, physical therapy shouldn't be a long-term thing for him. I'm sure you guys can manage to stay under the radar until his therapy is complete, can't you?"

I nod, knowing that's true. It's not like we'll need to worry about it forever. Still, there's always a taboo factor even after our professional relationship ends, and that still has the potential to tarnish what I've worked so hard for.

"What are you thinking in that head of yours, Pipsqueak? What are you afraid of that you're not saying out loud?"

Damn him and his weird intuition.

I roll around a cherry tomato with my fork. "Heartbreak, I guess. How do I know he won't break mine and Kai's hearts? How do I know he's as serious about this as he says he is? He's only twenty-seven."

Beckett purses his lips. "Yeah, I can understand that, and I can even see where you're coming from. I will say one thing, and then I'll leave you to figure out how you want to proceed." He rubs his jaw with his fingers. "I've met many types of athletes over time—arrogant, bold, loud, proud, intense. You name it, I'll tell you a player who fits the bill. But I've yet to meet one as sincere and well-intentioned as Slick. If it makes any difference, you should know you've got one of the good guys. Duck that, you've got one of the best ones."

CHAPTER 24
ROWAN

The crowd cheers as fans rise from their seats, hammering the boards with their fists. The din from the stands barely overpowers the pounding inside my chest as I take my position.

We're on fire tonight.

Play after play of near perfect shots, and we're already in the third period.

Aiden Langfield wins the face-off before passing it to me. The puck taps my blade before I rip it over to Rudenko, who's already past the blue line. I follow him with quick strides into the offensive zone before he sends it coasting back to me, and I shoot.

The puck whirs across the ice, finding the gap on the side of the offensive team's goalie, hitting the back of the net. *Swoosh!*

"Hell, yeah, baby!" I hear one of my teammates holler behind me as the high-pitched blast from the horn intermingles with the fans howling and clapping. New Jersey looks visibly rattled while their coach paces the sidelines, red-faced.

I throw my hands up, high-fiving my teammates as I make

my way back to the bench, reveling in our coach's commendation. "Great job, boys. This is what I'm talking about!"

We're up seven to one. Their one being the power play they won when our right winger received a two-minute penalty earlier in the game.

We're all razor focused on what could be the last play, having again won the face-off. Tracey passes the puck to me and I see our center in position for my pass. In one quick movement–a mere flick of the wrist–I send the puck soaring to Aiden, who sinks it in between the goalie's legs, getting the fans back on their feet and roaring right along with the horn.

The Bolts win 8-1 as music blasts from the speakers above, and I entertain the audience some more by rolling out a few dance moves.

I skate over to the boys as we wrap each other in padded hugs and helmet tugs, shouting out our cheers and waving to the crowd.

Fuck, I wish Shay and Kai were here to see this.

We've won a few games and lost a few too, but every time I've looked up at the crowd, no matter where I am–home or away–I've imagined them wearing my jersey and getting up to cheer for me the way they did the last time they were at my game.

The echo of Shay's words as she walked away from me–*"I need to think about everything."*–has replayed a thousand times inside my head. And though it's only been one day, the wait is already killing me.

I never did receive a response to the message I sent her, telling her I missed her, though she did send me a good luck text for the game. I responded, asking her if she was okay with me coming for Halloween, and she said yes.

I wasn't going to go, with her wanting space. But then Beckett Langfield called me this morning, saying Kai wanted to speak to me. I gathered he was nowhere near his mom, because I doubt she would have been okay with it.

In any case, with Kai's excited voice on the line, telling me he was looking forward to trick-or-treating with me, I couldn't renege. I'm pretty sure there's little I could refuse the kid–or his mom, for that matter.

But damn if it doesn't kill me not knowing where her head's at with all this, because as much as I told her the decision of our future lies in her hands, she'd be crazy to think I'll just roll over and accept it if it's anything but the one I want her to make. She'd be crazy to think I'll let her go that easy.

I'm just getting off the ice when I glance back up at the seats and, for whatever reason, my eyes connect with a pair almost identical to mine.

My spine stiffens as the man I call my father lifts his chin as the best greeting he can provide. *What's he doing here?*

With my good mood shot, I head into the locker room where the guys celebrate with whoops and yells. Someone turns the speaker up on their phone, playing one of our post-win songs, *All I Do Is Win*, by DJ Khalid.

Aiden criss-crosses his knees together, wearing his pads, while a couple of the other guys dance to the beat, smiling from ear to ear. I take a moment to post a selfie–even if my smile doesn't quite reach my eyes–on Instagram for my fans.

Left it all on the ice tonight and it paid off! #ComingfortheStanley

By the time I've showered, I've almost forgotten the reason my mood had plummeted, and make the mistake of checking my phone.

DAD

Let's chat after you're finished. I'll be waiting
outside.

I shove my hands inside my sweats as I amble over to the
man standing in our private parking lot. I'm not sure how he
got in here, but I suppose he's recognizable enough that he
could say the right things to get past security.

The truth is, I was already planning to head over to his
place one of these days—he lives about an hour outside of
Boston—and get a few things off my chest. He just made things
easier.

The chilly breeze skitters over my neck and the side of my
face, and I lift my chin to a couple of my teammates as the last
few cars leave the lot. They're all meeting up at the local bar for
drinks to celebrate tonight's win and, depending on how this
family reunion of mine goes, I might meet up with them. More
than likely, I'll be needing a drink.

My jaw tightens. "What are you doing here?"

Dad raises his arms. He's about as tall and broad as I am,
though with the lack of exercises over the years, he's gained
some weight around his middle. "Can't a father come watch
his son play pro hockey?"

I blink, not a hint of the humor that usually presides over
my expression. "Cut the shit, Dad. You haven't come to watch
me play since high school. Remember that last time? When

you called me a *fucking disgrace* in front of everyone because we lost the last game."

"Jesus Christ." My dad runs a hand through his short gray hair. "Are we on that shit again? When the hell will you realize I was making you tough?" He points a finger at my chest. "That's always been your problem, you know that. You've always been too soft, too fucking emotional, just like your mom."

My hands ball into fists inside my pocket. "I'm going to stop you right there before you go too far. Unless you like the taste of asphalt, because in that case, please continue."

Acrimony and outrage war over his expression. "I came here, putting my own ego aside, to support the son who doesn't even have the decency to text his father back. I came here even though you've been nothing but an ungrateful little bitch."

"What should I be grateful about, Dad? Tell me," I yell back. "Your shitty, degrading texts? You're *unwavering* support of my career? Or, hmm, let's see, the years you weren't present in my life?"

My dad laughs mirthlessly. "I *gave* you your career, son, don't forget that. It's my blood that flows through you and my genes that give you all that talent on the ice. Despite the fact that you have yet to win a single Stanley Cup, I *made* your career. I'm the reason they even drafted you—*my* name, *my* skills, *my* drive, and *my* resources are what got you to where you are today."

I nod. "Got it, Dad. Anything else you want to say, or were you here to count off the generous gifts you've bestowed on me over the years?"

He snorts, that same sinister glint in his eyes. "I get it now. I get why Audrey left you, why she'd find someone like Evan.

Even with all the talent he has, at least he's not an arrogant and thankless prick."

I walk away. Even though my hands are fisted so hard, I might break my own bones, and my head buzzes with uncontrolled, untampered adrenaline I walk away.

I've just placed my hand on the handle of my car door when I turn back to look at my pitiful father. A man who just lost the only thing binding him to the blood and lineage he seems to be so proud of.

Had he shown even one ounce of remorse, had he given me any indication that he was here to mend the rift between us and not make it wider, I would have caved. I would have pulled him into a hug, and we could have figured out a way to move forward.

But he didn't.

He might call me emotional or soft, but those aren't barbs at all; they're medals I wear with honor. But even I have limits.

"Oh, what? You're just going to walk away now?" he spits. "I give you one good dose of reality, and you can't handle it, can you, son?"

Despite hating myself for being goaded to walk back toward him, I decide to end this once and for all. "You want a fucking dose of reality, Dad? *You* are the reason you have no one. *You,* and solely you. You're toxic, lost, and delusional. You call me ungrateful? Go look in the mirror, old man. You had it all–a supportive wife, kids who loved you, and fucking dignity–but you threw it all away, blaming everyone else for your demise. And now, what, you're trying to get back into my life to bury the hatchet? Yeah, well, fuck you very much, but I'm done."

I turn to walk back to my car as Dad yells after me, "Rowan! Come back here."

Chuckling mirthlessly, I turn to look at him before getting

into my car. "Bestow upon me one last favor, Dad. One I'm *actually* asking for," I bellow across the breeze. "Lose my fucking number."

I tilt the glass tumbler to my lips, staring at the golden liquid for a moment before taking a sip. The caramel and vanilla notes dance over my tongue, erasing the acrid taste that had collected there after the run-in with my dad.

Picking up my phone, I send a text to Piper.

ME

I suppose we're both fatherless now. I blocked him today.

I wish I could say I was sad or laden with guilt—it would be the normal emotion after telling your dad to essentially go fuck himself. But, strangely, all I feel is a sense of relief, as if I'd finally taken a step forward in some direction—*any direction*—instead of being stuck in the same place like I had been for so long.

It wasn't the outcome I'd hoped for from our meeting, but it was one that reaffirmed my belief that I needed to walk away from toxicity, whether it came in the form of a cheating ex-girlfriend, a disloyal ex-best friend, or a mentally abusive father.

My phone lights up with Piper's response.

PEPPER

Good. I was waiting for you to make some
room.

I look at her response in puzzlement. *Make some room?*

ME

??

PEPPER

Make room in your head, in your heart, and in
your life for the right people. You can't do that
when you've got the wrong people taking up
space, little bro.

Pondering her words, I tap out a text.

ME

When did you get so wise and philosophical?

PEPPER

Born this way.

I chuckle, lifting my head and scanning the room.

The bar thrums with energy as my teammates cheer and
high-five each other, throwing back shots and belting out cele-
bratory chants.

I watch in amusement from my seat at the bar as Brooks
asks Rudenko to teach him the sun salutation. Rudenko's
entire face lights up like the sun he's about to salute as he
wobbles out of his chair and proceeds to guide my very inebri-
ated friend through the various poses, garnering the interest of
others at the bar. Soon, it's not just those two, but several
others who add themselves into the mix and make their way
through ill-formed gestures.

I snort as I take another sip of my drink before looking

down at my phone on the bar. It feels like an anchor. Every time it lights up, I find myself hoping it's her. The woman I can't seem to take my mind off of.

There's a tug-of-war inside my mind, between letting myself be selfish and calling her to hear her voice and respecting her wishes for time and space.

But, fuck, this has been a hellish twenty-four hours.

"Dude!" Sanders, our left winger, slaps a hand on my shoulder, dragging me out of my misery. "What the fuck is up with you today? If I didn't know better, I'd think we had lost tonight with the way you're moping by yourself."

I tilt my glass, still filled with a quarter inch of whiskey. "Just have something on my mind."

He waves a hand around the bar, showing off the various lingering women, either hanging off my teammates' shoulders or making eyes in someone's direction, including mine. "The world is your oyster, my man. Take your pick and clear that mind of yours."

I take another sip from my glass. "See, that's the thing. I have no intention of clearing my mind of this one thing."

CHAPTER 25
SHAY

I secure the elbow pads around his arms before studying his Bolts' hockey uniform from top to bottom with mild satisfaction. "I think between the shoulder pads, shin guards, and helmet, you should be safe."

"I'm going trick-or-treating, Mom, not to war."

I roll my eyes at my nine-year-old who's been talking more and more like a teen, and I have to wonder how much of that has to do with one of his best friends, Liam, being one. "Well, you can never be too safe."

Kai places his hand on my shoulder when I try to fix his shin guard once more. "Mom, I'll be fine. I'm going with Rowan, Bossman, and Cortney. They'll be with all the kids the entire time."

I try not to let my smile waver when I see the name on the back of his jersey—Parker.

Kai swings his hockey stick at an imaginary puck, making a *whooshing* sound. He dashes across the room and hits the puck again. "Langfield passes to Parker, who speeds toward the goal. Chicago's center, Louis, tries to intercept, but Parker keeps the puck close. He shoots and, *oh my God*, he scores!" Kai jumps up and down with his arms up in the air. "Parker wins the Stanley Cup finals!"

His joy is unparalleled, as if he's actually at the final game and, despite the way things have been between me and Rowan, I smile brighter, overtaken by my son's enthusiasm.

He's always been a reserved kid–more so after Ajay's passing–but watching him come out of his shell and be light-hearted again is something I wouldn't exchange for the world. So many of his smiles–*and mine*–have been because of the man I can't seem to stop thinking about, no matter how much I try. Truthfully, I've stopped trying, because I enjoy his presence in my thoughts.

The doorbell rings and Kai grasps my fingers, pulling me behind him. "Rowan's here, Mom! Let's go! I gotta show him my costume!"

"Okay, but walk slowly so you don't fall!" I holler after him as he breaks away from me, rushing through the back door in my office and ignoring me.

He bounds out just as Rowan comes down the stairs to the back patio, and I watch raptly as Kai runs toward him with full force.

As if he was already expecting him, Rowan bends down and picks him up, swinging my son over his head before gently placing him back on the ground. He and Kai bump fists, and Kai turns around to show Rowan his costume.

Kai's jaw drops as his wide eyes fixate on something on the ground in front of Rowan. I lean forward to catch a better glimpse. Rowan extends his foot, and Kai points excitedly, getting Winnie's attention. They both grin at Rowan, and I finally get a peek at what they were looking at–the same velcro shoes I've been begging Kai to wear.

Kai wraps his arms around Rowan in a quick hug, and

though I'm only a silent observer from afar, my heart feels inexplicably connected to their moment, their bond. As if my heart feels too big, I press my fingers against my chest, trying to ease the emotion.

A moment later, Rowan shakes hands with Cortney and Beckett, while Kai rushes over to the picnic table with the other kids dressed in their costumes.

Earlier today, when Beckett announced he was going to grill burgers, he told me he'd bought organic turkey burgers for me and Kai, but when I saw the wistful look on my son's face when he saw the burgers everyone else would have, I told him he could have anything he wanted today; no rules.

"Even all the candy?" He was a kid after all, and they were born with doe-eyes to manipulate parents into accepting their outrageous ideas.

I'd sighed but refrained from saying what I did every Halloween, which was a firm no. Instead, I told him he could have any five candies he wanted today and five more throughout the week. And though I wanted to take back my promise, I knew I'd done the right thing when I received the biggest hug I'd gotten all week from him.

I scan the patio once more from the confines and privacy of my office before straightening my pointy witch hat.

All four of us—Dylan, Delia, Liv, and I—are dressed in similar witch costumes, with the same green makeup and witch's nose on our face. We'd decided to stay indoors and greet the trick-or-treaters for our first Halloween in the house, while the guys took the kids out after our so-called *traditional* Halloween barbecue.

Beckett and Cortney are grilling burgers and veggies in the corner, while a green-faced Dylan is mixing something inside a large cauldron.

Dylan spoons an orange liquid into cups and hands them to Liv and Delia, who are sitting on chairs on the lawn with blankets over their laps. She looks so freaking adorable each day she gets rounder around her tummy. Recently, she even felt the baby's first flutters and said she can just tell based on the movement that this baby is going to walk early.

I slowly make my way out the door, catching Rowan's gaze first.

His golden-green eyes roam over me, starting at my pointed black shoes and snagging at my cleavage visible under the low V-neck of my black gown, before settling on my eyes. I may or may not have chosen the lowest V-neck possible and wore a push-up bra, but no one can prove it, and regardless, I'll continue to deny it.

Rowan pulls his bottom lip in between his teeth before leaning back on his heels. His hands are tucked into the pockets of his jeans, and his deliciously tattooed forearms are on full display under rolled-up sleeves.

"Hi," I manage out awkwardly, hoping the green paint on my face doesn't smudge with the drool threatening to slip out the corner of my mouth as my eyes feast on him hungrily.

His smile turns impish, telling me he very much read my thoughts. "You might not know this, Doc," he murmurs so only I can hear, "but I have a hell of a witch fetish. Especially for witches with short hair, plump lips, and stars tattooed behind their ears."

My lips twitch. "A witch fetish, huh?"

"A fixation, rather."

"I'm sure there will be witches out tonight who meet those qualifications."

He holds my gaze. "There's only one for me."

A warmth crawls up my chest. "Rowan—"

"Alright guys, here are your costumes," Delia announces, taking something out of a box and cutting off my words.

"Costumes?" Cortney asks skeptically. "I thought we were

just taking the kids trick-or-treating. No one told me we were dressing up."

"Well, you are," Delia reiterates, making it clear there is no room for arguments. She flings a lime-green jumpsuit in his direction, along with a purple nightcap.

Cortney catches it, looking at it with the same distrust as one would a ticking bomb. "The fu—" he catches himself, seeing that the twins have both raised their heads from their spot at the picnic table and are looking in his direction hopefully. "I mean, what the *heck* is this?"

"And you." Cordelia turns toward Rowan, giving him the same once over she'd give someone who was just released from federal prison. She throws a brown shirt with yellow sleeves and a golden cap in his direction. "You can keep your jeans on, but change your shirt to this, hockey boy."

Rowan catches the shirt in his grasp before mumbling, "*Hockey boy?* She really doesn't like me, does she?"

My soft giggle gets swept off in the wind. "Nah, I'd say that was Delia being *friendly*."

"Ah," he says with a nod. "So, that's Delia. We never properly got introduced when I came over last time, what with the humidifier *aromatherapy* incident."

Dylan brings over cups of the orange liquid for both me and Rowan. "Welcome back, Rowan. It's good to see you!" She hands me a cup, extending her green-painted hand. "That's a 'poison' apple sangria. Obviously, I'm not drinking, but Liv and Delia said it was pretty good, so try it and tell me what you think."

I take a sip, letting the tart apple cider and cinnamon sit on my tongue for a moment. "It's delicious."

She nods with satisfaction. "You've got quite the pink glow around you today."

I tilt my head. "Even though my face is green, and I'm wearing a black witch's costume?"

She shrugs, her lips red from the cherry Jolly Rancher she's been sucking on. "The aura of love really can't be weakened by a Halloween costume, Shay, especially not on All Hallows Eve. You should know that by now."

That heat that was crawling up my neck earlier sits on my cheeks as I try my damndest not to meet Rowan's gaze. Except, I can feel him searing my skin.

I finally look up to meet his smoldering eyes. "I think you owe me a conversation, Doc."

Freaking Dylan! I'm going to have to have a little chat with her later.

I look down at the grass under my feet, feeling all sorts of discombobulated. "Can we talk after?"

Rowan is about to answer when Beckett's voice snags our attention.

He holds up the red shirt, brown pants, and cap that Delia handed him, as if they were taken out of the nearest garbage. "I'm not wearing this. What even is it?"

"It's what we all decided," Delia retorts before Beckett can get started. "You guys are going to dress as three of the seven dwarfs when you take the kids out. Cortney is Dopey, Rowan is Happy, and you're Grumpy. Frankly, I'd rather you, in particular, be either Stuffy, Jerky, or Dicky, but alas, those costumes weren't available."

Beckett tilts his head at Delia. "Oh, har har. Is that the best you could come up with, Medusa?"

Liv chimes in before the two can get started with their unending jabs again, "It's what we decided, Beckett. Now, please go and change."

Beckett gawks at his wife, betrayed. He's just about to retort with something when Adeline claps gleefully inside

Liam's arms, regarding Cortney in his costume. Beckett's face morphs, all the hard lines softening at her reaction to the baseball star with his lime-green jumpsuit and purple hat.

"Yay!" She giggles, clapping again.

Beckett's shoulders slump and, despite the fact that he mumbles his irritation under his breath, I know there is absolutely nothing he wouldn't do for Liv or her kids. He waves a hand at the grill before looking at Rowan. "Mind taking over for me while I change into whatever this monstrosity is?"

Rowan grins, strolling over to the grill. "Not at all."

Liam hands Adeline to me since Liv and Dylan went back inside for something. "I'm heading to a friend's house. My other friend Scott's picking me up."

I tamp down my unease and the intrusive statistics swimming inside my head of the number of accidents that happen on Halloween night as I take Adeline into my arms. I'm not his mom, but my best friends and I have always played the part of second moms to each of our kids. "Be–"

"I know, Aunt Shay. I'll be careful."

I turn as he walks past me. "Remember to keep your phone on. And don't talk too much while this friend of yours is driving. Don't need him to be distracted."

Liam rolls his eyes. "Anything else?"

I narrow my gaze at him. "Don't you snark at me. You know I'll find a bunch of anything elses if you get me started. Oh, and I know you snuck into my office again."

"What? No!" He purses his lips, his eyes shifty. He's a worse liar than he thinks.

I tilt my head, narrowing my eyes at him in response, and he chuckles, flipping his too-long red hair off his forehead before ambling off.

I yell after him, "Next time you sneak into my office, try not to leave your death-by-sugar-overdose drink cups in there as evidence!"

I exchange a grin with Rowan, wondering what he thinks of all of us. He already got a pretty unique welcome the first time he came over, but I wonder if this is all too much for him.

As soon as Beckett comes back out, dressed like the character Delia assigned him and sporting the same grumpy look, Adeline flails in my arms, reaching for her favorite person.

Beckett gently grabs her from me and places a sweet kiss on her cheek. "I got you, little one."

"So, you told Rowan this was a Halloween tradition?" I ask him.

"Yup." Beckett winks at me. "And I intend to keep this going every year with the exact same people." He eyes Rowan and Cortney talking at the grill. "Your hockey player included."

"How do you know he intends to join every year? How do you know I will, if he's here?"

Beckett grunts in bemusement. "Pip, you might think you're fooling everyone with all the walls you keep up, but . . . you're only fooling yourself. Plus, if I can pull the strings to make you his personal physical therapist, think of all the other strings I can pull to make sure you guys end up together."

I cross my arms around my chest. This guy and his Earth-sized ego.

Beckett laughs. "Why do you think I created this whole Halloween tradition and *specifically* invited the man you're gaga over?" He leans forward. "Did you know I even had IceMan call Slick to personally invite him? I knew there was no chance he'd say no after that."

My mouth falls agape like a koi fish. This conniving piece of–

"And who do you think removed a lead from the spark plug

in your car so it wouldn't start that day Rowan came to pick you and Kai up for skating lessons?"

I take a step back, as if physically pushed by his blatant scheming. "You did, what?!"

"Don't worry, I put it back." Beckett shrugs nonchalantly. "If it was up to you, your friends would have all become ancient before you let them meet him. No way was I going to wait that long."

I shake my head in astonishment. "It's rare for me to be speechless, but I'm not sure I have words to describe the level of your manipulation."

Before he walks away, he taps his temple. "You call it manipulation; I call it strategy, Pipsqueak."

I giggle, recalling the three ridiculous-looking giant men in dwarf costumes, with the grumpy one pushing Adeline's stroller behind all the kids.

In spite of how unamused the three men looked, they were such good sports about smiling for the cameras when my besties and I insisted on taking a million pictures.

They even patiently let me reiterate the crucial items off my health and well-being checklist before they left.

I can't believe it's the same house behind me with how quiet it feels now that all the kids are in bed. I'm surprised they were even able to settle in, given the sheer amount of sugar they consumed. But I promised myself I wouldn't think about that today, and I'm going to stick to it.

Look at me, changing my "ball of nevers" ways, one confectionary catastrophe at a time.

"Thank you for taking Kai trick-or-treating tonight. I know how much it means to him," I murmur, clean-faced and in my pajamas, sitting next to the man currently dressed as Happy on the same steps we shared my last cigarette on weeks ago.

A cigarette that not only symbolized all the past hurt and frustration I'd been bottling inside, but one that, with its end, represented the start of something new.

A new me.

And he was there with me on the precipice of it all.

He nudges my shoulder with his. "You're welcome. I had a lot of fun. That kid of yours is something else, Shay."

"Yeah?" I ask, studying his profile, his square jaw, and the corners of his soft lips. How did the man manage to look so gorgeous, even dressed in a ridiculous costume?

He turns, finding my gaze. "Yeah, and I really like your family."

Something raw lodges in my throat, making my eyes prick.

He recognized their importance in my life—my crazy found family—and I can't quite put into words what that means to me. After years of marriage together, not even Ajay understood the love I have for my best friends.

A tear escapes from my lid. "Yeah. I really like them, too."

"Hey." A deep furrow extends between Rowan's brows as he takes my face in his palms. "What's wrong?"

I shake my head, reveling in the slide of his thumb over my wet cheek. "Nothing, I just . . ." I lift my watery gaze. "You might just be perfect for me, Rowan Slick Parker, and I might just be falling in love with you."

He stills, seemingly holding his breath.

I'm just about to apologize or cry or do something that doesn't make me feel like I said those words in a vacuum when his deep voice keeps me glued to my spot. "Take the mights and justs out, and say it again."

"You're perfect for me, Rowan Slick Parker, and I'm falling in love with you." I give him a wobbly smile. "I was scared of everything that could go wrong. That you might break my and Kai's heart. That the next time you get hurt on the ice, it could be worse . . . much worse. I was scared of being left alone again. But now," my lips quiver as I take another shuddering breath, "now, the only thing I'm scared of is not being there to experience everything that could go right."

He pulls my face toward him, pressing his lips on mine.

His tongue grazes over my lips, sliding in between my seam as I open my mouth to give him access. Our tongues tangle as my hands curve around his head, pulling him closer, and he hums his satisfaction.

Tilting our faces, he takes more, causing my skin to heat and my heart to drum. We moan softly, tasting each other as if the two days apart were akin to a century.

They were. They so fucking were.

"Fuck, baby, I missed you. Your lips, your taste, your laugh," he breathes, his velvety voice ghosting over my skin before he breaks away from me all too quickly. His chest rises and falls right along with mine as he stares at me with unspoken questions in his eyes.

I drop my hands from his shirt, knowing he needs those questions answered.

I take a breath, letting the last of the October breeze envelop my lungs. "This isn't a friends with benefits situation for me, either, Rowan. I know it's what I said, but I think that was my last-ditch effort to keep you at arm's length." I grab his hand, bringing his knuckles to my lips. "You're so under my skin, you're lodged in my heart. I couldn't stay away from you, even if I tried."

He raises my chin with a finger. "Then don't."

"I won't."

A satisfied smile lifts his mouth before it drops again. "I'm sorry about the online pictures, sweetheart. I wish they weren't something we had to deal with, but you're right. Those types of pictures will be taken again, and next time, they might be more incriminating."

My hand goes slack against his as I try to comprehend what he means. "What are you saying, Rowan?"

He entangles our fingers together, keeping me from shifting away. "I'm saying I'm firing you, Doc." At my creased brows, he continues, "It's not a foolproof plan, but it's the best I could think of to protect your job and reputation while finding a way to be together." He waggles his brows. "In any case, my groin is almost completely better, thanks to you." He's clearly not referring to physical therapy.

I grin, processing his words. It's not a bad plan. I could still get shit on if someone really wanted to make it a big deal, but terminating our professional relationship might be the only plan we have. And . . . I'm okay with taking that risk.

Because I'd be getting so much more in return.

"There's one more thing," he says, pulling me into his lap to straddle him. His hands rest on my ass possessively.

I run my fingers through his disheveled hair. "What's that?"

"That I'm positively, irrevocably, and insanely falling in love with you, too."

CHAPTER 26

SHAY

1 MONTH LATER

ROWAN

I'll be home in ten minutes. I want you completely naked and in the shower when I get there.

T bite down on my bottom lip, smiling at the lewd images scrolling through my brain of what he plans to do when he gets back to his place.

ME

You do know, most people generally get in the shower naked.

I laugh, imagining him clenching his jaw.

ROWAN

I think that smart mouth of yours just secured you a pink ass. And don't you dare even think about touching yourself or using one of your million toys in there until I'm home.

I run to his bedroom and take out my favorite toy from his

nightstand. Yes, I am now the owner of not one, but *two* over-priced, golden hoo-ha stuffers.

Rowan, being the generous and thoughtful man he is, insisted I keep one here for when I visit and one at home. The one at home only gets used when he's away at games, but I still have to adhere to our original stipulation–using it in front of him, as in while we're on a video call. And let me just say, the man likes to watch me pleasure myself more than he likes to watch Sports Center, and that's saying something because he *loves* Sports Center.

I turn on his shower before I unbutton my silky, long-sleeved top and drop it to the floor, before wiggling out of my pants.

Over the past month, we've continued seeing each other whenever he's home, and though I wish I could spend the entire night with him while I'm here, I always go back home to spend the evening with Kai.

This past weekend, Rowan came over to the house to cele-brate Thanksgiving with us, and after seeing the way he and Kai interacted–completely enamored with each other–I decided it was time to tell my son about us. He deserved to know.

Unsurprisingly, he was thrilled. In fact, he pulled us both into a hug and told me–and I quote–that I was "the coolest mom ever now that I was dating the most incredible athlete to have ever existed."

Also unsurprisingly, my boyfriend's ego inflated tenfold with those words. I literally thought my eyes were going to get stuck at the back of my head with how he preened and pecked like a damn peacock.

But despite the fact that Kai seemed happy, I made sure to dig deeper that night when I snuggled him before he went to bed. I reminded him that Rowan would never replace his dad, and that for me, Kai's happiness would always come first.

And because my son had proven time and again to be wiser than I give him credit for, he hugged me tighter and said, "I know how much you love me, Mom."

The steam from the shower has me coming back to the present.

I'm just about to drop my panties when I decide to place my toy—aptly named Wayne, after one of the greatest hockey players of all time, and because it pisses Rowan off to no end— under the seam with my finger on the button.

I click a quick picture and send it with a response to his last message.

ME

I was just going to let Wayne warm me up a little before you got here.

Giggling to myself, I drop my underwear and strut over to where he keeps his luxury bath products. I swear, the man has more bath products than a spa. I place my nose over a pink-and-yellow shower bomb, inhaling its light perfume. Peonies and vanilla.

Dropping it into the shower, I go back and check my phone when it vibrates.

ROWAN

You trying to get me in a wreck, woman?
Because that's what almost happened. I
swear to God, Shay, I will crush fucking
Wayne or Jensen or whoever, if you let that
thing touch you without me there.

Another message comes through as I'm giggling.

ROWAN

And what the fuck is up with the food emojis?
Please tell me you're not thinking about one of
your weird ass smoothies right now.

I've just gotten into the shower, immersing myself in the cascade of warm water and filling my senses with the flowery scent lifting with the steam when the bathroom door opens, and Rowan's form fills up the doorway.

A shiver runs through me, despite the warm vapor I'm surrounded by, as his stormy eyes bore into me before dropping to the golden object in my hand.

He's pissed.

And God, how a pissed-off, turned-on Rowan Parker is God's gift to my needy vagina.

Looking nothing less than the embodiment of sex and masculinity in his impeccably tailored suit, he stalks closer while slowly taking off his watch and unbuttoning his cuffs. With each stride, his eyes stay fixed on me while my mouth waters.

Silky streams of water slide over my curves, tracing every contour of my body the way his heated expression promises to do with his tongue.

His voice punctures the rhythmic hum of the shower as he unbuckles his belt. "Drop to your knees, Shayla. And get rid of what's in your hand."

My pussy throbs with anticipation as my breath skitters on an exhale, but I do what he asks, looking at him through the spray gliding down my face.

After making a show of taking off his suit and underwear, Rowan steps into the shower, his massive, bare form vibrating with need. His equally massive cock, with its beautiful mushroom head, taps my wet lips.

Rowan strokes his shaft once, twice, and my mouth falls open, impatient and longing.

He chuckles. "So needy. So ready for my cock."

I press my thighs together to relieve some of the want between them as my hand reaches for my clit.

"Don't even think about it." Rowan's firm command has me dropping it back to my side. "That pussy is mine to touch, eat, and fuck." He places his cock on my lips. "Now open up and suck."

A thrum of electricity rushes through me as I open my mouth, letting him enter. My lips wrap around his velvety wet skin as my hands come to rest on his thighs. I bob my head forward, taking him deeper. Satisfaction rolls through me when Rowan drops his head back, giving up his control.

"*Fuuuck.*" he groans, curving his large palm around my head. "That feels so fucking good, baby. God, I love your mouth."

I widen my jaw the best I can to accommodate more of him, while I run my tongue along the underside of his shaft before pulling my head back and teasing his tip, just how he likes.

It's a heady feeling to be on my knees in front of this enormous man but having all the control while doing so.

Placing my hand at the bottom of his shaft, I continue bobbing over him, licking and sucking him from root to tip. Rowan mumbles his appreciation, groaning as I thrust him into the back of my throat.

But before he can finish, he pulls out with urgency and hauls me up into his arm. I'm not surprised, given the man is all about delayed gratification.

Picking me up so my legs are wrapped around his torso, he leans my back against the wet shower wall, lining us up at my entrance. In one go, he sinks into me, so deep I scream in ecstasy. My walls expand to adjust to his girth, throbbing as he hits my G-spot.

"Watch, baby," he rasps inside my ear. "Look at my cock filling your greedy pussy."

And though I can barely lift my head from the wall, I watch as he pummels into me, hard and fast, focused and serious, like he's on an important mission.

My fingernails dig into his shoulders as I hold on to him for the ride of my life, while his lips devour mine. He kisses me thoroughly, delving his tongue into my mouth, while my back arches off the wall.

He drives into me again and again, cursing under his breath, before he withdraws almost completely and plunders into me again.

The swells of euphoria pull me under, and my body bows once more under him, gripping his cock with a chokehold.

Rowan presses his lips to my neck. "That's it, baby. Let go and fucking come for me."

He continues to drive inside me as I descend back to earth before his orgasm pulls him under. But even as he spills inside me, he continues to tell me how much he loves me, how beautiful I am, and how he can't live without me.

Turns out, my second chance at love might be my sweetest.

"I want you and Kai to move in with me." His Adam's apple

bobs, and I get the sense he's nervous. "I want us to be three peas in a pod."

The idiom is too cute at this point for me to correct.

I study the hard lines of his face and the soft curves of his lips as I lay naked under the blankets on his bed, facing him. Over the past hour, we've done nothing but talk and cuddle.

Okay, so we may have done a few more things that resulted in our sheets being a crumpled mess, but that's neither here nor there.

I find everything about him fascinating–from the way he checks in on his mom and sister daily, to the way he manages a stressful career in the limelight, to his views on life, as if nothing is out of reach. He's the most genuine and level-headed person I've met, and sometimes I'm shocked that he's only twenty-seven.

"We can't." The light dwindles in his eyes, and I rush to clarify, "It's not that I don't want to, believe me. It's just that my best friends and I specifically decided to raise our kids together. That's why I moved here."

Rowan squints. "So, is this a forever thing? Like you guys will all live together forever?"

I lift up on the shoulder not tucked under me. "Yeah, it's why Beckett and Cortney moved in with us . . . because that was our pact. At the time, none of us expected to find love again." I bring our entangled hands closer, brushing my lips over his rough knuckles. "I never expected to find you."

His lips lift into a soft smile. "But you did. You found me in that locker room and ogled my ass like it was a piece of organic, pasture-raised meat."

I giggle. "Your world-class ass sealed the deal for me."

Rowan chuckles. "I don't know if I should be flattered or worried that *that's* what did it for you."

"Oh, definitely worried." I nod teasingly.

He and I both laugh again before the mood gets more serious, and I want to clarify a bit more. "Kai is a quiet kid, and it takes him time to come out of his shell. I'm proud of how far he's come with the other kids in the house. He's made incredible connections–specifically with Winnie and Liam–and I want to make sure they stay close, you know?"

Rowan whispers, "Yeah, I know."

"I don't want to uproot him again. As much as he loves your house, his family and friends are in that house, and he would miss them if he didn't get to see them every day. I'm afraid he'd become closed off and reserved again. I see how happy he is right now, and I don't want to risk that."

Just the thought of my little boy's smile dimming makes my chest feel tight.

Rowan cups my face, making sure he's got my attention. "I understand one hundred percent, baby."

I take in a relieved breath. "Would you . . . consider moving in with us?" It's a lot for me to ask, and I'll understand if he says no.

"Yes," he responds so fast, I'm left wondering if he even heard me. He chuckles, seeing the surprise on my face. "Yes, Shay, I will move in, if everyone else is okay with that. I want to be in both your and Kai's life. I want to spend every minute that I'm in town at *home* with you."

"What about this place, your apartment?"

"I'll sell it."

My jaw goes slack. "You'd sell it? Wouldn't you miss the view of Boston Harbor?"

I'm in shock that it took him less than two seconds to decide that, like there was nothing to it. And the fact that he made such a big decision so fast clues me in to how serious he is about us. That he's all the way in this–no escape hatch, no exit route.

"Baby, the only view I'd miss is of waking up next to you every morning. And that's non-negotiable."

God, this man . . . Do I even deserve him?

I kiss him with abandon. "I just might be in love with you, Rowan Parker."

His eyes heat. "Take the mights and justs out, and say it again."

I giggle at what's become our common exchange. "I'm so in love with you, Rowan Parker."

Minutes later, we're wrapped around each other, him kissing and nipping my neck, when I recall our plans for tomorrow. I need to get going so I can spend time with Kai. "So, are you still okay with taking Kai and Winnie skating tomorrow?"

Rowan chuckles softly. "I'm one hundred percent okay. The question is, are *you*? I know it's worrying you that I'll be taking them to a public outdoor ice rink, but Kai is so excited. He's become such a great skater over the past month."

I nod, biting the corner of my lip. "I know they'll both be safe with you. It's just, with the conference I have to attend tomorrow night, I won't be able to come with you guys and . . . I'm just a little nervous, is all."

"Do you want us to reschedule? I can take them another day."

I shake my head. This is something Kai and Winnie have been looking forward to all week, and it would really dishearten them if they rescheduled. Plus, Rowan will be on the road for the next ten days. It will be hard to find time again with his busy schedule.

The old me would have rejected even the idea of letting Kai skate in a public rink–let alone go skating, period!–but I'm making strides to control my anxiety and opting to stay positive, knowing he'll be in good hands.

"No, don't reschedule. I want this for them." I give him my most confident smile. "I can't wait to hear all about the fun you guys had afterward."

"It'll be like you were actually there," he says, assuaging my worries. "We won't leave out a single detail."

But of course, the first time I take my eyes off my son, the universe throws in a twist, challenging me to tackle all my fears at once.

CHAPTER 27
ROWAN

"I heard you'll be joining this wild brigade soon." Beckett Langfield indicates behind him with a wave of his arm as Kai and Winnie make their way out of the house.

I'm here to take them skating at the outdoor ice rink while Shay's at her all-day conference.

"Looks like it. I'll be moving in, in a couple of weeks." I look over my shoulder at the home with the for-sale sign a few doors down. "So, what's going on with real estate in this area? It's been skyrocketing the past few months."

While I'm still happy to move into this house with Shay and Kai for the time being, I don't know how viable that is forever. It would be nice to have our own place, too. But since I don't want to take her and Kai away from their best friends, I've been looking into buying a property in the neighborhood.

"For the love of God, not you, too." Beckett closes his eyes, taking a breath. "I'm assuming you're looking to buy in the area?"

I give a nonchalant shrug but don't say much more. I don't

want Beckett to say anything to Shay before I've had a chance to speak with her, since it's something I only started researching recently.

"How about you, me, and Cortney talk sometime soon?" he asks, sliding his hands into his pockets. "We've got some plans in the works, but our last chess piece is proving to be the most difficult one. And she comes in the form of a woman with venomous snakes in place of her hair." He rubs a hand over his jaw, muttering as if he's speaking to himself. "And since she tends to turn most men into stone, it's going to take someone really ducking patient. Someone almost as stubborn as her . . ."

I eye him suspiciously. Has he been smoking the ganja? Or maybe living in this place has just driven him mad? Because, really, what the fuck is he talking about?

He waves his hand at me. "Nothing for you to worry about, hockey star. Just know, we're on the same page."

He follows his statement by pointing two fingers at his eyes before turning them toward me, repeating the movement a few times.

Yeah, he's definitely high.

I squint. "What are you doing?"

"Telling you with a universal hand gesture that we're on the same page."

"That's not the universal hand gesture for being on the same page. That's the gesture for 'I see you.' The universal hand gesture for 'we're on the same page' is waving your pointer finger between two peoples' chests." I demonstrate the gesture.

"That's absurd. I've been using this gesture my whole life, and no one has ever had a problem with it."

"Your *whole life*? Really? When would you ever need to use that gesture?"

"I just did!" he barks.

I pinch the bridge of my nose. "Well, you've been using it wrong for your whole life."

"No, I haven't. No one waves between chests. That looks idiotic."

I can see we're going to clash, what with both of us being overconfident assholes and all.

I'm just about to argue again when Kai and Winnie whine, "Can we go now?"

I point my index finger between Beckett and me. "This isn't over."

He points two fingers at his eyes and then mine, doing his stupid, incorrect gesture. "We're on the same page about that."

"Alright, buddy, I want you to stay near the edges of the rink, in case you need to hold on to something, okay?"

We're standing outside of the fairly busy ice rink, surrounded by shops and trees glimmering with holiday lights, fully bundled up in warm winter gear, with our skates on. Both Kai and Winnie haven't stopped chatting about how excited they are to finally go skating together, with Kai telling her how good he's gotten over the past month.

It's true, he's taken to skating really well, but he's still a beginner, so while he has a good grip on the basics, he's less confident with the more complicated moves.

Kai puts his thumb up to me, his nose pink from the crisp breeze. "Got it."

Kai, Winnie, and I step onto the ice, with me holding Kai's hand. He releases it in lieu of the edge of the rink as soon as we enter, giving me a sheepish shrug. I get it. He's got a reputation to maintain in front of his friend and doesn't want to be known as the kid who has to hold an adult's hand while ice skating. Still, I make sure to keep an eye on the two of them as they skate ahead.

Winnie seems to have a good grasp on skating and Kai's not lagging too far behind. He only wobbled for a few seconds before he got his footing and started to glide around right next to her.

A few strangers pass by us, eyeing me curiously, likely wondering why I look familiar. I nod at them before following behind the kids, making a mental note to tell Shay how well Kai is doing.

It's a beautiful but chilly end of November day, and though it's technically a workday for most people, there's quite a lot of bustle amongst shoppers around the square.

Winnie makes a big circle on one foot, gliding with her hands lifted while Kai watches her, grinning. Puffs of steam rise in front of his face when he giggles.

"Bet you can't do this, Kai! Don't worry, you'll be able to one day when you get as good as me."

Kai's smile wavers slightly as he recovers from the hit to his ego. "Rowan says I'm already pretty good. He also said I was the fastest learner he's ever met. And he would know. He's the best hockey player in the nation. Probably the world. Maybe even the universe."

Geez, kid. Talk about raising me up to the sky.

Go on, though, I don't mind one bit.

They skate around for another ten minutes, giggling and talking, while I stay a few feet behind them, thinking about everything over the past couple of months.

Thankfully, there haven't been any more pictures posted online of me and Shay, but I'm sure the media frenzy will start when news gets out of us moving in together. But given she's no longer my physical therapist, we're ready to handle things as they come. We have nothing to hide.

I'm just thinking about the move as soon as I get back from being on the road–what life will be like living with so many other people–when, all of a sudden, a couple of oblivious teenagers skate toward Kai and Winnie. She moves out of the way, and I'm preparing to tell Kai to watch out when his face morphs into surprise, and he narrowly misses running into them.

But in that effort, he tumbles backward, trying to right his footing. I reach out for him, but I'm not close enough to catch him.

I hear him grunt and the unmistakable *thud* as his body crashes onto the unforgiving ice, his hands desperately trying to break his fall.

Fuck!

"Kai!" I holler, rushing to his side, my heart flapping like a hummingbird's wings inside my chest. "Are you okay?"

God, please tell me you're okay.

My stomach drops when I see the pooled tears in his eyes and the pronounced frown pulling down his lips. He holds his wrist with his other hand, trying to straighten up his face after seeing Winnie's concerned gaze on him.

Sniffling, he swallows. "I . . . I hurt my wrist."

I nod, though my throat feels like it's closing. I've seen tons of injuries on the ice. Hell, I've broken my nose, gotten plenty of cuts and bruises over the years, and have even broken my wrist. But the look on this kid's face, coupled with the way he's holding his wrist, makes me feel like I'm experiencing the pain myself.

Careful not to jostle his arm and wrist, I haul him up into my arms, laying a kiss on his temple before telling Winnie to follow close behind me. "I got you, buddy. Just hang tight for a minute."

Placing him on a bench outside the rink, I examine his wrist closely, asking him to move it this and that way to study his range of motion. It's swelling up fast, and based on the way he's wincing–not letting me even touch it–I need to take him to the hospital to get it checked out.

Given the way Kai is more wincing than crying and the minimal bruising, I don't think it's broken, but there's no way to know for sure until I take him to see a doctor.

My stomach drops, thinking about the phone call I'm going to have to make to Shay on my way.

Jesus. The *one fucking time* she trusted me to take care of her kid, and I messed it up! The *one fucking time* I was supposed to protect him, he ended up hurt.

What the hell was I thinking bringing the kids here, outside the safety of a private rink? What the hell was I think-ing, convinced I knew how to take care of kids? I'm not fucking fit for this; I'm not fit to raise a child with her if I can't even anticipate obvious accidents like these.

I don't have the time to think about the repercussions for our relationship when Shay finds out. Right now isn't the time to think about us, not when my priority is Kai.

But given how important Kai's safety has always been for Shay, could I blame her for faulting me for not taking care of him today?

Could I blame her for walking away from me, if that's what she chooses to do?

I pace around the small room, chewing on my thumbnail.

"It's a good thing you put ice on it so quickly," the emergency room nurse says, moving around to check Kai's vitals. I'd had the wherewithal to get a small bag of ice from a street vendor as we were leaving the rink. "The doctor will come see you in a minute and determine if you need X-rays."

Kai nods, but his eyes soften when he sees my face. I must look as scared as I feel.

He opens his mouth to say something when there's a knock on the door and Shay enters. Her eyes brush over me and Winnie before she rushes toward her son, her hands reaching for his face. "Oh, gosh, Kai-bear, are you okay?" Her lips quiver as she regards his wrist under the ice pack. "Is it just your wrist or are you hurt anywhere else, too?"

My breath skitters on each exhale with her questions.

I was supposed to keep him safe. I was supposed to show him he could have fun when he was with me. I was supposed to help relieve her fears of anything happening to him when she wasn't around.

And I failed every step.

There's another knock on the door before the doctor enters, taking us all in. Given how small the room is, and the fact that I'm having a hard time breathing, I clear my throat, speaking to Shay's back. "Winnie and I will just get out of your hair." I turn toward Winnie on one of the chairs. "Why don't we sit outside for a bit until they're done?"

She nods, and I note that Shay doesn't even look over her shoulder to acknowledge my words. It's almost as if I'm not there, but then again, I can't hold that against her. She's stressed and has more important things to deal with at the moment than my feelings.

Still, it doesn't change the sinking feeling that envelops me.

CHAPTER 28
SHAY

"Oh, gosh, Kai-bear, are you okay?" I rush to my little boy's side, my chest feeling tight as I regard the ice pack on his wrist. "Is it just your wrist or are you hurt anywhere else, too?"

When Rowan called me to tell me they were heading to the emergency room because Kai had gotten hurt, I swear, my heart felt like it came to a stop. I scrambled out of the conference room, asking him a million questions as I got to my car.

Let's not even mention how fast I drove here. It's a miracle I didn't get caught breaking traffic laws in the process.

And when I walked inside this room and saw the morose expression on Rowan's face, I actually wanted to go to him first and console him. But it was more important to check on Kai.

"It's just my wrist," he answers softly. "But, Mom, you don't even understand how much fun I had today."

I search his worried eyes. He's not concerned about his wrist. I know him well enough to know that's the last thing on his mind. It's his fear that I'll tell him this is the exact reason I don't let him do sports.

And the old me would have said that. The old me would have leapt for a chance to prove that staying home and taking part in only safe activities was the way to go.

And though the new me wants to fall back on her tried-and-true crutch, she knows that's not going to help her keep her promise to herself. To grow. To live. To stop being a "ball of nevers".

I rub a thumb over his cheek as we wait for the doctor to come in. I can't be sure, but I don't think it's broken. There may be a hairline fracture the doctor needs to assess through an X-ray, but it doesn't seem to be a more significant fracture.

"I'm glad you had fun, sweetheart."

I'm just about to turn to talk to Rowan when there's a knock on the door and a bit of commotion as the nurse asks Kai a few more questions. I know Rowan has said something–I believe asking Winnie to follow him out–but I was so distracted, I couldn't hear properly.

Once he and Winnie have left, Kai speaks to the doctor, telling him what happened again. And another forty minutes later, once X-rays have been taken and looked at, the doctor confirms my original suspicion, that Kai has sprained his wrist.

Nothing we can't manage, and nothing I don't have experience providing therapy for. Moreover, Kai doesn't look too uncomfortable, though it'll take a couple of weeks for him to heal.

Rowan straightens up on his chair in the waiting room, next to Winnie, as soon as Kai and I exit.

Winnie squeals, rushing over to us. "What did they say? Are you okay, Kai?"

My son shrugs, looking up at me with a sheepish grin, before answering her, "The doctor said he'd never seen someone as strong! He asked if I had mutant powers." He shows her his wrapped forearm nonchalantly, as if this type of thing happens to him all the time. "They took X-rays and said my bones were made of adamantium, like Wolverine." He rubs his nose, knowing he's telling a tall-tale. "Anyway, they said it's just a sprain. I'll be better in no time with how quickly I heal!"

"Wow!" Winnie responds, stepping closer to him to examine his wrist. "That's so cool, Kai."

I giggle under my breath. Only kids would think having a sprained wrist would be *cool*.

I'm just about to make my way over to Rowan–who looks relieved at hearing Kai's update–when Delia rushes in through the doors of the waiting room, heading toward Kai. Her sharp eyes assess him quickly. "Hey, buddy. Are you okay?"

Kai waves his arm at her. "I'm fine, Aunt Delia. Honestly, it doesn't even hurt that much."

She ruffles the mop of hair on his head before finding me. "Hey! I was in the area and saw your message in our group chat about Kai, so I decided to swing by and check on him."

I give her a hug. For all the outward displays of strength, she's a big softie on the inside. "He's going to be okay."

"And how are you?" She eyes me curiously. "Seeing him hurt like this can't be easy."

I suppose her assessment is valid, considering this is one of my biggest fears coming to fruition. "Surprisingly, I'm not freaking out," I tell her, glancing at Rowan in his chair, looking dazed. I imagine this whole ordeal must have been stressful for him, given the anguish marring his face. "Rowan did the right thing by bringing Kai here to get examined. He called me on his way and stayed calm while I asked him a million questions." I smile at her. "Honestly, I felt relieved he was there with Kai the entire time, and I know Kai feels the same way."

Delia's eyes soften on Rowan for a moment before she squeezes my hands. "I'll disown you as a friend if you breathe a word of this, but even I have to admit, you have one of the good ones, Shay. In fact, my besties might have snagged the last three decent men left on the planet."

My brows rise. *Now I've heard it all.* "Wait, is Cordelia Masters, CEO of 'Men Are Just Apes With Smaller Brains and Dicks' club, calling for a ceasefire on the men her friends' love?" I tease.

She purses her lips. "A *temporary* ceasefire. Don't get hung up on it."

I giggle. "Well, I have a feeling there's still one more good one out there. And I bet he's going to show up at our doorstep one of these days and whisk you right off your feet."

Delia snorts. "Right, and pigs will fly and unicorns will dance in our backyard." She tilts her head toward a forlorn-looking Rowan. "Have you spoken to him yet?"

I shake my head. "I was just about to."

She nods. "He looks like he needs a hug. I'll go chat with the kids for a few; you carry on."

I close the distance between me and Rowan, and he rises to his feet, his shoulders tense.

"Hey." I reach out to grab his hand. "Are you okay? I'm so sorry you had to–"

"No, don't apologize, Shay." He waves a hand, his mouth tightening as if he's trying to stop a quiver from passing over his lips. "I'm the one who should be apologizing. I feel terrible." He disentangles our hands, running his fingers through his hair. "I'm so sorry I let this happen. I failed you both."

I take a step closer. "It happens, Row–"

"One moment we were laughing and skating, and the next . . ." He squeezes his eyes shut. "I should have anticipated this could happen. I should have given him more lessons before I took him out onto a public rink–"

"Rowan, listen to me." I fist the lapels of his coat to get his attention. "You did *nothing* wrong. You couldn't have anticipated this, and I am not blaming you for it in the least."

He finally looks at me, his eyes glistening. "So . . . you're not ending things with me?"

My mouth opens and shuts as I process his question. *Ending things with him?* Is that how feeble he thinks my love is for him? Is that what I've shown him? That one mistake, one event that wasn't even his fault, could lead me to leaving him?

God, how shitty that he lives in that kind of fear, and it's all my fault.

I swallow as tears prick my eyes. I feel like such an asshole for not doing a better job of showing him how much I believe in us. "No, Rowan, I'm not ending things with you. Yes, it's unfortunate that Kai got hurt, but he'll get better. And this little incident won't be what he'll remember from today. What he'll remember is how much fun he had hanging out with his best friend Winnie, and his favorite person," I press a finger into his chest, *"you."*

I gaze into his eyes, hoping he sees how much he means to me. "I'm sorry I've made it so difficult for you–*and everyone in my life*–to not be able to have fun with him without all this worry looming over your head. I'm sorry I've made you feel like if he got hurt, it would all be on you."

He cups my cheeks. "Don't apologize."

I shake my head. "I need to. I *want* to. You have been the best thing that's happened to both me and Kai, Rowan. You've shown us how to have fun, how not to take life so seriously. In every moment I've spent with you, I've learned, I've laughed, and I've lived. *Truly lived.* And I can't tell you how grateful I am for you. I was a hot mess only a few months ago–"

"Well, you're definitely still hot," he adds, making me laugh.

"I was an emotional wreck after everything Kai and I dealt

with over the past few years, smoking to find a reprieve from my thoughts." I slide my hands over his shoulders. "You changed all of that. You changed my life, Rowan Parker. You helped me find a new version of me, and I have no intentions of going backward, no intention of letting you go."

He pulls me toward him, his eyes smoldering. "Well, that's good to know, Doc, because I have no intention of letting you go, either. Though," a sly grin plays on his lips. "I may have some intentions of tying you up to my bed tonight."

I giggle, blinking away the mist in my eyes. "You better seal that promise with a kiss, then."

He bends, skating his lips over mine, and pulling me into a heated kiss, as a succession of *eews* and *grosses* is loud-whispered behind us, garnering the lifted brows of some others in the waiting area.

Both Rowan and I turn to see Winnie peeking at us through her fingers and Kai's nose scrunched in disgust. Delia chuckles next to them, looking from the kids to us.

"Get a room, you guys!" Winnie chides and Kai repeats, though I can tell he's feigning the revulsion. I know how much he loves this for me—*for us*.

Rowan chuckles, looking back at me, before placing another kiss on my lips. "Believe me, I intend to do just that."

"Oh, yeah? How about we send the kids home with Delia? Then, I want to know all about that tying-up thing you were talking about."

"Sounds like the best plan you've ever had, Doc. But fair warning, I'm not sharing you with any of your toys."

I chuckle. "That's okay, I like Keanu the best, anyway," I tease, referring to the name I've given his cock.

"Shay, I swear to—"

But he doesn't get a chance to finish, because my mouth is on his again.

EPILOGUE
ROWAN - 7 MONTHS LATER

I pride myself for my ability to stay calm during the most crucial times, especially when it comes to hockey.

That ability to ignore the thumping of my heart against my chest and compartmentalize the pressure while playing in front of eighteen thousand fans usually comes easily to me.

Today, though? Not so much.

Today, not only is the Stanley Cup on the line—*what with us at game seven and the series tied at 3-3!*—but so is my future with the woman of my dreams.

With just a minute left in the game, and our team on a power play—with us having a 5-on-4 advantage—and our score tied at 2-2 with St. Louis, the pressure has never been this high. One more goal and we'll clinch the win.

The tension in the arena could be cut with a knife, the crowd roaring so loud, it'd be deafening if I was actually listening.

One mistake and we'd lose the championship. The one

thing we'd worked so hard for and poured our blood, sweat, and tears into over the past months.

With the seconds ticking away, I position myself at the point. I watch the puck move swiftly between our forwards, testing the St. Louis' penalty killers. Seeing a clear pass, Aiden slides it over to me, and I fake a shot, causing a scramble amongst the penalty killers.

My head swivels to the right, seeing our sniper, Sanders, open. I send the puck gliding over to him, and he catches it easily, winding up for a slapshot, and unleashing his power against the puck. I track it, soaring between the mass of legs and sticks, and my heart practically stops when, by some fucking miracle, it catches at the back of the net.

Holy fucking shit, he did it!

The crowd explodes, the stands thundering, as the buzzer signifies our game-winning shot.

For a second, time freezes as I process what just happened. Is this even real?

We just won the Stanley Cup!

We just won the motherfucking Stanley Cup!

My eyes swivel over to the stands, connecting with Shayla and then Kai, who are both wearing my jersey. My fucking family, my hearts.

She places all her fingers to her mouth and throws me a kiss before her and Kai—along with the rest of my new friends from the brownstone—jump as if they're on a trampoline, screaming and crying as if they'd won the Cup themselves.

Within an instant, I'm wrapped inside of large arms— Whose? I couldn't tell you—as my teammates crowd me in a hug, screaming with actual tears streaming down their faces.

Shortly after, the Bolts are presented with the Stanley Cup in a ceremony on the ice with our fans cheering, each player getting a moment with the coveted cup. I lift it up in my hands, showing it off to the kid who's anticipated this moment for me almost as much as I have–my buddy for life, Kai. He jumps up and down with his arms in the air, knowing I'm looking at him and only him.

It's been an incredible, albeit interesting, few months living in the same house with everyone. There's no shortage of daily–if not hourly–shenanigans, laughter, and fun. I can't deny I don't crave the quiet from time to time–a place for just Shay, Kai, and me–but I won't complain as long as I get to wake up next to my girl when I'm not on the road.

"You ready, stud?" Sanders is in my ear, speaking above the din. He nods, and we both look back up at Shayla in the stands. "One victory down; now, go get the next."

I hug him before skating over to the edge of the arena, motioning to Shay and Kai to meet me there. Kai and I exchange looks, and he hurries his mom toward me while people around them watch.

As soon as I meet them with a short metal gate between us, separating the crowd from the players, I pull them both into my arms, placing a kiss on Kai's temple.

"You did it, Rowan!" he squeals. "You were amazing out there. The best of the best."

I run my hand through his unruly hair, looking down at him with so much fucking adoration, I honestly never thought I'd be capable of loving a kid as much as I love this one. "The only people I want to be the best for are you and your mom, little man, and I'll try every day to make you both proud."

With that, I slide my hand into my pocket and take out the game-winning puck. Kai's eyes practically fall out of his sockets, his mouth agape, as he stares at what's in my hand.

"For my biggest fan and the coolest kid I've ever known."

"Rowan . . ." Kai's hand trembles as he takes hold of the

puck, looking at it as if it's the most precious jewel in the world. "Are you serious?"

"It's yours, bud. Maybe later I can take you back to the locker room and get it signed by all the players?"

He nods so enthusiastically, I'm afraid he's going to get a neck sprain.

I look at Shay, taking in our entire exchange with a smile. Curving my hand around her neck, I place my forehead on hers. "What do you say, Doc? Can I get my daily kiss a little early tonight?"

She giggles, leaning forward to place her lips on mine, and I take the opportunity to deepen our connection, letting the softness and sureness of her lips quell my heartbeats. I can feel the pride and happiness swelling inside her, and damn if that doesn't make me love her even more. This woman who chooses and supports me every day.

Rounding my arm around her back and pulling her to me, I say, "I love you, sweetheart."

"I love you so much, Rowan. I'm so proud of you, and so happy I got to be here to see you achieve your dream."

"I thought the Cup was my dream. I thought it was the only thing I wanted; that my life would be fulfilled if I had it." I shake my head, pressing one more kiss to her lips. "Turns out, I was wrong, Doc."

She pulls back with a confused expression. "What do you mean?"

I look down at Kai, who is smiling from ear to ear.

Taking his cue, just like we'd talked about when I'd asked for his blessings yesterday, he pulls out the little velvet box from his pocket, making Shay gasp.

Her hands cover her mouth, and as onlookers watch, I get down on one knee, right there in front of her. "Rowan . . . oh my God, yes!"

I throw back my head, laughing. "You gonna let me at least *ask*, Doc? I've been prepping this speech for weeks!"

"Yes!" She nods, her eyes tearing, while Kai hugs her around her waist, and her best friends–more like her sisters– come up behind her, smiling just as broadly. "I mean, yes, I'll let you ask, but just know my answer is yes, too."

Talk about making a guy feel like he's on top of the fucking world.

I open the box for her to look at the two-carat diamond solitaire I got her during Christmas but wanted to wait until we were both settled in together before giving it to her. "Shayla, before you ask, yes, this is an ethically-sourced, conflict-free diamond."

She giggles, her eyes sparkling.

"Baby, I have loved you from the moment I saw you through my phone camera–"

Somewhere behind her, Dylan chimes in, giddy and bouncing on her feet. She and Cortney had just had their baby girl, Willow, three months ago. "Oh gosh, this might be the first insta-love romance I've loved in a long time!"

I don't really know what that means, so I continue, "I love your spirit and your heart, but mostly, I love the way you share them with those around you. I love your fears and your doubts, but mostly, I love the way you work through them. I love your quirks and everything that makes you unique, but mostly, I love the way they make you stand out in a world where it's hard to. I love your wit and your sass, but mostly, I love that you know how you keep me on my toes.

"From the mole on your cheek to your always-painted toes, I love everything about you, Shayla Kumar. So much so that I've even grown to love the swamp sludge you make for my breakfast every morning.

"You're my source of inspiration, and the only woman who

can handle me—all of me. Even my newsworthy rear end." She rolls her eyes, as expected, but my eyes have filled so I can barely see. "So, will you do me the honor of marrying me and let me love you more with each passing day, sweetheart?"

"Yes!" She's nodding before I've even finished, jutting out her left hand so I can wiggle her ring over her finger, speaking over the cheers all around us. "Yes, I will marry you."

I pull her in for another kiss, groaning into her mouth as I take a mental selfie of the best fucking day of my life.

Two wins in one night. Feeling on top of the world as I hold the Cup in one arm and my future wife in the other. Life couldn't get any better. #StanleyCupBaby #SheSaidYes

BONUS EPILOGUE
SHAY - 2 YEARS LATER

I tap the button on my phone to bring up my camera, raising it to take a picture of my son playing his first hockey game.

Though he's hard to follow, speeding across the ice and focused on the puck, I zoom in to capture a photo of him.

"Yes!" Rowan roars, standing with both arms up, yelling toward the ice as if Kai can hear him. "Great defense, buddy! Way to block that shot!"

I turn the camera and take a picture to capture the glee and pride emanating from my husband's face. He couldn't be more excited to be here, sitting in a private area of the stands, to watch my son play. After all, he's had a huge hand in helping Kai realize his dream. From teaching him to skate, to convincing me–ahem, *begging* me–to let him play hockey, to then teaching him the sport himself. Rowan's been more of a dad to Kai than I could have ever expected.

And he's the same way with our daughter.

As if she knows I'm thinking about her, our three-month-old baby girl, Kiara, whines inside her carrier, waking up from her nap. Her tiny fist finds her mouth, her lips smacking around it, while she blinks up at the lights.

Her head tilts this way and that, following the noises around the arena before her golden-green gaze finds mine, and she coos at me with a toothless smile. God, is there anything more heartwarming than that smile?

I'm just bending to pull her out of her carrier when Rowan's hand lands on my shoulder. "I'll get her. You relax." He turns his soft gaze toward our daughter. "Hey, sleepy head! Glad you're awake. Now you won't miss your brother's first game!"

Rowan unbuckles our daughter, taking her into his arms before nuzzling her neck. She giggles when he does it again, blowing a raspberry on her cheek.

I rise, putting her shoe back on her foot–she'd wiggled it off earlier–before looking up at Rowan. He cups the back of my neck with his free hand and bends to place a kiss on my lips. "You're incredible and the love of my life, Mrs. Parker."

I close my eyes, smiling into his kiss.

It isn't the first time I've heard those words from him; in fact, he says them every chance he gets–and I'll never tire of them. The man comes pretty damn close to perfect.

He's been the most attentive and supportive father and husband. From taking care of me–practically waiting on me hand and foot throughout my pregnancy–to waking up to take care of our baby, even more than me some weeks, to spending time with Kai and taking him to his practices, I have been in awe of his dedication. Even with his busy travel schedule, he's made it clear that we're his priority.

But that doesn't mean I haven't needed my best friends.

They've been my rock, helping me while Rowan's on the

road. They've even babysat Kiara and Kai full days to give me a chance to have me-time. Most of those days have started with a quiet bath using all of Rowan's expensive bath products, of course. The man loves his bath products.

Kai bounds up the metal stairs after his game. His team lost, but I haven't seen a bigger smile on his face since the day his sister was born.

"Did you see me make that pass to our center?" He gleams at Rowan, his chest puffed out with pride. "The coach said I'm getting better every day!"

Rowan tousles my son's hair. "You are, bud! I saw you flying on the ice."

Kai smiles, taking Kiara's hand in his and pressing a kiss to it. She peers down at him with the same affection. Somehow, I already know how close these two will be. He's going to be one hell of a protective brother, but I have a feeling she won't mind it all too much.

"Now, how about we get home, and I'll make you some lunch," I say to Kai, brushing back the hair over his forehead.

He nods and it makes me happy that he actually looks forward to eating the food I make for him these days. Another great change, courtesy of my husband, since I'd now consider myself a decent cook. He's helped me find my confidence in the kitchen and around food in a way I never thought was possible. I'm no longer worried about every ingredient, or obsessing about Kai eating a few junk-filled snacks. I'm more concerned with us living fulfilling lives where we enjoy ourselves in the way we all deem right for us.

"Can we pick up an ice cream shake on the way?" Kai turns his hopeful eyes at me. "I feel like it'll help me get over our team's loss."

Both Rowan and I laugh. At almost twelve, the kid still knows how to turn on the charm so I can't say no.

"Okay," I respond. "But only if you promise to balance it out with a chicken and kale salad later."

He sighs, but gives in. "Deal."

It was about four years ago that I moved to Boston, nervous and broken. I had no idea where life would lead us, but I was content in the knowledge that I'd at least get to raise my son with some of my favorite people on earth—my best friends. The family I chose for myself and the one I continue to choose every day. We've grown over the years—having added a few more people into our mix—but one thing has remained the same . . . our unwavering affection and dedication to one another.

And as I look up at my husband with our daughter inside her carrier in one hand and the other placed around my waist, his broad smile rivaling his broad shoulders as he looks at my son on my other side, I'm struck once again at the way my life took a turn for the better in every way since the moment I met him.

There's not a day that goes by where I'm not smiling in his presence; not a day where he doesn't tell me—*show me*—how much I mean to him. Some days, like today, I have to pinch myself and wonder if I'm dreaming. Because it's exactly what it's been over the past four years.

A dream full of inside jokes and spontaneous adventures. A dream where every day brings a new reason to laugh, another reason to make love.

A dream I never want to wake up from.

Your review matters! Please consider leaving a review for Mother Pucker on Amazon.

. . .

*BE sure to read **the entire MomComs Series**. You won't regret the laughs :)*

*LIKE SINGLE MOM **romances with swoony heroes?** Read **ASCEND**, a marriage of convenience, single mom, forced proximity romance by Swati M.H.*

ABOUT THE AUTHOR

Swati M.H. writes stories full of humor, heart, and heartbreak. She lives in the Bay Area with her incredibly patient husband, two beautiful daughters, and her pitbull, Sadie Sapphire. Her days start with caffeine and sometimes end with a glass (or three) of wine.

Swati loves staying in touch with her readers. Find her at www.swatimh.com or through Facebook and Instagram. Be sure to join her Sweeties reader group for daily fun.

Read all books by Swati M.H.

About the Series Authors

Brittanee, Jenni, Daphne, and Swati started their writing journey roughly three years ago. And since we're also all moms who love each other's books, we thought it would be fun to write a romcom series based on four friends who end up living together with all their kids.

Oh, what a thrilling ride this has been!

Acknowledgments

What an incredible adventure it has been to write this book! The entire series started off as a "what if" in our heads and evolved into something we're all so very proud of. So, if you've come this far with us, I want to thank you from the bottom of my cinnamon-roll loving heart.

While most of my books contain humor, I tend to write angstier, slower-burning books. I didn't think I'd ever write a sports romcom because, it's a lot of pressure, y'all! But, Shay and Rowan made it easy. As did the crazy clan living together in the dilapidated Boston brownstone. I hope you enjoyed them and their shenanigans as much as I did writing them.

I want to give a huge thank you to my friends and the fellow co-authors of this series, Brittanee Nicole, Daphne Elliot, and Jenni Bara for inspiring me to write this book. You all are truly talented women and I'm grateful for your friendship.

A huge thank you to my husband and the true cinnamon-roll hero in my life. Your patience and love are immeasurable. I don't know how you do it but please continue doing it :)

Thank you to Suhani and Sanika. You aren't just my daughters—though there is nothing I love more in the world than that—you're my friends, my guides, and even my inspirations. I love you to the ends of the infinite universe.

Thank you to my lovely parents. I've said it a million times and I'll say it a million more: I'm the luckiest girl on the planet to have the type of unrelenting support that I do from you. Thank you for always cheering me on.

Thank you, Stephanie, for being so much more than my PA. Thank you for your friendship and support. I'd be a hot mess without you.

Additionally, thank you to Sara for being so instrumental in the promotion and marketing for the Mom Coms. You're amazing!

Thank you to my incredible alpha and beta reader team—Rachael Poxon, Rachel Childers, Michelle Mastandrea, Melissa Schmidt, Manda Laclair, Amarilys Santiago-Maldonado, Kerri Bonvie, and Anna Lewis. Thank you for the chats, the feedback and all your encouragement. I couldn't have done it without you.

Thank you to my friends, Emily Silver, Rin Sher, and Monica Arya, for listening to my long messages and smacking sense into me when needed. Thank you for being so inspirational, supportive, and for constantly making me laugh. I love you guys so much.

Thank you Madison Lee for taking the time to speak to us about our vision and for bringing the Boston brownstone to life on the Mom Coms covers.

Thank you, Kristie Lynn, for taking the time to chat with me and for giving me so many ideas when I was just starting to write Rowan and Shay. That first sexy tub scene—Shay's pivotal shift into the woman she's about to find within herself again—is dedicated to you.

Thank you to everyone in my reader group, Swati's Sweeties! I love hanging out with you.

And most importantly, thank you, my readers! You guys make this journey incredible. I absolutely love writing stories for you and I'll continue to do so for as long as I can.